MURDER CHECKS INN

A MAIDEN HARLOW MYSTERY - BOOK 1

CAMILLE SHARP

CONTENTS

Chapter One

"That one is going to be a nightmare."

Maiden Harlow sat behind the reception desk of her family's inn and glanced over at her older sister, who had made the terse comment.

She had been looking over the notes from that morning and preparing herself for the rest of the day when her sister joined her. Vonny walked out of the office and pointed an accusing finger at the computer screen. The name she'd picked out was a certain Ms. Vera Randall.

Maiden obligingly had a look. Ms. Randall appeared to be traveling alone and had booked a room for four nights. Maiden shrugged and turned back to her.

"So, what's the problem?" she asked, hoping that Vonny was just indulging her slight tendency to be critical.

"She's a cranky old cow, that's all." Von rolled her eyes. "She was rude about everything when I took her booking and got furious when I told her all the rooms are non-smoking. She said we must be a bunch of oversensitive hicks."

"She actually said that?" Maiden gave her a patiently skeptical look.

"Yeah." Vonny folded her arms over her small bust and arched a pale brown brow. "She wheezed it out like a horse stepping on a set of bagpipes. I could almost smell the smoke over the phone.

When I asked if she still wanted the booking she just said yes and hung up."

"You do bring out the best in people," Maiden laughed quietly and propped her chin in her hand.

Rude guests were an unfortunate part of life in their business; time and experience had helped her to toughen up when it came to verbal abuse and excessive demands. Vonny had improved as well, but she was touchy by nature, and it was rare that an offense got past her without comment.

"Since we have no other option, let's give her the benefit of the doubt," Maiden said with a shrug. "Maybe she was having a bad day and took it out on you. No one's perfect."

"Vera Randall certainly isn't," Von said under her breath and rolled her eyes again. "Well, you're the calm one. So, you can deal with her, talking to her on the phone was enough for me."

"Thanks a lot." Maiden gave her a wry look but let it go as Von stalked past and headed upstairs to the apartment they shared with their parents.

She went back to checking the bookings and saw that two more guests, besides the infamous Vera Randall, would be arriving that day. They were a married couple, Mr. and Mrs. Robert Gilford, who had booked their room a few weeks ago. They had no notes warning about chain-smoking or sweeping insults impugning the honor of the town, so that was a good sign. Not that there was much that could be said against the lovely little town.

Golden Glen was a popular tourist destination in the heart of northern Michigan, and it was also the home of the Harlow House Inn. The small family business had a hard-earned reputation for its classic charm and elegant atmosphere. Gloria and Alfie Harlow had run it for years, but these days their two daughters were carrying a fair bit of the workload.

Maiden stepped away from the computer and looked around the foyer to ensure everything was clean and in order before the new guests arrived. Like the rest of the inn, the lobby was warm and welcoming. Ornate pink and ivory paper embellished with gold filigree lined the walls, disappearing behind gleaming white wainscoting. Plush area rugs softened the pale, marbled floor tiles, and a beautiful chandelier tastefully crowned the room.

On the right side of the foyer was the reception area, with the door to the private office behind it. To the left was an arched entryway that led into the large dining room, with the kitchen nestled beyond it. Straight ahead was the library, which they occasionally hired out for intimate gatherings and small corporate events.

Everything looked to be in order that morning, but Maiden's watchful green eyes narrowed slightly when she spied the little round table that sat beside the library door. They used it to display brochures so that their guests could take advantage of the many local shops, bakeries, restaurants, and vineyards. There was also a booklet about the Addison Theater; a handsome old concert hall where small-time musicians and theatrical troupes performed. Maiden loved the beautiful little town, and she loved sharing it with those who came to stay at the inn.

But the normally helpful display of brochures had been left in a chaotic pile that had spilled onto the floor beneath the table. She knew the family that had checked out yesterday had two sweet but rambunctious children who weren't shy about making a mess. She also knew that Vonny was on duty when they left and she wasn't big on keeping things tidy.

Maiden sighed, grateful that the friendly but inattentive parents had taken their adorable little turd-monkeys and traveled on, and started straightening the display. She rearranged the brochures and sorted a few stacks of business cards that had been shuffled together before heading back to the desk.

She checked the clock. There was plenty of time before the next guests arrived, so she picked up the morning paper. And immediately regretted the decision. An uneasy scowl creased her forehead as she read the front page.

Westfield National Bank Robbed at Gunpoint!

Yesterday morning the doors of Westfield's largest and oldest bank opened for business as usual. Two men wearing black coveralls, ski masks, and carrying rifles entered and demanded that the staff open the safe.

The bandits reportedly escaped with over $300,000. They were last seen climbing into separate cars and speeding away from pursuing authorities. Both men are to be considered armed and extremely dangerous.

The article went on to describe the horrified reactions of the unsuspecting staff. It was the first violent crime in the bank's long history, and the whole community was in shock.

Maiden set the paper back on the desk and stared at the picture on the front page. The old bank looked ominous with half a dozen police cars parked in front of it. Her heart beat a little faster. Westfield was about half an hour away, and that suddenly felt uncomfortably close. She quickly reminded herself that Golden Glen was smaller, and it was a tourist town. Banks didn't get robbed here.

Despite that attempt to be rational, Maiden was still picturing masked men bursting through the front door, brandishing

Tommy guns. She jumped and made a tiny squeaky noise when the door to the office swung open and her parents came walking out. Her mother, Gloria, smiled at her as she reached her side and gave her shoulders a squeeze.

"You all right, angel?" she asked in her heavy southern tones.

Gloria had been born in Kentucky, raised in Tennessee, and defied the odds by falling in love and marrying a Yankee. Alfie Harlow had swept her off her feet in their youth and whisked her away to the freezing cold winters of Michigan. She bemoaned this cruel fate whenever it snowed, but she loved her husband and their life together in the beautiful little town.

"Yeah, I'm fine." Maiden smiled at her overactive imagination and pushed the paper aside.

"Good," Gloria murmured and rummaged through one of the many drawers before pulling out a stack of papers. "I need to have a look at next week's menus; we'll have a lot of people to feed."

"Um, isn't that Kylie's job, Mom?" Maiden asked tactfully. Kylie was their new chef.

"That woman," Gloria scoffed. "She can't handle that much organizin'. And horror of horrors, she might have to actually speak to people. Sour as a lemon!"

"She's very organized and she's a great cook. Which is why we hired her," Maiden pointed out. Again. "She's just shy, Mom."

"She's not 'just shy'; she's rude!" Gloria sniffed. "Every time I talk to her she won't even look at me, and then she scuttles away like a cockroach the first chance she gets. What happened to tryin' to impress your boss?"

"I guess that goes out the window when your boss is a scary old southern broad," Maiden said under her breath.

"We've all worked very hard to make a good name for Harlow House," Gloria began a well-practiced lecture that caused her husband and youngest daughter to look at each other with commiseration. "I'm not about to let some uptight little snip blow it apart by walking around with her nose in a cookbook offendin' people right and left. Only the other day a guest told me to compliment the chef on her strawberry soufflé, and Kylie looked at me like I'd thrown one of them in her face!"

"Firstly, I doubt that," Maiden said mildly. "Secondly, who cares how she acts when the guests never meet her? The food is great, everyone loves it, can't we just leave her alone and let her do her work?"

"I'm bein' very patient, girl," Gloria reminded her with a grim expression.

"In that case patience sounds a lot whinier than I realized." Maiden smirked and quickly dashed around the desk before her mother could swat her backside.

"I'll just go and see Billie and ask her if any of the cleaning supplies need restocking," Maiden said sweetly as she ducked through the door between reception and the staircase and on outside.

It was about 2 pm when Maiden heard the bell above the front door tinkle. She glanced up and smiled politely as a man walked in, carrying a suitcase in one hand and a briefcase in the other.

She watched as he approached with a friendly smile and set his cases down at his sides. He had a kind face; his hair was dark and curly, and he wore a thin mustache that looked like something from an old Errol Flynn movie.

"Good afternoon," she said nicely. "Welcome to Harlow House. My name's Maiden; how can I help you?"

"Robert Gilford." He inclined his head in greeting and pulled out his wallet. "I believe my wife, Anna, booked us in."

"Ah yes, just give me a moment," she murmured as she turned to the computer and started tapping away at the keyboard. "Booked in for two weeks?"

"We are." Robert nodded. "Is that long enough to see the best of Golden Glen?"

"No, but it's a decent start." She smiled. "I just need your driver's license and the credit card you want to pay with please."

He dutifully presented both cards and looked around the foyer as she entered the information into the computer.

"This is really nice." He gestured to indicate the room. "My wife will love the atmosphere."

"Excellent, thank you," she said and flicked him a quick glance. "Is your wife joining you later?"

"Yes, in a day or two." He nodded and rested his elbows on the desk. "She got caught up in a business trip that took longer than it was supposed to. But she promised me she'll be here by Thursday at the latest. I'd never call her a liar to her face, but we'll see."

Maiden smiled at his wry expression and was about to ask what she did for work when someone flung the front door wide open.

They both looked over sharply to see a tall, slender blonde standing in the doorway. The bright afternoon light poured in around her, emphasizing her long legs and small waist.

Also emphasizing her legs was the neon yellow miniskirt that obscured little below her underwear. Her black and white zebra print blouse was something out of the 80s, complete with some impressive shoulder pads.

The woman whipped off a pair of oversized sunglasses and ran a disdainful gaze over the room. Her lip curled and her eyes narrowed critically as she strolled inside and closed the door loudly.

Maiden's heart sank when she saw the pale lavender suitcase she wheeled along behind her; she was a guest. She nodded to the woman and was about to finish booking in Mr. Gilford when the stranger approached the desk and slapped her purse down on top of it.

"I'm checking in," she said imperiously.

"How nice." Maiden managed a polite smile. "I'll be with you in a moment, but this gentleman was here first."

The woman harrumphed ungraciously and planted a fist on her hip. Maiden ignored her and turned back to the computer, but saw Robert shift from the corner of her eye.

"I don't mind waiting," Robert gestured toward the woman standing beside him. "Ladies first."

"Aren't you a gentleman!" Her bright pink lips stretched into a smile, showing sharp, slightly yellowed teeth. She gave Maiden a cool look and tossed her credit card on the counter. "Vera Randall."

Maiden picked up the card and set about checking her in quickly just to get her out of the room. Even if the woman hadn't given her name, she'd have known her by the sickly stale waft of cigarette smoke that mingled with her musky perfume. Maybe Vonny's warning had been accurate after all.

Vera looked quite harsh up close; as much from her unfriendly expression as from her physical appearance. She was heavily tanned, and her hair was bleached so severely that it looked stiff and dull, like cotton. Her low-cut blouse revealed deep creases between her breasts and a dense scattering of sunspots.

While she waited, Vera turned to the man at her side and smiled slowly as she looked him over blatantly. He cleared his throat and edged away a little, pretending to study the pegboard of room keys that was mounted on the wall behind the desk.

"The name's Vera," she said warmly and stepped closer, in no way discouraged by his visible discomfort. "So nice to meet you."

"Robert Gilford." He looked a bit startled by her sudden friendliness. "Likewise, I'm sure."

"Yes, what a charming little place to make a new friend." She favored him with a predatory smile. "Been here before?"

"No, I haven't." He cleared his throat again. "My *wife* heard good things about the town and Harlow House in particular, so she booked us in."

"How cute." She didn't appear at all put off by the mention of a wife. "I'm here all by my lonesome, unfortunately."

"Well, I'm sure you'll find some means of occupying your time." Robert shifted awkwardly. "I know I'll be looking forward to seeing the sights once my Anna gets here."

"Your key, Ms. Randall," Maiden interrupted and set her credit card and her room key in front of her. "Room 9. It's up the stairs to the second floor and the second room on the right. If you're dining in, lunch is available from noon and dinner from 5:30. Welcome to Golden Glen, have a wonderful stay."

Vera didn't spare her a glance as she collected her things and turned towards the stairs. She stopped long enough to give Robert a slow, *friendly* look.

"Let me know if you get tired of waiting alone," she said with a coquettish smile and sauntered away.

Maiden stared after her like an...oversensitive hick.

I guess I might have to give her that one, Maiden thought wryly.

She glanced at Robert to find him gawking as well, which made her feel a little better. He closed his mouth and adjusted his tie uncomfortably as he reluctantly faced her again.

"Nice shy girl, that one," Robert said lightly, but Maiden caught sight of a faint blush. "I'll be careful to lock my door tonight. Maybe even hook a chair under the knob!"

She could see that he was embarrassed, so she just chuckled at his joke and went back to finishing his check-in. She then handed him a large and ornate metal key.

"There you are, Mr. Gilford." She smiled nicely. "You're in room number 8."

"Uh...isn't Ms. Randall in room 9?" he asked uneasily.

"If you feel unsafe at any time just let us know," she said reassuringly.

"Yeah, I'll be sure to run and do that. Thanks, Maiden." He smiled ruefully and walked rather cautiously towards the stairs.

Maiden watched him go with a faint smile; she felt bad for him, but there wasn't much she could do about the situation. Vera might be a bit pushy, but she hadn't behaved in a threatening or intimidating manner. Besides, there weren't many other rooms to be had at the moment.

Even though about half of their rooms were currently vacant, that would change in the next day or two. It was early summer and nearly all of their standard rooms were booked out.

Golden Glen was quaint, picturesque, and famous in a small way. So much so that several movies had been filmed there. It had a reputation for attracting and nurturing talent; writers, musicians, and artists all went there for inspiration.

It was a scenic and tourist-friendly town that usually offered plenty to do. The local powers that be encouraged this by hosting big events and festivals throughout the year.

The ever-popular Summerfest was fast approaching. It was their annual town fair and featured a large carnival, baking contests, and one of the biggest outdoor markets in the state. Tourists always flocked in, and that meant the hotels around town were booked out well in advance.

Maiden was looking forward to it; life had been a bit dull and predictable lately, a touch of excitement would brighten things up nicely.

CHAPTER TWO

That evening Vonny was sitting alone behind the reception desk. She preferred the closing shifts since she hated getting up early. Maiden was the opposite and nearly always woke up an hour or two before the rest of the family. Therefore, Vonny would often volunteer to take the late shift. It also got her out of helping with dinner, so it was a win-win situation in her opinion.

The evening had been peaceful, boring really, but that was fine by her. Most of the guests had had their dinner, and either gone to their rooms or out to enjoy the quaint nightlife that Golden Glen had to offer.

Vonny twirled a few strands of her long, chestnut hair around her finger and checked the clock. It was close enough to 7:30 to set the automatic door lock and head upstairs for the night. The fancy locking gadget, as her father called it, was one of a few modern features they had installed for security's sake. Paying guests all had their own keys and could let themselves in whenever they wanted.

She walked towards the front door and shivered as she listened to the wind howling outside. Despite the warm time of year, it was Michigan, which meant that nothing was out of the question weather-wise. At the moment, a storm sounded as if it was about to pass through. It didn't surprise her when a heavy rainfall started just as she reached for the keypad to type in the code.

But before she could touch it, the latch rattled, and a man shoved the door open, nearly hitting her with it. Vonny gave a startled gasp, but then scowled at him.

"Watch it!" she huffed. "Are you trying to break our door down?"

"Sorry, honey," a surly man muttered as he pushed his way in. "The wind must've caught it."

"The wind's blowing the other direction, *toots*." She folded her arms, not appreciating his condescending address. "What do you want? We're closed for the evening."

"I need a room for the night," he said as he shut the door firmly.

Von looked the man over with a distinct lack of enthusiasm. He was fairly tall and had a wiry build. His clothes were rumpled and looked like they needed a wash. He said nothing else, just watched her expectantly with his cold, dark eyes and ran a hand over his slicked-back hair, and then his unshaven jaw.

"Try one of the bigger hotels downtown," she suggested with a shrug. "We're full."

"You must have *something*," he said implacably and made no move to leave. He nodded over his shoulder. "Listen to that storm, you can't send me out into that."

"There's nothing I can do about the weather, sir." She added the 'sir' as an obvious afterthought. "You should've called ahead and saved yourself the walk."

"Look lady!" he snarled and took a step closer. "It's late and pouring down rain! I just need a bed for tonight, that's all. If you chuck me out into that weather, I'll leave the worst review you can imagine on every travel site there is!"

"I don't appreciate being threatened!" she snapped, but he was making her uncomfortable, and she knew she wasn't hiding it well.

"Then show some basic decency and help a guy out," he said grimly. "I just need a place to sleep tonight, that's all."

It was clear he wasn't going to leave, so Vonny begrudgingly stalked back around the desk to the computer and had a look. They had a window of availability for room 6. As much as she didn't want to do the creep any favors, she didn't want to deal with him anymore either. She glanced up to find his eyes roving over her figure and for a split second was tempted to throw the stapler at him and run.

"Fine," she spoke up quickly and started typing. "You can stay in room 6, but it's a 2-night minimum and its due in advance."

"Fine, honey. Absolutely fine." He smirked and dug a hand into his pocket. "How much?"

She named a price that was higher than the normal rate and watched with a frown as he counted it out in cash and pushed it across the desk to her.

"Can I get a name for the reservation?" she asked.

"Creevey," he said in a tone that didn't advise asking any more questions.

Vonny slapped the key to room 6 in front of him and grabbed the money.

"Upstairs on the right-hand side," she said tightly.

He offered her a mocking salute before heading for the stairs. Her frown deepened as she watched him go. He had no luggage; only a tattered old backpack slung across one shoulder. It matched his wrinkled and dirty clothes.

Vonny gave him a minute to get to his room before she moved. Thoroughly unnerved by the unpleasant man, she went to the front door and set the lock before scampering upstairs to the safety of her family's apartment.

The storm raged through the night, but in the early hours of the morning it finally calmed and gave way to clear skies and bright sunshine. Maiden was downstairs early as usual. It was 8 am, and she'd already answered several phone calls and changed three bookings. She glanced up and smiled as the front door opened and Tony Ferris walked in with his hands full of the day's mail.

She and Vonny had gone to the same school as Tony, although Maiden was a year and a bit younger than both of them. But they were all close enough that being in a different grade had never been much of a boundary.

Not that things had always been straightforward or even peaceful between her and Von. Maiden had developed much earlier, and the boys around them noticed. That, along with a considerable difference in temperament, caused some tension and strained their relationship for years.

It had taken a while, but Vonny did stop resenting Maiden for the attention she got from their small circle of friends, and they finally grew closer. But Tony had been a good friend to both of them ever since they'd all met in elementary school; regardless of the sisters' sometimes tumultuous relationship with each other.

He walked up and laid the stack of letters in front of Maiden before leaning forward over the desk. His dark eyes twinkled; he had news to share.

"What's up?" She quirked a brow and smiled at him.

"Plenty." He grinned and set his cap aside, but his tightly curled hair retained the shape of it.

"I thought you were getting a haircut." Maiden started flipping through the stack of envelopes.

"Don't start, *please*," he jokingly pleaded. "Mom's already calling me a hippie. She said I'm starting to look like Jimi Hendrix."

"She's mistaken, but you could do a lot worse," she laughed. "So, what's the latest news? I doubt you came here just to show off your rebellious streak."

Tony had been a straight-A student throughout high school and joined the postal service right after graduation. He had been a dedicated employee ever since. 'Rebellious' wasn't a word that would typically spring to mind in his company. But 'gossip' was.

"The new head of the police station has arrived and he's already making some waves," Tony informed her.

"How exactly?" she asked.

"Apparently he's looking to modernize the place." Tony leaned closer. "He's supposed to be some hot shot from the big city. I'll bet he thinks Golden Glen is way behind the times."

"Well, it probably is," she conceded. "Where's he actually from?"

"Stanton." He waggled his eyebrows. "And not the nice part."

"*Is* there a nice part?" Maiden blinked owlishly. Stanton was a sprawling city on the other side of the state; largely industrial, it had a reputation for crime and a history of high-level corruption. That tarnished legacy was supposedly in the past, but who really knew?

"I couldn't tell you; it's not my sort of town." Tony shrugged. "But this guy is here now and looking to make changes."

"That's brave, I guess," she allowed. "But he'd be better off learning to adapt to us than trying to twist the place into something else. Golden Glen is iconic, and people won't put up with some big city wannabe trying to ruin it."

"You're one to talk," he laughed and pointed toward the computer. "Didn't you force your parents to adopt all these godless modern do-dads?"

"I'm not sure a computer booking system is an earth-shaking revelation," Maiden said. "Besides, that's different. I can do anything I want to; I'm a local."

Tony chuckled. "Anyway, from what I've heard from Nancy, the receptionist over at the station, all the officers are on their best behavior until they figure this guy out."

"Is he that bad?" she asked with a questioning frown.

"They don't know yet," Tony murmured. "Captain David McAlister, he's called. No one knows much about him, but he only got here a couple of weeks ago. They say he worked in some pretty dangerous places and no one knows why he's decided to settle here."

Before she could offer any further comment, Kylie, the chef and perpetual source of annoyance for Gloria, walked through the front door. She entered without a word and just barely acknowledged them with an instant of eye contact and a nod before shuffling quickly towards the kitchen.

"Good morning, Kylie," Maiden said with deliberate cheerfulness.

Kylie looked over at her and then away again. "Good morning."

She then walked straight through the archway and into the safety of the dining room. Maiden pulled a face and sighed.

"I wish she'd warm up a little," she confided discreetly. "Mom really doesn't like her."

"Why not?" Tony shook his head and glanced at the doorway she'd disappeared through. "She seems harmless enough."

"She *is* harmless. She's just so shy that Mom thinks she's stuck up and rude," she murmured, resting her chin in her hand. "They barely speak to each other, but it's still getting harder to keep the peace."

They heard footsteps coming from the side door. Only staff ever used that entrance, so it was no surprise when Billie walked in with a cheerful wave.

"Morning all!" Billie's smile was bright, and so was her tone, which only emphasised Kylie's unfriendly manner. "How are we all today?"

Billie had been the housekeeper at the inn for nearly a decade and still enjoyed her job. She was a small but muscular woman who was addicted to running, cardio kickboxing and, curiously, scrapbooking.

She was clutching a cloth in one hand and a can of wood polish in the other as she came and propped her elbows on the desk.

"Hi, Billie." Tony shifted his cap out of her way. "We were just talking about your chef. Apparently, Gloria doesn't like her."

"No shock there," Billie snorted. "She's the anti-Gloria. They couldn't be more different."

"That's not a crime," Maiden said.

"She's weird." Billie pointed her rag at her in some gesture of emphasis. "I asked Kylie to join me for a drink after work yesterday. She turned purple! You'd have thought I'd invited her to a strip club! I wouldn't dare ask her to have dinner with my family; she'd spit in my face. What an iceberg."

"A slight exaggeration," Maiden sighed, more hopeful than convinced. "She'll warm up to us eventually. She'll have to."

"I doubt it." Billie propped her chin on her fist. "She's been here for three months already and I can't get a full sentence out of her. Maybe she's hiding out. She could be in Witness Protection or something."

"Yes, that's the most logical conclusion." Tony gave her a wry look. "She's probably been kicked around a few times and struggles to make friends. A lot of people have baggage."

"Well, is she gonna carry it with her and not have any friends for the rest of her life?" Billie challenged; her blue eyes flinty.

"Why ask me? I don't know the woman," Tony reminded her with a shrug. "Sounds like you don't know her either."

"Sounds like *no one* does," she said with a hint of triumph.

"Come on, Billie, there's no actual issue here. Kylie does her job and the food is great," Maiden said in a tone that she hoped would end the topic. "Please don't give Mom any more reasons to dislike her. She hasn't done anything wrong and I can't just snap my fingers and make another trained chef appear to take over."

"Fine, fine." Billie waved it away and checked her watch. "It's time for coffee anyway. See you guys later."

"I'd better get going too," Tony said as he slapped his cap back over his springy curls. "I'll let you know more about this McAlister guy when I hear something."

"I'll be holding my breath." She smiled down at the letter she'd picked up.

Tony left with a wave and a cheerful whistle that faded as the front door shut behind him. Maiden started leafing through the rest of the mail and soon forgot all about big-city cops and anti-social chefs. The peace and quiet was abruptly spoiled, however, when a muttered argument resounded along the hallway.

Maiden glanced over towards the library; behind it was the long passageway that led to the ground-floor guest rooms. She spotted two of their guests, Mr. and Mrs. Varney, who had been staying with them since late Monday afternoon.

They had booked the entire week, but Maiden couldn't imagine them lasting that long; every time she had seen them so far they were squabbling. This was no exception, but as soon as they rounded the corner and entered the foyer, they saw her and fell silent.

Maiden smiled and politely pretended to have heard nothing. They returned the forced pleasantry and became absorbed in rifling the pamphlets she'd tidied so carefully the day before. She studied them subtly as they browsed.

Reg Varney was a barrel-chested man, not too tall and only a little fat. She guessed him to be in his fifties; his dark hair was still thick and wavy but heavily dusted with gray. His crisply ironed button-down shirt and a bushy mustache gave him an air of stodginess.

His wife, Emily, looked much younger, maybe only in her mid-thirties. Her smooth brown hair fell in a shoulder-length pageboy. She wore very little makeup, something that would have shocked and perplexed Gloria, and seemed to favor cotton dresses and busy floral prints.

Maiden had only spoken to them a handful of times but had found them pleasant enough to everyone but each other. They loitered for a moment or two before selecting a few brochures and heading out into the bright morning sunshine.

Several minutes ticked by. The phone hadn't rung, and the foyer was quiet, so Maiden decided to get another cup of coffee and make another attempt at talking to Kylie.

She slipped into the dining room and made her way toward the kitchen. None of the guests had come down to breakfast yet, but that wasn't surprising because the hot food wouldn't be served for another half hour or so.

She pushed the door open and peered inside. Kylie was hard at work whisking a large bowl full of what were probably eggs, judging by a slightly smaller bowl of cracked shells that sat nearby.

Maiden glanced around; the room was unpleasantly dark since the shades were pulled down over the large windows. The only illumination came from the cold, sterile lights overhead that bounced off all the stainless-steel countertops. She rubbed the goosebumps that had risen on her arms and edged carefully closer.

"How's it going, Kylie?" Maiden tried to keep her voice gentle, but the other woman still jumped and nearly overturned the bowl. "Oh sorry! I didn't mean to startle you."

"It's all right." Kylie took a deep breath and then resumed her whisking. "I wasn't expecting anyone, that's all. Breakfast will be ready on time, don't worry."

"I wasn't really worried about it, but okay." Maiden fought back a frustrated groan.

Kylie was quickly going from painfully shy to just painful. It had never been this hard for a staff member to gel with the rest of the team before. They were a small business, one that was friendly and welcoming; they didn't go through a lot of staff. Ones that had left in the past had gone because they moved out of state or got married and started families.

They were nice to work for; Maiden knew that, she made a point of it. But Kylie didn't seem to care about that, and it was starting to feel like she wasn't even trying to fit in or be happy there.

But Maiden was still inclined to persevere since Kylie was good at the job itself. Capable staff wasn't the easiest thing to replace; it would be a lot of extra work if she grew dissatisfied and moved on.

"Do you need a hand with anything?" Maiden tried again, hoping to start a conversation.

"No. No, I don't, no...thank you, but no." She shook her head for a few seconds longer than she spoke.

She looked so severe, so serious. She wore her pale hair pulled back in a tight bun that was shellacked to her head; it shone like yellow glass in the bright lights above them. Her chef's whites were perfectly pressed and almost glowed with pristine cleanliness. Maiden felt an urge to throw a pudding cup at her, just to see if it would stick or bead up and roll off.

"Cool," she said quietly and glanced around for something else to say. "So...what's for lunch today?"

"Havarti and shaved ham on grilled sourdough." Kylie set the bowl aside and started deftly mincing a bundle of herbs. "With roasted pepper and tomato bisque."

"That sounds amazing." Maiden ignored her rumbling stomach and reminded herself that she'd already had breakfast. "I can't wait. Will you be joining us? It'd be nice."

"What?" Kylie gasped as she nearly sliced off her fingertip. She took a steadying breath and set the knife aside, finally managing to meet Maiden's eye. "I really wouldn't feel comfortable eating with the guests."

"I'm talking about the rest of the staff. Me and Von, and my parents." Maiden gave her a patient but wry smile. "You aren't too good to have lunch with your boss, are you?"

"Of course not but...look, you're very kind, but I have a lot to do." She shifted her gaze away and resumed her mincing. "Thanks anyway, Maiden."

Maiden exhaled quietly and nodded. Nothing was working. Poor Kylie was running out of slack and probably didn't even know it. The woman was all business, but it seemed more out of a desperate fear of forming relationships than a dedication to her art. Looking at her gave Maiden a sad little pain deep inside; she was increasingly convinced that Kylie was just awkward and lonely.

For now, however, she decided to retreat. She'd have to give it more thought.

She returned to the dining room and stopped at the coffee station long enough to make a cappuccino. As she walked back towards reception, she looked up and gasped. A strange, scruffy-looking man was standing behind the desk, scowling at the computer as he tapped away at the keyboard.

"Hey!" Maiden said loudly and angrily as she rushed to the desk. "Get out of there!"

The man's head shot up with a snarl, but he quickly hid it and stepped back with his hands peacefully raised.

"I said get away from there." She glared at him until he walked out from behind the desk.

Maiden hurried to the computer and set her coffee aside. She looked at the screen and was relieved to see that he hadn't gotten past the security page; she turned back to him coolly.

"Who are you and what are you trying to do?" she demanded.

"I'm a guest," he said, as though expecting an apology in return. "The name's Creevey."

"We'll see about that," she muttered as she typed in the password, making sure he couldn't see it, and studied the register. "Creevey...checked in last night. Fine, so why were you trying to hack into our computer?"

She forced herself to hold his intimidating glare and turned the screen away from him when he had the audacity to try to look at it. He narrowed his eyes at her and said nothing.

"That's it then, I'm calling the police." She pulled out her phone and held it up, ready to dial.

"Calm down, lady!" He scowled and took another step back. "Like I said, I'm a guest here, and I don't like being talked to as if I were some kind of criminal."

"Mr. Creevey you are incredibly close to a chat with the cops," she informed him. "I think you'll find them even harder to talk to!"

"All right, all right." He made a visible decision to relax. "I thought I saw an old friend walking out earlier, I just wanted to check the names of the other guests to see if it was him."

"Most people would have waited for them to come back and asked them personally." Her tone was dry, and her expression unconvinced. "In any case, we're required to keep the personal information of our guests confidential. If you try to break into our system again, I'll call the police."

"Nice place, friendly staff!" he mocked with an ugly snarl. "I'll be sure to include that in my reviews! You treat me nicely or I'll see to it no one will want to stay in this hovel!"

"I doubt that, Mr. Creevey." She folded her arms across her chest and eyed him coldly. "If you slander my business, I will throw you out right now and sue you for libel. Or you can behave yourself and stay out of our computer. What would you prefer?"

He looked furious, and he balled his hands into fists at his sides. Maiden was used to putting up with demanding guests, but she didn't tolerate threatening behavior. She raised her phone and started dialing. His demeanor immediately changed.

"Hey wait!" he said quickly and forced a contorted grimace that may have been an attempted smile. "Let's not get hot under the collar, okay? My mistake, all right? I'm real sorry."

Maiden paused but still eyed him watchfully. She lowered the phone a fraction and saw him instantly relax. A suspicious scowl settled over her features.

"Do you have any ID, Mr. Creevey?" she asked in her most professional tone. "Nothing seems to be entered under your booking. I'll need to see a driver's license at least."

"Um…" He looked around like a cornered rat and patted his pockets. "I haven't got it on me, no. Sorry, honey, but don't worry about it, eh. I'll mind my manners, don't you worry."

He turned and hastily slipped outside without another word.

Maiden frowned at the closed door; despite her bravado, the man was unsettling. She hated confrontation, but working reception had forced her to learn how to handle herself; in professional settings at least.

Whoever this Creevey guy was, he was shifty. She didn't believe his flimsy excuse for trying to get into the computer either. In retrospect, she wished she had told him to go and find another hotel.

Chapter Three

The morning passed slowly. Maiden looked at the clock; it was only 11. She pulled a face and went upstairs to grab her purse. She'd been cooped up for a few days and was hoping to go out as soon as Vonny turned up to take over the reception duties. Both of their parents were out as well, so she was stuck.

When she came back downstairs, she glanced down the hall that led to the ground-floor rooms. She faltered slightly when she spied Vera Randall having a heated discussion with Reg Varney.

At least it looked heated on his side. She was cool as anything as she brushed her stiff, over-teased hair off her shoulders. Fuchsia lips stretched into a jaded smile as she spoke, and whatever she said sent Reg into a whispered fit. His face was flushed, and he even stomped his foot before stalking to his room and closing himself inside.

In that unguarded moment, Vera's look of sophisticated amusement faded into one of quiet disappointment. She looked rather fragile.

Maiden frowned at the uncomfortable encounter but walked on before she was spotted. She could only imagine why the pair were having a whispered argument, and the last thing she wanted was to get involved.

She went to the desk and sat down again, hopeful of a quiet hour or so to finish her workday. Maiden had agreed to stay until Vonny returned from getting her hair done and had been promised that it wouldn't take all day. She glanced around and, left with no other viable option to while away the time, pulled her library book from the top right drawer.

For a moment she stared down at the cover of perhaps the worst book she'd ever tried to plow through, and she wasn't even halfway in. What had started out as an enthusiastic recommendation from a librarian who had known her since she was in elementary school had now descended into a mind-numbing obligation.

It was a rather torrid and completely frustrating historical novel about a disgraced Scottish nobleman and the buxom young waif that was certain to turn his life around. It had quickly become annoying. The waif in question absorbed ridiculous amounts of insults and general abuse and yet continued to trail after him like a Labrador with low self-esteem.

By now she'd invested enough time to keep persevering through to the end, but her hopes that the idiotic heroine would strangle the creep with his perfectly starched cravat had been dashed. It was the sort of book she hated.

Maiden had barely had a chance to open it and start reading when she heard angry voices approaching.

"Just stop sniffing around our room!" a woman hissed angrily.

"I told you I got lost, that's all." Vera rolled her eyes as she rounded the end of the hallway and took long strides to get away from a furious Emily Varney.

"I wish you would 'get lost'!" Emily snapped, her cheeks flushed and her hands gripping her purse strap as though it were the other woman's throat.

"Hilarious." Vera applauded sarcastically. "Listen sweetie, if you spent more time trying to look half-decent you wouldn't have to swipe your little claws at innocent strangers. If you're worried about your husband's wandering eye, that's hardly my fault."

"'Innocent'?!" Emily repeated incredulously. "You wouldn't know the meaning of the word! You're just another selfish hag that can't keep a man of her own so you try to steal someone else's! I've seen your type before, you're *pathetic*."

Maiden's eyes rounded; she hurried out from behind the counter before a full-blown catfight could erupt. Vera wasn't smiling now; her pale eyes were cold and furious, and her hands were clenched so tightly she was at risk of piercing her palms with her hot pink acrylics. Sharp, nicotine-stained teeth gnashed together in a snarl. Emily looked briefly triumphant, but she took a step back when she saw Vera's face.

"Ladies, please!" Maiden stepped between them and attempted a soothing expression. "I'm sure it's only a misunderstanding, there's no need to argue."

"I understand perfectly," Emily said stiffly, though she seemed relieved she wasn't facing Vera alone now. "This *person* was hanging around our door like a lost dog."

"Don't you call me that!" Vera shrieked and lunged at her.

Maiden was in the way, however, and managed to hold her back. Vera shoved her away and stared daggers at Emily. Maiden heard a few of the doors to neighboring rooms crack open and knew this needed to end immediately. She held up a hand before either of the angry women could speak.

"Enough!" she said firmly and, she hoped, authoritatively. "You are both disturbing the other guests! No one wants their vacation tainted by this sort of spectacle. *Please* settle down now."

"I was looking for the dining room; I want a coffee before lunch," Vera said tightly, trying to regain some dignity. "I only arrived yesterday, and I turned the wrong way, that's all."

"And you got all the way down to our door at the end of the hallway before you figured that out?" Emily folded her arms. "All that bleach you dump on your hair must've soaked in pretty deep."

"Mrs. Varney, please." Maiden frowned at her. "We're all grownups, let's act like it. Are you two actually planning to come to punches right here in the lobby?"

"Of course not." Vera sneered and pretended to study her nails. "Some boring little housewife isn't worth ruining my manicure."

"The dining room is right over there, Ms. Randall," Maiden said sternly as she pointed to the large room beyond the woman's shoulder.

Vera followed her gaze and then gave them both a disdainful look before turning and walking away, the sway of her hips exaggerated in her leopard-print miniskirt and black back-seam stockings.

Maiden gave a silent sigh of relief; she wasn't sure what she would have done if the women had come to blows. Trust Vonny to skip out and leave her to deal with all the drama. She glanced at Emily to find her looking embarrassed; she took a step closer to Maiden and managed an uncomfortable smile.

"I'm sorry about that," she said quietly. "I rarely get that worked up, but that horrible old trout really got under my skin! Imagine chasing after a man who's here celebrating his wedding anniversary! It makes me sick."

"I can understand your frustration, Mrs. Varney." Maiden smiled politely, very aware that she had seen Vera and Reg talking only a few moments before. "Where is your husband, incidentally?"

"In our room, hiding probably." She glanced heavenward. "I can't really blame him, a couple of angry cats going for each other's throats."

"He might've been more helpful considering the nature of the argument." Maiden knew as soon as she said the words that she possibly should've kept the thought to herself.

"Excuse me?" Emily's eyebrows rose sharply.

"I'm sorry," she quickly placated, clasping her hands daintily before her. "It's just very difficult to see you so upset, and knowing he was nearby but didn't help, well...it's not for me to say."

Emily looked embarrassed again, perhaps because she secretly agreed with her. She soon recovered, and her expression mellowed.

"Let's forget the whole nasty business, okay?" she said pleasantly enough and gave her arm a little squeeze. "Thank you for stepping in to help though, I do appreciate it."

Maiden smiled as the woman turned and escaped back down the hallway.

Well over an hour later, Vonny breezed in. Her long brown hair, now blown out straight and shiny, boasted a few dozen golden blonde highlights. She removed her sunglasses with a dramatic flourish and posed before the desk.

"What do you think?" She fluttered her eyelashes.

"I think you took more than two hours," Maiden replied, but then smiled fondly at her sister. "You look good though."

"I can't help it!" Vonny grinned and came around the long desk to join her. "Thanks for covering Mae, I'd have gotten my nails done too, but I thought that would be pushing it."

"The way today's gone, it certainly would've been," she said and stood, gesturing towards the chair. "It's all yours."

"Well hold up." Von dropped her leather jacket on the coat rack and sat down. "What happened?"

"Oh, not much. Vera Randall and Emily Varney almost fought to the death over Emily's husband, who was conveniently nowhere to be found," Maiden sighed as she draped her hands on her hips. "And I had the joy of meeting the creepiest man that's ever stayed here. Who's Mr. Creevey anyway?"

"Oh, that guy." Von pulled a dour face. "He pushed his way in last night and acted like a total jerk. He kept threatening to say all sorts of nasty things about the inn if I didn't give him a room."

"That sounds like his favorite threat." Maiden frowned. "I'm surprised you let him bully you like that."

"Well, it was pretty cold outside," she said with unusual patience, and then smirked. "But I did make him pay for two nights in advance."

"Yeah well, the joke might be on us. I caught him trying to get into the computer this morning."

"What?!" Vonny sat up straighter and looked at the screen as if expecting it to be smashed through. "That stupid creep! Did you kick him out?"

"No, he skulked out quick; after I called his bluff about the bad reviews and threatened to call the police," she replied and gave her a look. "Why didn't you get any ID from him? There's nothing entered in the system. You know that's a massive no-no."

"I was on my own and he was weirding me out," Von admitted, hugging herself. "I just wanted to lock up and get into the apartment as fast as I could."

"You could've stalled him and called us." Maiden pointed to the ceiling and the family's apartment that sat above it.

"Well, I didn't, okay?" Von bristled.

"Fine, forget it." Maiden kept her tone mild, knowing that pushing her further wouldn't achieve anything. "Did you have lunch while you were out?"

"No, I didn't want to take that long," she said, still sounding churlish.

"Well, let's go eat then, Kylie's menu sounded awesome." She turned and led the way, assuming Von would follow at some point.

She loved her sister, but she could be prickly. According to the whispered conversations she had overheard between her mother and her aunt, they believed that was a big reason Von had never had a serious boyfriend.

Vonny was an inch or two taller than her and more fashionably slender. Maiden herself was on the curvy side, and it didn't always go unnoticed. She'd been asked out for the first time when she was barely old enough to be in high school. Maiden had found the encounter awkward and embarrassing, especially when the guy realized he was on the verge of breaking the law.

Vonny had a bolder personality and wouldn't put up with anyone that didn't like and respect her. Maiden admired that example and tried to follow it, but had still stumbled into a couple of disappointing relationships. She had yet to meet anyone who both held her interest and treated her well.

Von claimed similar reasons for continuing single despite turning twenty-eight a month ago. But it was a hard sell to their mother, who had been married at nineteen and believed that enough mascara and red lipstick could make any dream come true.

Maiden thought her mother's notions were old-fashioned and quite silly. She and Vonny weren't about to be rushed into anything; they would each date when they found someone they liked. It was occasionally lonely, but quite straightforward.

In any case, she was certain that Vonny could've been with a few different guys by now if she'd really wanted to. The trouble was that she had already found the guy she wanted, but he hadn't returned the interest. Not yet, at least.

Von could be a lot sweeter than she sometimes let on, but Maiden wondered if her sharp tongue scared people off. She'd certainly been challenging to grow up with.

Vonny had gone through a long phase in their teens when she didn't want Maiden around her, or her friends. That rejection had been painful, but Maiden also knew her sister would come roaring in like a lioness if anyone else was that mean to her. And fortunately, it was all ancient history now.

Maiden entered the dining room and studied the area out of habit. Her family had owned the Harlow House Inn since she was in her early teens; she was used to taking an active interest in the day to day running of the place. Her eyes flitted over the dozen or so tables, almost half of which were occupied by guests eating lunch.

From what she could see, Kylie's soup and sandwiches were a hit. That was a relief since it was only the quality of the food and Maiden's constant efforts to mollify her mother that kept the bashful chef in a job.

Her eyes quickly found Reg and Emily Varney sitting at a table near the far wall. Before she could turn away, Emily looked up and caught her eye. She looked as uncomfortable as Maiden felt, but dredged up a kind smile. Maiden returned the silent acknowledgment and glanced away. She sank into a chair at the nearest table, which also happened to be closest to the door.

As she waited for Vonny to join her, she picked up a discarded magazine and pretended to thumb through it while subtly looking over the rest of the room. Three of the tables were taken up by young families, who were chatting happily; the only other occupied table was being used by Robert Gilford. He was sipping coffee and reading a newspaper. The empty plate that sat beside him was evidence that he had enjoyed his midday meal as well.

Maiden gave a satisfied nod and glanced at the doorway when she saw a flash of movement from the corner of her eye. Expecting Vonny, she held back a startled gasp when Vera Randall strolled in like she were treading a catwalk. Sort of.

Her bright yellow hair was now pinned up in a French twist, though her bangs were so feathered they looked like a poodle's tail. More eye-catching was her skin-tight pink mini-dress. Cut so low that her darkly tanned cleavage threatened to spill over with the first deep breath and stopping so high on her long, slender legs that the slightest misstep would spell disaster.

She walked with confidence—completely assured that every man in the room was watching—straight to the Varney's table. The ensuing discussion was indiscreetly loud. Maiden tried to hide her interest behind her magazine as she listened to every word.

"Well, well, it's the *happy* couple." Vera smirked as she perched on the edge of a chair and leaned closer, displaying her cleavage boldly. "Are you feeling any better with the poor man in your sights, dearie?"

"Still wobbling around like mutton dressed as lamb, I see," Emily retorted. "Are you drunk as well this time? A sober woman certainly wouldn't be seen dead in that getup. Not once she reaches *your* sort of age."

Vera glared and flicked her gaze over Emily in disgust. Maiden also studied her; the two women were quite a contrast. While Vera's favored style was obvious, Emily Varney seemed almost prudish by comparison. Every time Maiden had seen the woman, she was wearing loose, floral-printed dresses with very high collars. The only thing that broke up the monotony of the wallpaper-like patterns was a thin brown belt cinched around her waist.

"At least I don't dress like a Victorian schoolteacher," Vera bit back with a nasty smile. "No wonder you're so worried about old Reg looking elsewhere."

"That's *Mr. Varney* to tramps like you!" Emily started to stand when Reg grasped her arm and held her in place. He shifted his coldly irate eyes to Vera.

"You are being deliberately rude, Ms. Randall," he muttered. "Please go somewhere else!"

"Oh really?" Vera looked shocked and angry. "Well, suppose I want to stay so we can chat a bit more? I'm sure we'd all find it interesting!"

Reg shot to his feet. His face was thunderous, and his hands were curled into fists.

"Get out of here," he said through clenched teeth.

Vera flinched almost imperceptibly and stood. As she took a few steps back, she glanced around at the other patrons; most of them looked away, but they had all seen everything. Vera's long legs faltered; she quickly recovered, but her eyes now held a hint of desperation.

Her gaze rested on Robert; he smiled benignly before turning in his chair until he was facing away from her as much as possible. Anger and self-pity showed briefly in her countenance, but she rolled her shoulders back and lifted her chin high as she turned to walk away.

Maiden saw Emily Varney smiling as the brazen woman went. Vonny finally arrived, again missing the drama between the squabbling pair, and sat across the table from her sister. She started to speak, but Maiden put a discreet finger to her lips and mouthed the words, *wait a minute.* Von gave her a look but followed her gaze.

Vera had stopped at the coffee station, probably to avoid looking as if someone had chased her off, and now she headed out clutching a travel cup, her bright pink lips pursed irately.

As she'd almost reached the doorway, Mr. Creevey appeared and stood surveying the room. He still looked like some sort of thug, but perhaps her opinion was biased by their earlier discussion. His eyes were cold and shifty, but became very interested when they landed on Vera and took in the view.

"Oh yuck!" Vonny grimaced, but fortunately kept her voice low.

Vera was so bolstered by his admiring stare that she seemed inclined to ignore his sweat-stained clothes and the scruffy stubble that darkened his angular jaw. She gave him a friendly smile that he returned as he approached.

He ran a hand over his hair, which was long on top and slicked back from his forehead but trimmed short on the sides. Maiden and Vonny's table was near enough, and they both listened to every word as they engaged in a bit of crass flirtation.

After some suggestive comments from each, the conversation hit a sour note when Mr. Creevey edged closer. He was leering openly as he mentioned he had cash on him and asked how much it would take. Maiden barely swallowed a gasp and saw Von clap a hand over her mouth and stare at them with rounded eyes.

Oh, no way! Maiden groaned internally.

The look of mortification on Vera's face was painful to see, and Maiden couldn't help feeling a bit upset for her. Vera gripped her coffee in a shaking hand and hissed a scathing refusal. She looked as though she wanted to spit on him, but just pushed past and stormed out. Maiden turned to watch her go and saw her duck into the library. She and Von both peeked subtly at Mr. Creevey.

He had also watched Vera's retreat with a quietly surprised expression, but then he shrugged and turned back to the room. He stilled and his smile grew. Maiden tried to see what he was looking at but saw only Reg Varney sitting red-faced and silent while Emily muttered something to him.

Mr. Creevey walked over and sat at one of the tables on the opposite side of the room. He settled in and disappeared nonchalantly behind a newspaper.

"Order for us, will you?" Maiden murmured as she stood. "I'm going to check on Vera."

"You do like looking for trouble," Vonny said dryly as Maiden rushed out.

Chapter Four

Maiden took a few steps into the darkened room. It was mostly used as a library. Bookshelves lined the walls, and there were plenty of places to sit and read, but there was also enough room to accommodate a large desk, a few potted palms, and a grandfather clock that had been in her father's family for generations.

Skimming her eyes over the elegantly masculine decor, the tufted leather couches and dark wood wainscoting, Maiden found Vera standing with her back to the door and her head bowed. She bit her lip and wondered if she ought to interrupt after all; the poor woman was obviously trying to stop herself from crying.

The decision was made for her when Vera tensed and looked back at her sharply. Maiden blinked in surprise when the other woman glowered hatefully.

"Um..." She didn't know what to say in the face of such obvious dislike. "I just wanted to make sure you were all right."

Vera looked dismayed and quickly glanced away. Maiden shifted uncomfortably towards the door again, but Vera rallied. She stood straighter and squared her bony shoulders.

"I'm fine," she said with a twist of cynical amusement. "I'm no stranger to being admired. *Obviously*."

"Okay," Maiden said slowly. "Well, that's good then."

"It is!" Vera rounded on her and braced a fist on her hip. "I'll bet you think you've got it all, don't you? The prettiest little peach on the tree. Well, let me tell you a few hard truths, honey! I happen to be *Vera Randall*, I've stolen men from fashion models, I've seduced ski instructors that didn't speak a word of English, I've broken up engagements that were years in the making!"

Maiden stared at her. Vera held her head high as if she'd just claimed to have climbed Everest or won an Academy Award. Even in the darkened room, her jaded and haughty expression made her look predatory and harsh. Maiden couldn't believe this complete stranger was trying to drag her into some bizarre, imaginary contest.

"I'm happy to say I haven't done any of those things," she said simply. "But how nice that you're feeling so pleased with yourself."

She wondered if she sounded patronizing; it wasn't entirely unintentional, but she supposed it was impolite. Vera clearly agreed. Her face went red, and she slammed her coffee down on the desk behind her.

"I'm *very* pleased with myself!" she hissed. "Why wouldn't I be? Especially here, in this squalid little hole full of crass bumpkins!"

"You don't seem fond of our lovely town." Maiden put on the special smile she saved for the most difficult guests. "I wonder that you booked four nights here. Business trip perhaps?"

"'Business'," Vera scoffed. "Yes, I suppose my work is my life...but I do sometimes wish...I guess like anyone, I'd like someone to share it with."

That somberly spoken sentiment took Maiden by surprise. For a moment, Vera's hardened exterior faltered, and a glimpse of a tired, lonely woman showed through. It didn't last long, however, and her thickly painted lips curled into a smug smile.

"The trouble is," Vera laughed coldly, "I've really never been good at sharing anything."

"That's...a shame," Maiden said mildly, unsure how she was meant to respond to such a remark; it hadn't exactly been laced with humility.

"No, it isn't!" Vera's eyes narrowed grimly. "I have a great life, a bright career and no shortage of *worthwhile* men. But this town is full of brainless hicks."

"Mm." She folded her arms loosely. "What about Mr. Creevey? I don't think he's from around here and he certainly seemed...interested."

"That pig!" Vera spat. "I've never met anyone so disgusting! How dare he talk to me as if I were a—"

Her tirade was cut short by an involuntary sob. She was so insulted and humiliated that Maiden felt her dislike of the woman waver. When she wasn't boasting and preening, or talking at all, Vera Randall was a rather sad creature.

Maiden had known women like her before. They always thought they were better, prettier, and exempt from the rules that applied to everyone else. Hurting others meant nothing, but their own pain was all-consuming. It was unfair, but they truly believed it, and it was still hard to see someone suffer.

"Did he threaten you, Ms. Randall?" she asked, mostly to show concern rather than pity.

"No." Vera rolled her eyes and dug a crumpled tissue from her tanned cleavage. "Let's just say he thought I was on the menu. In any case, I'm not about to tell all my troubles to a nosy employee...I think I'll eat out tonight, the food here is disgusting."

Maiden felt all the intended offense thrown her way, but rather than rise to the bait, she stepped towards the door.

"Suit yourself, Ms. Randall." She shrugged as she slipped back into the hall.

"I always do!" Vera's petulant reply followed her.

Maiden shook her head as she stalked back to the dining room. She hadn't met anyone as deliberately unpleasant as Vera Randall in a long time, and she hadn't missed the experience.

That evening the Harlows tucked themselves away in their apartment. Dinner was always their best opportunity to catch up and share the details of their day. Kylie had made tacos for the guests, and Gloria succumbed to the temptation of bringing a platter upstairs and having a night off from cooking. The family then sat around the kitchen table and chatted over dessert.

"Have all you want girls. There's plenty." Gloria smiled at her daughters even as she served herself another slice of apple pie.

"Stop trying to fatten me up." Vonny smirked, patting her flat stomach.

"Oh please, scrawny little brat." Gloria chuckled. "Trust me sweetie, men like a bit of somethin' to get hold of. Look at your sister!"

Maiden, who had been minding her own business, looked up to find her mother pointing a long, peach-colored nail in her direction. She then turned to her equally startled but far more amused sister and gestured towards her half-eaten pie.

"Here, you need this more than I do, apparently," she said. Vonny sniggered and waved it away.

"Don't start that sort of talk again, Gloria." Alfie gave her a stern look. "I won't have my beautiful daughters driven to eating disorders by your thoughtless comparisons."

"Eating disorders?" she exclaimed and flung a hand towards Vonny. "I'm tryin' to *get* her to eat!"

"Maybe if you didn't try to force grits down her throat every morning, she'd have more of an appetite," he replied dryly.

"There ain't nothin' wrong with grits, mister!" she retorted, her accent deepening with cultural outrage. "They made me the woman I am today!"

"So how was your afternoon, Vonny?" Maiden asked loudly, more than ready to change the subject.

"Easy. I don't know what you do to stir up all the drama. My shift was fine." Von shrugged, but then smiled wryly. "But I suppose it helped that the delightful Ms. Randall stayed out for the rest of the day. The last time I saw her she stormed towards the stairs with a snooty look and a couple of bottles of wine."

"Oh dear." Gloria glanced heavenward. "I hope she won't get drunk and make a scene."

"I hope she'll get bored and behave herself. For the novelty if nothing else," Von replied with a huff.

"What's she done?" Alfie asked, relieved that the conversation had diverted from discussions about his daughters' weight.

"For a start, she and Mrs. Varney almost had a fistfight right in the foyer." Maiden shook her head. "It was awful. I get the impression that old Vera's a bit of a man eater."

"Who told you that?" Alfie pulled a face.

"*She* did!" Maiden said a tad defensively.

"Sorry, precious," Alfie replied with a fond smile.

"Well, did anyone complain?" Gloria looked annoyed. "I won't have our other guests disturbed by that skinny trollop."

"I thought *I* was the skinny trollop?" Vonny asked, ever ready to be needlessly difficult.

"You're not the only star in the sky, little girl." Gloria gave her a patient look and turned back to Maiden expectantly.

"I broke it up pretty quick. Ms. Randall seems to have formed an interest in Mr. Varney, which his wife understandably took exception to," she explained with a shrug. "As long as they avoid each other it should be okay...hopefully."

"I don't know what brought her here anyway." Vonny pulled a face. "She complains about everything. Nothing and no one seem to be good enough for her."

"Yes, she doesn't seem to think well of anyone other than herself." Maiden poked at a bit of apple with her fork. "And Reg Varney for whatever reason...She certainly hates me."

"Jealous." Gloria shrugged, casually summing up the woman's feelings and motives despite never having met her.

Maiden smiled a little, but said nothing. Her mother was biased, but the earlier discussion with Vera suggested she might be at least partially right this time. It didn't matter. Maiden had been hated by a lot of the other girls throughout high school, not that she'd ever done a thing to any of them; she was used to being unpopular.

"Don't let her bother you, dear." Alfie scowled protectively at his youngest. "If she starts being rude just tell me; I'll ask her to leave."

"*I'll* throw her out so fast she'll bounce off the sidewalk!" Gloria fisted her pudgy hand around her fork and took an angry bite.

"I doubt that'll be necessary." Maiden smiled at her parents and resumed eating. "But thank you for your loyalty."

CHAPTER FIVE

T he following morning, after another night of wild weather, Maiden was up early. She rarely slept in, and on the few occasions that she did, she felt as though she had wasted the day. On the other hand, Vonny would still be in bed, thoroughly unconscious, and it would be another half hour before Gloria had consumed enough coffee to apply the day's makeup and face the world.

Maiden went downstairs and unlocked the front door. She looked around the foyer, pleased to see that everything was tidy and no water had seeped under the door and soaked the rug during last night's storm.

She walked around the reception desk and switched on the computer. As it flickered to life, she glanced over at the row of hooks that held the keys to the rooms.

They were large, old-fashioned keys that looked as though they'd open a secret door in an ancient castle. While a far cry from the modern swipe cards that newer hotels used, they fit the whimsical, romantic feel of Harlow House.

She quirked a brow when she saw the key to room 6 sitting on its hook. Mr. Creevey was in room 6. Maiden smiled; she knew he was due to check out today and hadn't been keen to see him off. It appeared that it wouldn't be necessary now.

Most guests who left outside of reception hours dropped their keys in the box on the desk that was labeled for that purpose; she briefly wondered if Mr. Creevey knew how to read before chiding herself for being ungenerous.

The important thing was that the man was gone, and the room was free in plenty of time for the family that had booked it a few weeks ago. She was entering some notes under their booking when she heard the office door open. She glanced up and smiled as Billie walked in, shivering from the crisp morning air.

"What a storm last night! I thought our roof might blow off!" She pretended her teeth were chattering as she slipped out of her light jacket. "And I swear it feels like winter out there already."

"We have a few months to go yet." Maiden laughed and then nodded towards the stairs. "It looks like room 6 is free. After it's cleaned we'll need to pull out a few roll-away beds, the next booking is a family of four. They aren't due for another couple of days, but we may as well be ready. I can give you a hand."

"All right, I'll just put my things away and go have a look." She nodded as she slipped behind the desk and into the office.

Maiden was still writing up her notes as Billie walked out, clutching a long feather duster and tying her crisp white apron around her waist, and headed up to the second floor. A few minutes later Maiden glanced over when Billie returned, looking sheepish.

"Uh, Maiden?" She winced. "Can you come and help me?"

"Yeah, what is it?" Maiden asked, swiveling the chair to face her.

"The guy in room 6." Billie wrinkled her nose. "He's passed out. I don't deal with drunk guys, not on my own."

"What?" Maiden blinked. "He's still here? But his key's on the hook."

"Yeah well," Billie shrugged, "his face is on the floor."

"Is he okay?" Maiden's eyes widened as she pushed to her feet. "Did you try to wake him?"

"I jabbed him a few times, but he didn't budge." She held up her duster to show the slight bend the tip had sustained. "I think he's out cold. Should we leave him for a bit?"

"No!" Maiden almost laughed as she walked past and headed upstairs.

She led the way down the hallway to room 6; Billie had left the door open. Maiden paused in the doorway and peered inside.

As promised, Mr. Creevey was lying face down on the floor just inside the room. Maiden scowled; his arms were at his sides, and he was incredibly still.

Billie stood beside her and grimaced as she looked at the prone form.

"Kinda weird," she offered.

"He doesn't look...right," Maiden said quietly as she crept through the door and tried to see Mr. Creevey's face. "Should we try to push him onto his back? It can't be easy for him to breathe like that."

"You do it, I'll keep watch. It could be a trick." Billie did a few shallow squats to warm up. "If he grabs you, I'll start kicking him."

"Thanks." Maiden swallowed as she knelt at his side. "Mr. Creevey? Are you all right?"

He didn't move, and he didn't utter a sound. Maiden glanced at Billie, who was now scowling anxiously.

"Maybe he's not okay." Billie risked edging closer.

Maiden turned back to Mr. Creevey and braced her hands against his side. She pushed as hard as she could, but he was heavier than she had expected. She took a deep breath and tried again. When she finally managed to roll him onto his back, she gasped loudly and quickly pulled her hands away. His eyes were wide open, and there was a bloody gash on his left temple.

Billie let out a terrified scream.

"He's dead! I can't believe you touched a dead body! That's so gross!" she shrieked, and then screamed again when she looked at her duster as if it had turned into a severed limb and flung it into the hallway. "*Ew!* I poked him!"

"Calm down!" Maiden said unsteadily, unable to look away from Mr. Creevey's lifeless eyes. "Go call the police."

They heard rapid footsteps running down the hall a moment before Robert Gilford appeared in the doorway.

"I heard shouting," he said by way of explanation. His hair was mussed from sleep, and his robe was tied crookedly. He looked at the body and sucked in a sharp breath. "Oh hell, who's that?"

"Jim Creevey," Maiden replied numbly. "He was staying in this room."

"Okay," Robert's eyes were wide and horrified. "W-what happened?"

"I don't know. We found him like this," Maiden said shakily as she pushed to her feet and staggered back a few steps. "Billie, the police. *Please!*"

Billie nodded jerkily, but her gaze remained fixed on the corpse in macabre fascination. Maiden looked over and scowled when she saw that she still hadn't moved.

"Hurry up, Billie!" she exclaimed. "We don't know what happened here!"

Billie started at that and obligingly ran past Robert and scampered down the hall. He stepped closer and gently tapped Maiden's shoulder. She glanced over at him with wide, frightened eyes.

"Maybe step away a bit more," he said kindly, getting a handle on his own distress now that he could focus on hers. "You look shaky."

"I might throw up," she admitted, pressing a hand to her stomach.

"Probably best not to do that on the body," he pointed out pragmatically. Maiden woke from her petrified shock enough to slide him a speaking look.

"Thank you, Mr. Gilford." She spoke in a deliberately steadier tone. "I'm sorry you had to walk into this. It's fine, everything's under control. Sort of."

"Yikes. 'A' for effort, Maiden." He almost smiled and shook his head at her. "Look, I really feel like I should put pants on. I'll go get dressed, please be careful and don't throw up in here."

"I won't." She shuddered and folded her arms. "But you should probably wait in your room until the police get here." He nodded and slipped out.

Maiden watched him go and then turned back to Mr. Creevey. She'd never seen a dead body before; even at her grandfather's funeral she had avoided the casket. She had an incredibly vivid and sensitive memory; she always had, and she knew that if she looked at him in death, it would be the only way she'd ever remember him.

This was different, of course; she hadn't even liked Mr. Creevey, but she certainly didn't wish any ill on him.

Maiden's initial shock and the resulting nausea were starting to ebb. She looked him over more carefully, searching for anything out of place apart from his injury, but nothing stood out. She then slid her gaze around the room and tried to figure out what had happened to him.

On the heels of the shock came the worry, worry that something in one of their rooms might be unsafe. She looked at the spot where Mr. Creevey lay motionless; there was nothing nearby that he could have hit his head on. The desk on the other side of the room looked as though it could be the most likely culprit. She edged closer to it.

He could have struck his head and staggered across the room, but there was no trace of blood on the pale wood. Her gaze strayed to the few other pieces of furniture; they looked undisturbed as well.

As she studied his position, she realized it was very unlikely that he'd fallen and hit his head anyway. He was lying only a step or two inside the door, and looked to have fallen forward into the room. It was all so bizarre...and sinister.

Maiden bit her lower lip and hugged her waist; she hoped the police would get there soon.

Gloria and Alfie had also heard Billie's screams and eventually wandered out in their pajamas to see the source of the commotion. Maiden had managed to convince them to stay out of the room and go get dressed.

Apparently 'getting dressed' meant stopping to make a pot of coffee because she hadn't seen them since. She reminded herself that it hadn't truly been all that long, and her parents didn't move fast at the best of times, but she was tired of being alone in her grim vigil.

Several minutes that felt like the gaping jaws of eternity passed before Maiden heard heavy footsteps on the stairs. By this time, she had stationed herself outside in the hallway where she could monitor the door without having to stare at the body.

Two police officers approached with a pale and fidgety Billie trailing behind them. They both appeared to be in their mid-twenties, perhaps only a few years younger than her. The men looked her over quietly when they reached her side and then peered into the room.

Maiden glanced from Mr. Creevey's corpse back to the cops when she heard them gasp loudly; it wasn't a promising start. Their expressions made it clear that they hadn't believed Billie's claims of a suspicious death. They both looked shocked.

As they entered the room and took a closer look at the body, with its glaring wound and staring eyes, the officers snapped into action. One of them pulled out a phone and started frantically dialing while the other ushered her out into the hallway and shut the door behind them.

"Okay." He swallowed hard and looked them both over more carefully. "Is everyone else safe? You're both all right?"

"Yeah, I think so." Maiden rubbed her arms and let out a shaky breath.

"Good...good." He looked like he was trying to remember what he was supposed to do now. "Is there someplace quiet where we can talk? I need you to tell me exactly what happened and how you found the victim."

"Oh, of course." Maiden gestured towards the door of their apartment. "Um, come through here."

Maiden opened the door and led the way inside. She and Billie sat at the kitchen table, leaving room for the young officer to sit between them. She studied him for a moment while he settled himself and pulled out a notebook, jotting a few things at the top of the page.

His pale blonde hair was almost white and cut very short. His lean, angular features looked like they were of Scandinavian descent. He was nice-looking but clearly overwhelmed. It didn't instill confidence.

When he turned to her, she met his gaze and waited. And waited. Finally, she lifted her dark brows a fraction and shook her head a little.

"Are you okay, officer?" she asked. He was kind of staring, and it was getting awkward.

"Oh, yes. Sorry." He shut his eyes briefly and cleared his throat; he fixed his attention resolutely on his notepad. "Please describe your movements from when you woke up to when you found the body."

Maiden was thrown off completely for a heartbeat or two. She was uncomfortably sure that the cop had been checking her out, something that couldn't have been weirder or less appropriate at the moment.

She pulled herself together and fumbled through her account. There wasn't much to tell. She'd gotten up and had breakfast, then gone downstairs and found the key on the hook. Everything else had happened so quickly but was so significant; it felt odd that she had so little to say about it.

The officer asked one or two questions and jotted down her responses. He then smiled briefly and shyly and turned to Billie. Maiden sat back a bit, trying to put some polite distance between them. She was way too stressed to deal with any extra complications.

By the time Billie finished her far more dramatic telling of the same meager bits of information, Alfie and Gloria had emerged from their room and hurried to join them.

"All right," Gloria clasped her pudgy hands together and looked at the young officer, "first things first. Do you want some coffee, honey?"

"No, thank you." He started to smile but quickly stopped himself and sat up straighter at the table. "Now then, your names please?"

"Alfred and Gloria Harlow," Alfie said stoically. "Owners of Harlow House Inn. And you are?"

"Um, Officer Jeff Briggs." He blinked and glanced at Maiden. "Sorry, I thought I mentioned that."

"Not to me, but pleased to meet you anyway." Alfie tolerantly waved away any perceived slight.

"Okay. Um, yes." Briggs collected his thoughts and went back to the notepad he'd been scribbling on. "Did either of you see anything unusual leading up to the discovery of the body?"

"We haven't seen the body." Gloria shrugged. "We were both asleep."

"We don't usually go hunting for bodies until after breakfast," Alfie chuckled dryly. "Or at least coffee."

Both Maiden and Officer Briggs gave Alfie an uncertain look; the man folded his hands and glanced away. Maiden knew her father would be startled by the whole business, and he sometimes expressed his nervousness in odd ways. Her only hope was that he'd answer the questions succinctly, but there was little chance of that happening.

"Miss Harlow and Mrs. Lewis have given their version of events," Briggs resumed steadily. He seemed to be getting a better handle on his role with more potential witnesses present. "Please tell me your *exact* movements since you woke up this morning, and don't leave anything out. We'll start with you, Mr. Harlow."

Maiden shut her eyes and tried not to writhe as Alfie described his scant hour of wakefulness in appalling detail. She supposed the officer had asked for an exact description but doubted he'd bargained for the graphic account that washed over them.

"Dad," Maiden murmured patiently when he concluded his tale. "I know he said *movements*, but I think he was after something a little more general."

"He said *exact*!" Alfie protested with a scowl. "And not to leave anything out."

"Good lord, honey." Gloria wrinkled her nose distastefully as she studied her husband. "I thought I heard you get up a few times through the night."

"It was those darn tacos!" he grumbled. "You and your 'theme nights'. Why can't we serve regular food like everyone else?"

"Tacos are hardly exotic these days, Mr. H," Billie pointed out.

"My toilet bowl would beg to differ," he said dryly.

"Dad, for the love of—" Maiden stopped herself mid-sentence and then dared another look at Officer Briggs.

He was watching them all with a slightly bemused expression. He met Maiden's uncertain wince and cleared his throat.

"I'm not sure what to write down, to be honest." He twirled his pen between his fingers. "I certainly don't look forward to typing up my report."

"Well, frankly, I found your question intrusive!" Alfie sniffed. "I *chose* to take the high road and not make an issue of it."

"I've given my statement, can I go now?" Maiden turned to Briggs with a mildly pleading expression.

"Aha, you too!" Alfie pointed at her and smirked in triumph. "I said it was the tacos."

"*Dad*! I didn't mean that!" Maiden glared at him and then stood. "No one is stationed at the desk or answering the phone,

I need to get back to work. That's where I'll be if anyone needs me."

"I'll come too," Billie piped up eagerly as she hopped to her feet.

Maiden and Billie slipped out into the hall. Maiden shut the door and took a few steps away from it. Her mind was reeling and her stomach was in knots; it was a total disaster on top of an enormous problem.

"Well, that won't have helped us," Maiden muttered under her breath, and then stopped and turned to face Billie. "Tell me the truth, is there any chance at all that my father hasn't come across as a nut?"

"What do you mean?" Billie shook her head mildly. "I thought he sounded all right."

Maiden just stared at her for a moment before turning and starting back down the hallway. "Never mind, it's fine."

As they headed downstairs, they heard more voices coming from the end of the hall. Maiden glanced back and saw three more officers, two in uniform and one in plain clothes. She caught only the briefest glimpse as they walked into Mr. Creevey's room and shut the door firmly behind them. She sighed and started trying to come up with an acceptable explanation for the other guests for why the Harlow House Inn was suddenly crawling with cops.

Chapter Six

Captain David McAlister stood in the middle of the crime scene and looked around. He'd been in his office for about half an hour when the call came through about a body being found at a local inn. His receptionist, Nancy, a quiet but very watchful and intelligent person, passed the message along somewhat dubiously.

When she informed him that the caller was hard to understand and borderline hysterical, he sent a couple of officers over to take a look. He'd been expecting an accident or natural causes. That wasn't the case, unfortunately.

So, he now found himself standing in a room at the Harlow House Inn, dealing with a homicide. He'd been in town less than a month, and this was not the welcome he'd been hoping for.

He studied the walls, which were painted a dark shade of cream, and some prints of country landscapes hanging in vague patterns across them. It was simply but nicely furnished with only a bed with a square table on either side, a desk with a matching chair, and a small TV sitting on a tall but narrow cabinet.

There was a window over the bed and on the far wall a glass door that appeared to lead out onto a balcony. Overall, it had a warm, inviting atmosphere. Until you noticed the guy on the floor with his head bashed in.

David sighed as he looked the body over once more. He had already sent a few officers to question everyone who was onsite. The forensics team hadn't arrived yet, and most of the guests were purportedly still in their rooms.

In his previous assignment, he would have walked into a similar scene on a daily basis. But judging from the undercurrent of excitement he noticed in the younger officers; this was big news around here. That would doubtless lead to gawkers, snoops, and a lot of counterproductive attention, but he couldn't complain.

After almost 10 years of dealing with the worst that a large city had to offer, everything from small-time hoods to drug dealers to heartless killers, he needed a change. When he learned of a position opening up in a small town he'd never heard of, he jumped at it.

Golden Glen, Michigan, was a quaint little tourist trap. Surrounded by apple orchards and vineyards, the town was filled with cafes, gift shops, and wineries. Nor was there any shortage of B&Bs and themed hotels. But Harlow House seemed distinct for its heritage and aspirations towards elegance.

Rumored to be one of the oldest houses in the area, it was on three floors and boasted thirteen guest rooms. Room number 6 was where he now stood, staring down at his first real test as the head of the Golden Glen Police Department.

Investigating a homicide was an unwanted reminder of what he'd come here to escape.

It was done, though, and he needed to sort it out quickly. One thing he knew about small towns: the locals stuck together and regarded outsiders with suspicion. He had a lot to prove.

His attention returned to the body; it was a certain Mr. Creevey, according to the hotel staff. The room was in order; no signs of fighting, nothing looked to be out of place. He'd already checked the balcony door; it was locked from the inside. The cause of death appeared obvious, but he knew better than to make assumptions in this line of work.

The victim's eyes were wide open; David followed his unseeing gaze to the blank ceiling but then scowled when he recalled that the body had been shifted. One of the first officers on the scene told him that the woman who found the victim rolled him onto his back, which explained why the blood that had dried on his temple hadn't dripped back through his hair. The stain on the floor was also a little too far away. Annoying.

He hated it when people touched crime scenes; it added needless complications.

"Captain McAlister?"

He glanced over at the door as it opened and another young officer poked his head inside.

"What's up, Briggs?" he asked.

"I finished interviewing the Harlows." He stepped further in and looked down at his notebook.

"Good," he murmured. "Did they have anything useful to say?"

"Not really, sir. No," he admitted apologetically, as though it was his fault that they saw nothing.

"Great." David rolled his eyes. "Which one found the body?"

"The youngest daughter," Briggs said rather quietly, and let his gaze drift back to his notes. "Maiden."

"'Maiden'?" David gave him a skeptical look. "That's actually her name? Right. And what was she like?"

"Really nice." He started to smile but caught himself and tucked it away. "She was very helpful, and a bit more level-headed than the parents, I'd say."

David nodded as he held his hand out for Briggs' notes and quickly skimmed them. He pulled a face.

"What's this about tacos?" he asked.

"Oh! Not that part, sir!" Briggs reached over and flipped to an earlier page. "Here, these are the notes from Miss Harlow's interview."

"The cleaner found the body...asked her to help...Mr. Gilford came running when he heard screams," David mumbled to himself as he read through the officer's scratchy shorthand. "Where's this Gilford guy?"

"Two doors down, sir, room number 8."

"How many other rooms are occupied on this floor?" he asked as he handed his notepad back.

"Only two at the moment," Briggs dutifully replied. "Rooms 8 and 9."

"All right." David nodded towards the door. "Let's go talk to them."

By the time they'd questioned the other two guests on the floor, the coroner had arrived and was hard at work. David's discussions with the guests were less productive.

Mr. Robert Gilford had gone to bed early and hadn't heard a thing until the first scream, and Ms. Randall in room 9 was so hung over that they couldn't get a sensible sentence out of her. Room 7, which was right next to the crime scene, was unhelpfully vacant.

David was turning to join the coroner back in room 6 when a flash of movement from the corner of his eye got his attention. He noticed that the only door on the left side of the hallway was open a fraction. He walked straight over and opened it wide, nearly hitting a woman who hurried to get out of the way.

Her pale eyes rounded, and she was pressing her lips together nervously, looking as caught as she was. She quickly recovered from her shock, however, and a cool look settled over her features. Her expression was hostile and off-putting.

"Good morning," David said grimly. "Looking for something?"

"No, I wasn't." She shrugged. "I was just looking."

"Were you?" His tone cooled further. "And what makes a police investigation any of your business?"

"The fact that it's happening in my home, maybe?" she replied caustically.

"What's your name?" David asked as he pulled out his notebook and pen.

"Miss Harlow," she muttered crisply.

"What?" His dark eyes snapped back to hers. "Are you the one that found the body?"

"Uh no, sir." Briggs, who'd been hovering in the hall behind him, quickly spoke up. "That's not Maiden Harlow."

"*Vonny* Harlow," she said, folding her arms. "And I haven't seen the body at all."

"So, why were you creeping around in the shadows?" David quirked a brow.

"Because I heard that someone was killed in my home." She spoke as though he were a simpleton. "What would you have done, Inspector?"

"*Captain,*" he replied stonily. "Captain McAlister. Look for that written on the door when you come to my office for further questioning. I'll see you at 1 o'clock this afternoon. Have a lovely morning, Miss Harlow, and stay away from room 6."

Maiden had taken refuge in the office the moment her mother came downstairs. The police systematically questioned all the guests, and as soon as the interviews were done, they invariably called reception demanding to know what was going on.

Gloria, being well-rested and also having been spared the unpleasant experience of finding Mr. Creevey, was happy enough to field the questions and let her daughter find a moment of solitude to collect herself.

It was all too horrible to be real. A murder. There had been an actual murder at their sweet little inn. Maiden had never been so close to a crime of this magnitude, and it was a chilling experience.

As she worked through the shock, however, her mind started exploring the situation more fully. There was a murderer on the loose, and possibly staying in one of their rooms. She thought about the guests that were currently lodging with them and, ironically, the only one she would have guessed to be capable of such a deed was Mr. Creevey himself.

He had been such a shifty, unpleasant man. Why did he have to come to their inn? Why didn't Vonny demand ID and send him scurrying? Why didn't *she* throw him out when she caught him trying to break into their computer?

Maiden shut her eyes and took a steadying breath. It was pointless to look at what they could've done. She needed to focus and think about damage control. The other guests would be unsettled naturally, and she wasn't sure they had grounds to refuse if any of them demanded a refund and left.

She blinked as another thought occurred to her. They probably wouldn't be free to leave, and that presented other problems. Almost every room was booked out for the next several weeks. If the current guests weren't allowed to go, where would the next lot of guests stay?

Maiden rubbed her eyes; they were sore and her head was spinning. So many things were up in the air and beyond their control. She was also quietly waiting to be called in to answer more questions. Officer Briggs hadn't asked her very much; he'd just gotten a quick rundown of what she'd seen.

Although he had been a bit tight-lipped when she described what happened when she found Mr. Creevey lying on the floor. She wasn't sure why; she thought she'd behaved as rationally as could be expected under the circumstances. But then she remembered one of his few questions—*You touched the body?*

He hadn't looked happy when she confirmed that. Maiden chewed at her lip. What else was she supposed to have done? She'd never seen a dead body and hadn't noticed the bloodstain on the rug until she had pushed him over onto his back. She certainly hadn't been expecting to find him murdered.

She was shaking her head and grumbling to herself when the office door opened and Vonny slipped inside. She looked pale and anxious. It occurred to Maiden that her sister had slept through most of the morning's drama; she wasn't sure how much she knew.

"You've heard about Mr. Creevey then?" Maiden asked gently as Von came and sat in the chair opposite her.

"Uh, yeah." She rubbed her slender arms. "A bit."

"It's pretty awful," Maiden said solemnly. "I didn't honestly like him but...yeah, it's bad."

"Mm," Vonny grunted and stared down at the table.

"What's up?" she asked carefully; even under the circumstances, Von was a little too subdued.

After a self-conscious moment, Vonny finally, and rather quietly, told her about getting caught trying to eavesdrop. And by the new captain of the police department, no less.

"Oh, that's..." Maiden paused and tried to come up with a tactful way to proceed. "Did you explain to him that you hadn't been aware of much of the situation and were worried when you saw all the police officers around?"

"I...yeah, basically." She wouldn't look up and absently picked at her cuticles. "I didn't say it quite like that though. I guess I should've."

Maiden squeezed her eyes shut but withheld a groan of frustration. She could easily guess how Vonny responded to being caught and told to explain her behavior. Not for the first time she wished she could shake her sister and tell her she made things so much harder for herself when she was aggressive.

"Well, that's unfortunate," was all she ventured aloud.

"To put it mildly." Von pulled a face. "I was told to report to the new cop's office at 1 pm today."

"Why?" Maiden felt her stomach sink.

"Because he's a suspicious jerk with nothing better to do!" She folded her arms and sat back in a sulky posture.

"Von," Maiden said in a warning tone that her sister bristled at. She ignored her reaction and pressed on. "You have to calm it down this time. This is no joke; a man was murdered here and we don't know why or who did it. None of us can afford to be hostile towards the police. *Please!*"

"I know, I know," Von relented, but still wouldn't meet her eye. "I'll be more careful."

Maiden looked at the glossy top of her older sister's head. Von's big mouth had gotten her into trouble more than once, but never with the police before. She could tell she was scared this time, but she was sickeningly sure that Vonny would still make a mess of it.

A heavy silence stretched between them. They both started and glanced at the door when it eased open a fraction. Officer Briggs looked inside and smiled faintly when he saw Maiden.

"Hi again, Miss Harlow," he said nicely. "Captain McAlister has asked that you come to the police station around 2 o'clock today. Just for a little more clarification around the events of this morning; it's nothing to worry about."

"Of course, Officer Briggs," she replied with a small nod. "I'll be there."

"Thank you, have a good day, Miss Harlow." He was at least subtle as he looked her over, but his eyes sobered uncomfortably when they flitted to Vonny. "And you too, Miss Harlow. We'll see *you* at 1 o'clock. Bye for now."

CHAPTER SEVEN

David had just finished eating lunch and was sitting at his desk looking over the coroner's notes. It was a large office; the largest he'd ever had. The station in general was a decent size, but it was old and needed refurbishing. Of course, that sort of frivolity was rarely accommodated in small-town budgets.

It didn't bother him; everything worked and served its purpose. His office was located in the rightmost corner of the building and was at least twice as big as the one he'd had in Stanton. He also had a large window that faced the street, another luxury that made the age of the place easy to ignore.

His desk sat on the side wall, giving him a view out the window to his left while also allowing him to see the door and a glimpse of the hallway to his right.

Across the hall and down a bit was the large communal office space where several of the officers did their paperwork. He sometimes left his door open, which allowed him a candid insight into the discussions of the officers in his charge. He'd already heard snatches of a few interesting conversations over the last few weeks.

The coroner, Doctor Jenkins, served a few of the surrounding towns but had an office in their station. He was therefore able to have his notes written and hand-delivered along with a bit of additional detail. It was handy, particularly now that they were dealing with a murder.

Jenkins' preliminary findings confirmed that Mr. Creevey had died from a blow to the head, likely between 1 and 2 am.

David was typing this into his report when he heard a rap on the door. He glanced at the clock on the wall and smiled; at least the little sneak was punctual.

"Come in," he said impassively and went back to his typing.

Vonny Harlow slipped inside and looked uneasily around the room. She had changed into a sunny yellow dress that seemed to clash with her cranky expression. She was holding a small brown purse so tightly that her knuckles were white.

"Please have a seat, Miss Harlow." He pointed to the chairs in front of his desk and kept typing.

Vonny looked at the hard wooden chairs for a moment before walking over and dropping into the one nearest the door. Her knees bounced up and down nervously, and her death-grip on her purse tightened.

A show of nerves wasn't unexpected under the circumstances, but he thought her a little too anxious, unless she had reason to be worried.

He finally sat back and met her gaze; she held it for a moment but then pretended to look around the room again. He'd guess her to be in her mid-to-late twenties, tall, attractive, but hostile and emotionally driven.

"Thank you for coming in, Miss Harlow," he said evenly, trying to put her at ease a bit in hopes she'd be more helpful. "Is Vonny short for Yvonne?"

"Yeah." She took a deep breath in an obvious attempt to relax. "It was my grandmother's name."

"Very nice." He typed a few more lines.

Her eyes settled on the door she had left open when voices carried down the hallway. He ignored it but kept watching her from the corner of his eye as she tried to see who was coming. One voice rose above the rest as it drew closer; when Vonny heard it, she made a face of utter disgust and slumped back in her chair.

David found her reaction curious and looked over when the door was pushed wide and two officers walked inside. It was Sergeant Ramirez, one of the more experienced and competent individuals he'd encountered there, and Greg Smith. Officer Smith was in his late twenties, a few pounds overweight and eager to impress his new commanding officer.

David didn't mind the slightly younger man. His buzzed blonde hair, wide-set blue eyes, and heavy smattering of freckles made him look like a classic hayseed, but he paid attention and did what he was told.

Today, his usual attentive countenance darkened when he and Vonny Harlow looked at each other. Smith's lip curled in distaste, and Vonny glared at him.

"Well, well, it's little Greg Smith." She folded her arms across her chest. "We're all safe now that the ace is on the case."

"Ugh! It's *you*," came Officer Smith's disdainful reply as he glanced at Ramirez. "You said 'Miss Harlow' is here, you didn't tell me it was only Vonny."

"He should have told you that a witness is here for questioning," David pointed out. "It's not for you to worry about who it is, this isn't a social event."

"Yes, sir." Officer Smith all but gulped as he stood straighter. "I'm sorry, sir."

"Wowzah," Vonny chuckled and turned to David with more interest. "That's a good trick. I wish I could shut him up so easily."

"Miss Harlow." David's eyes narrowed minutely at the abrasive woman. "You aren't here to offer a running commentary on my officers, you're here to account for your own actions. And you may as well get started. Where were you last night from 8 pm to 5 am?"

"Nice." She pulled a face, but then settled back in her chair to think. "I helped clear the dining room after dinner and then I was in the kitchen until, oh…8:30 maybe."

"'Maybe'?" he pressed.

"Yes, Captain." She gave him a look. "Had I known Mr. Creevey was going to be cracked on the skull I would've synchronized watches or something."

"Go on." He refused to be goaded.

"I went up to the apartment and hung out with Dad for about an hour after that." She shrugged. "Then I went to bed."

"Alone?" he asked.

"Yeah." She glared at him.

"So, no one saw you until the following morning?" David asked as he flipped through his notepad.

"Not unless that peeping tom is lurking around again." She smirked.

"He'd be after Maiden, not you," Greg sniggered just loud enough to be heard.

Vonny's smile shriveled.

"That's not helpful, Officer Smith," David sighed, feeling more like a referee than a policeman at the moment.

The young officer paled and gave Vonny a look as he clamped his mouth shut. David shook his head as he went back to his notes. He really wasn't used to small towns, and the level of banter was startling under the circumstances. He shifted his attention back to the angry woman sitting in front of him.

"How did you learn about the murder?" he asked politely in an attempt to smooth over Smith's rude quip.

"Mom told me when I woke up," she replied in a more subdued tone.

"You didn't hear anything through the night?"

"No, I'm a heavy sleeper," she said. "And the storm was pretty loud."

"Did you hear the housekeeper scream?"

"I'm not sure. I may have heard something at one point. I looked at the window and saw it was light outside," she rubbed her arms, "but I fell back to sleep."

"Did you know who Mr. Creevey was?" he asked.

"Yeah, I was on shift when he checked in," she admitted. "And I saw him a couple of times after that. I didn't know anything about him though. I didn't even talk to him again."

"Did you observe any strange behavior? Anything to suggest that he might be in danger?"

"No." She scrunched up her nose as she considered that. "He was more like the type to cause the danger."

"Why do you say that?" he quirked a brow.

"He was a jerk," she said plainly. David looked at her until she rolled her eyes. "He was rude and insistent when he checked in. He turned up right at closing time and threatened to badmouth the inn if I didn't give him a room."

"Did he threaten you in any other way?" He watched her expression for any sign of distress.

"No, but he was creepy." She hugged herself and appeared to be sinking into a grim mood.

"Could you be more specific, Von?" Smith grumbled, bracing his fists on his hips. "You called *me* a creep last week!"

"You *are* a creep!" she shot back with another glare.

"Did he ever express any fear of the other guests?" David interrupted loudly and gave Smith a warning look. The younger officer obligingly quieted.

"No," Vonny said flatly.

"Did he threaten the other guests?"

"No."

"Did you notice anyone unusual hanging around the inn yesterday?"

"No."

David watched her for a moment; she didn't budge. He could see she was going to be uncooperative, but he wasn't too concerned at this point.

"All right, Miss Harlow." He kept his tone placid and turned to his keyboard. "We'll record an official statement and then you can go. Just detail your movements from yesterday evening until we spoke this morning."

Vonny rattled off an emotionless recounting of her actions. David asked a few questions, some to get clarification when she was deliberately vague and a few to annoy her when she was rude. After about half an hour of unhelpful back and forth, he'd had enough.

"That's fine, Miss Harlow," he murmured. "You can go now. But don't leave town until I give you the okay."

Vonny pushed to her feet, gave them all an icy look, and stalked out without another word. David released a silent whistle and rubbed the back of his neck.

"Not the friendliest person I've spoken to today, that's for sure," he sighed.

"Don't let Vonny get to you, sir," Smith said mildly. "She's okay, but she can be a jerk sometimes."

"You didn't help the situation." He gave him an irritated look, but then his expression turned curious. "You obviously know her."

"Yeah, I went to school with her and Maiden, but mostly Maiden. Von's a year older than we are." He shrugged. "She's always been a little cranky."

David considered this and then dismissed them with a wave. Smith and Ramirez shuffled back into the office across the hall, but left the door open. He listened as one of them started making a pot of coffee. Before long he saw Briggs walk down the hall and slip inside, and the chatter resumed.

"Hey Briggs," Ramirez said.

"Afternoon," Briggs replied.

"So...what did you think of Harlow House?" Smith asked slyly. "Nice 'scenery', eh?"

"It's a nice place, I guess," Briggs replied. "What's so funny about it?"

"C'mon," Smith sniggered. "You interviewed the Harlows didn't you?"

"Mr. and Mrs. Harlow, yes." Briggs cleared his throat. "I also spoke with the daughters. A bit."

"And?" Smith laughed. "Don't tell me you got that close to a private conversation with Maiden Harlow and blew it? What a waste."

"I was only taking her statement," Briggs said after a telling pause.

"It doesn't matter." Smith's grin was clear in his voice. "You wouldn't have a chance with her anyway."

"What's all the fuss about Maiden Harlow?" Ramirez's tone was bemused.

"Officer Smith is bordering on obsessed with this woman," David called out dryly from across the hall. "I'm not sure why, but I'm confident that it isn't helpful."

Smith went abruptly and awkwardly silent. His desk was the closest to the door, and he was clearly unaware of how far his voice traveled.

"Sorry sir," he said a little louder, though he didn't dare approach the office door. "I really don't have that much of an interest. Just chatter, sir."

"Just stick to your duties, Smith."

David stopped paying attention to the men as their voices dropped self-consciously. He re-read his notes and tried to make sense of them. They had a murder that took place in a hotel full of people, and no one admitted to seeing or hearing anything. But Creevey died in the early hours of the morning, so that wasn't impossible.

The victim had had little by way of identification on him. The only things in his wallet were an expired driver's license, a business card from a Chinese restaurant in town, and several hundred dollars in cash. There was no luggage in the room, not even a change of clothes.

Vonny Harlow hadn't told them anything very useful; she'd also been more hostile than was reasonable. Despite Smith's knowledge of the family, he found her reticence suspicious.

David set his notes aside and eased back in his chair and stared out the window as he let his mind wander over what he knew so far. There wasn't much to go on yet, but he'd ordered a background check on Creevey. Hopefully, that would produce some leads.

Time ticked by. Lost in details and possibilities, he was vaguely aware of someone stepping into the doorway. The dainty click of heels tapped across the floor and stopped before his desk. David looked over slowly; his eyes widened and his breath caught.

No way, he thought to himself. *I must've nodded off; there's no way you can be real.*

One of the most beautiful women he'd ever seen in the flesh was standing right in front of him. She had long dark hair, big green eyes, and a lot of curves arranged so perfectly that he forgot his own name for a heartbeat. She met his gaze and held it without difficulty, even though he knew he was staring; she lifted her fine brows a fraction.

He quickly recovered and sat up, absently straightening his loosened tie. He never used to wear the damn things, but he had wanted to cement the look of professionalism that came with his new role. It was a short-term nuisance.

"Excuse me, are you Captain McAlister?" the lady asked.

It occurred to him that he hadn't spoken yet.

"I am, yes, sorry." He stacked his hands on his desk and smiled. "How can I help you, miss?"

"I was asked to come and see you." She brushed her long hair off her shoulder. "I'm Maiden Harlow."

The scrape of chairs being hastily pushed back across the hall was startling; so was the sight of two men suddenly jammed in the doorway. Maiden recognized one of them immediately.

"Hi, Mae!" Greg smiled broadly and waved to her.

"Hey, Greg, good to see you." She smiled more sedately and then noticed the other man bunched up next to him. "Hello again, Officer Briggs."

"Miss Harlow." Briggs nodded politely.

Maiden stared as Captain McAlister stood up from his desk and calmly shoved the men back into the hallway without a word. She hid a smile as he shut the door behind them. He was quite tall and, as evidenced by the way he cleared the room so easily, very fit. She caught sight of him rolling his eyes and shaking his head at the officers as he turned to her again.

"Miss Harlow." He smiled as though they'd never been interrupted and pointed to the chairs before his desk. "Make yourself comfortable, please."

Maiden lowered into the hard wooden chair directly in front of him and studied this new policeman. He was younger than she'd expected, maybe thirty, and carried himself far more confidently than Briggs had.

Vonny had called her to complain as soon as she'd finished giving her statement. Maiden wasn't at all surprised to hear that it hadn't gone well. Von said little about her own behavior but went on for several minutes telling her that it had been an infuriating and degrading interview. She also criticized the entire police department because Greg had been allowed to be there too.

Greg Smith was another friend from school. She'd always gotten along well with him, but he and Vonny had squabbled from almost the moment they met. The passing years and the shuddering march towards maturity hadn't made much difference, apart from fewer spitballs being fired.

Maiden dismissed the old fight and her sister's irate criticisms. She was at the police station, about to answer questions about a murder; she needed to focus. She looked the captain over subtly.

Von didn't mention that you were this good-looking, Maiden mused and then suppressed an ironic smile. *Nice focus, Maiden, this is gonna go great. But he is actually...wow, yeah. The second cop today to peruse the real estate. You guys must not get out much.*

Having no idea what a person ought to wear when questioned by the police about a murder, Maiden had simply aimed for being dressed nicely. She'd worn her favorite pair of jeans and an electric blue shirt, which the new captain was struggling to drag his eyes from. She actually didn't mind his interest, but did self-consciously tug the neckline of her top a little higher over her full bust.

McAlister seemed to realize what he was doing and scowled to himself as he sat up straighter and forced his gaze back to her face.

"Thank you for turning up, I appreciate your time," McAlister said as he turned his notebook to a blank page and fiddled with his pen. "Your sister seemed quite put out over being questioned."

"That's Von." She shrugged and waved it away. "She can be a bit touchy, but she didn't mean anything by it."

"Are you sure about that?" He drummed the tips of his long fingers on his notepad. "She was a bit rude, to be honest."

Maiden met his richly brown gaze as she considered that. Captain McAlister held eye contact easily, as if gauging her honesty. His jaw was strong, square, and clean-shaven. She glanced at his broad shoulders before reminding herself that she'd seen handsome men before.

"Was she rude to everyone?" she asked carefully. "Or just Greg?"

The briefest smile escaped into view before he tucked it away under a more impassive expression. He turned his pen in his hands and studied her expression; she hoped she looked calm.

"I won't say she saved her venom for him exclusively," McAlister allowed. "But he certainly caught the brunt of it."

"That's pretty normal for them and always has been," she said with a shrug. "I wouldn't pay too much attention to it."

"I'll decide what I pay attention to, Miss Harlow." His eyes narrowed a fraction.

Maiden sat taller at his stern tone. *Uh-oh. I hope I don't owe you an apology, Von.*

"Whatever you say, Captain McAlister." She crossed her legs and rested her hands on her knee. "I'm sure you're very busy, shall we get on with your questions?"

"Yes, thank you." He glanced briefly down at his notepad as he seemed to gather his thoughts, his pen poised above the page. "How long have you lived in the area, Miss Harlow?"

"In Golden Glen?" She quirked an ebony brow. "About twenty-two years."

"And has your family always worked in the hospitality sector?" He met her gaze once more.

"In some form or another, yes." She wondered at the line of questioning. It didn't seem relevant. "We've owned the inn for about twelve years."

"And before that?"

"I was still in high school." She shook her head. "Does it matter?"

"Your educational background? No, not really." He tapped his pen on the page, but had yet to write anything. "How's business?"

"Good." She found his manner strange and felt no inclination to volunteer much information.

"Is the inn typically busy?" he persisted.

"There are usually several people staying with us, yes." She nodded once. "Some months are busier than others. It's all affected by tourism and seasonal events, that kind of thing."

"Are you fully booked at the moment?" He sounded companionably interested.

"You must have seen the books by now, Captain." She draped her arm across the back of the chair and settled into it. "Why ask me?"

"I didn't memorize every detail," he replied somewhat dryly.

But you asked about it; something you could check yourself. Do you think I'd lie, or did the question not occur to you until now? You're overthinking this, Maiden.

"Yes, we're fully booked for the next few weeks," she told him. "Assuming that we can make use of room 6 again anytime soon."

"I'll see what I can do, Miss Harlow." He scribbled something. "Did you know Mr. Creevey?"

"No."

He glanced up at her brief and tepid reply. She met his gaze easily, even when shadows of suspicion darted through their golden-brown depths.

"You didn't know him at *all*?" He sounded skeptical.

"I met him; I didn't know anything about him though," she explained, not sure why that would seem strange to him. "I did have words with him when I caught him trying to break into our computer system."

"You didn't mention that in your statement." His eyes narrowed slightly.

"My statement pertained to his death," she pointed out. "No one asked me about anything beyond that."

"And you honestly don't think it's relevant?" he asked.

"I have no idea, Captain." She shook her head.

"A man was killed in your place of business after trying to hack into your computer," he murmured steadily. "But it didn't occur to you to mention it when Officer Briggs questioned you?"

"No, and it's not as though it happened immediately after," she replied honestly. She didn't want to mention that Briggs had been too flustered and distracted to ask her very much or put her at ease enough to recall any extra details to mind. "Is it okay that I told you instead?"

McAlister didn't answer at first. His eyes were trained on hers as he tapped the end of his pen against his lower lip. "Tell me exactly what happened."

She briefly related the unpleasant encounter, trying not to be too concerned that she'd potentially given herself a motive. She knew it would have been worse to try to conceal the argument; things like that had a way of coming out.

"So, he threatened you?" McAlister asked.

"Essentially. But I told him I'd call the police if he kept it up," she replied. "And he backed right off when I asked to see some identification."

"He checked in without any ID?" The captain frowned and shook his head. "How?"

"Look, I didn't check him in," she sighed, again wishing that Von had just called and asked for help that night. "But apparently he arrived quite late and paid in cash."

"Is that unusual?"

"Yes, it is." She nodded.

McAlister studied her for a moment. She knew she would've looked far more at ease than her sister had, and she held his gaze with no trouble. Some of it was a bluff; she wasn't exactly enjoying being there. The captain let the silence stretch a bit longer, probably trying to play on her nerves. It worked a little, but she refused to let it show.

"So, what was your overall impression of Jim Creevey?" he asked.

"That he was a thug and a creep," she replied candidly. "But I'm still sorry he's dead."

"Did you notice anything strange after he'd checked in?" he murmured. "Did he act like he was afraid or watching his back?"

Maiden considered that as she glanced across the room and replayed what she'd seen of Mr. Creevey in her mind. The man had been downright belligerent at times; he certainly hadn't acted as if he thought his life was in danger. She drew her brows together broodingly and shook her head.

"No, he wasn't nervous or anything. He was pretty ballsy." She shut her eyes and visibly chided herself. "*Gutsy*, sorry. I don't usually talk like that; it's been a strange day."

She risked a glance at McAlister to find him looking quietly amused as he scribbled away.

"That's all right, Miss Harlow, I've heard worse," he said with a smirk lingering in his voice.

Immediately feeling stupid, Maiden stacked her hands in her lap and tried to look confident.

"Where were you last night between 8 pm and 5 am?" he continued.

"I worked in the office until around 10 o'clock, then I went to bed," she replied.

"That's a late finish, isn't it?" He started writing again.

"One hazard of a family business. I had to catch up on some bookkeeping." She shrugged. "I'm used to it. And it'll be even busier in a month's time when Summerfest starts. There'll be tourists everywhere."

"I suppose a guest dying in his room is bad for business," he mused, looking her over subtly.

"It's probably not great for it...I guess we'll find out," she murmured, resisting the urge to adjust her shirt again.

"You don't seem worried," he pointed out.

"Well, there's not much I can do about the situation." She gave him a curious look. "Have I done something to make you suspicious, Captain McAlister? Besides willingly telling you about a minor tiff with the deceased?"

"Not necessarily." He smiled faintly. "I'm told you were also the first to reach the body."

"Yeah, I suppose I was." She inclined her head once and shut her eyes at the disturbing image that floated through her mind with crystal clarity. "Billie actually found him, but she thought he was passed out so she didn't check to see what had happened."

"But you did?"

"I didn't know he was dead until I pushed him onto his back." She fought a shiver at the memory. "I was afraid maybe he'd had a heart attack or had fainted or something...I never thought he had been killed."

"'Killed'?" he said very carefully. "You don't think it could have been an accident?"

"No, of course not," she almost scoffed, but then stilled and blinked at him. "*You* don't think it was an accident, do you?"

"Why are you so sure of murder?" he asked, ignoring her question.

"Well, there was no blood on the furniture, he didn't hit his head on anything in the room," she explained pragmatically.

"How can you be so certain of that?" McAlister's eyes narrowed. "Did you search the room?"

"No, I didn't touch anything." She shook her head. "But I looked things over while we waited for your officers to turn up."

"You should've waited outside," he replied rather tightly.

"Ah. Well, I'll have to remember that," she said as mildly as she could. "It wasn't a situation I've ever encountered before."

"I do understand that, Miss Harlow." He lowered his gaze briefly and made an effort to speak more patiently. "Bear in mind that you could have overlooked something. Or even forgotten what you saw. It's not uncommon in traumatic circumstances."

"I don't forget those sorts of things, Captain," she said very seriously. "Not even when I want to. I see that room and that man exactly as they were when I walked in."

"Do you?" he asked dubiously.

"Was that all?" She uncrossed her legs and pushed to the edge of her seat.

"You seem to be in a hurry," he said.

"To be honest, you're not the most pleasant company I've ever had," she told him bluntly, but her breath caught when she realized how rude she'd sounded. She was pretty sure it wasn't smart to insult cops. "Plus, I have a lot of work to do."

"Miss Harlow. You expect me to take your word for it?" He only smiled at her candor and searched her face once more. "You're claiming that you remember the scene so vividly that you're convinced you didn't miss a thing?"

"Try me." She arched a brow and folded her arms across her chest.

McAlister grinned at her challenge and gave a conceding nod. He turned to his computer and pulled up the crime scene photos with a few clicks of his mouse. He looked it over and regarded her with a confident smile.

"All right," he said. "Impress me. What was the victim wearing?"

"A rumpled pair of navy-blue trousers, the left leg of which needs re-hemming. A brown leather belt and scuffed brown shoes. His shirt was off white, missing the top button and had sweat stains under each arm." She held his gaze as she rattled off the facts. "No wristwatch but a tan line where one used to be. His hair was parted to the right and matted with blood above the left temple. He was unshaven, had bushy eyebrows and a hole from an old piercing on his left ear."

McAlister stared at her, clearly stunned, but just slid his gaze back to the screen.

"For extra points, he was laying on a reddish-brown plush rug that was slightly turned to the right. He had been laying face-down in a heap a few steps inside the door." Maiden spoke calmly and coolly. "No blood on the corners of the desk or tables, not that he was anywhere near them, and not even a bedside lamp overturned. As I said, he was killed."

The captain looked a little more circumspect as he faced her again. His expression was difficult to read. She found herself doubting he was the sort of man to apologize even when proven wrong to his face, but she wasn't in a generous mood either. After looking between her and the picture a few more times, he folded his hands on the desk and cleared his throat.

"Remarkable."

"Yes, it is." She shrugged it off, knowing he hadn't meant it as a compliment.

"An unusual...talent," he ventured cautiously.

"A fact of life for me," she corrected. "It's not always nice to remember details, and it's a challenge to forget them again."

"You'd be a great waitress." He smiled faintly. "Wouldn't need to write anything down."

"You're genuinely awful at this," Maiden informed him and stood. "If you have any *real* questions for me, Captain McAlister, you know where I work."

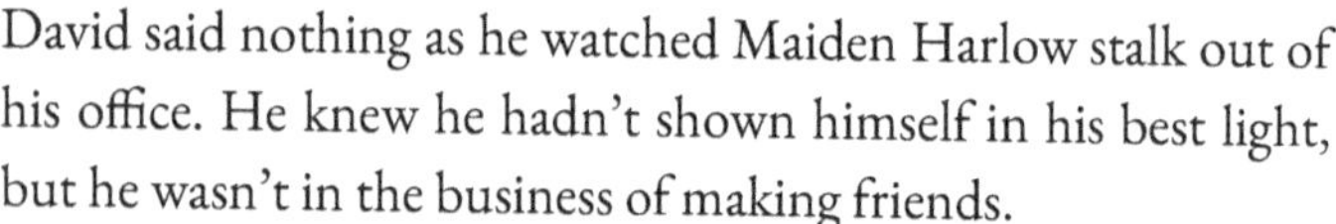

David said nothing as he watched Maiden Harlow stalk out of his office. He knew he hadn't shown himself in his best light, but he wasn't in the business of making friends.

He glanced back at the picture that Miss Harlow had described so accurately.

The color of the man's clothes wasn't such a difficult thing to recall, but the other details were. He wondered if she might have known the victim better than she claimed. Perhaps his prodding had annoyed her into betraying too much under the guise of some freak talent. He needed to find out for certain.

"Smith!" he barked loudly and waited.

A moment later he heard rapid footsteps before Greg Smith came to the door and poked his round face inside.

"You called me, sir?"

"Sit down."

Smith sat and waited with the alertness of an obedient terrier. David leaned back and tented his fingers.

"Tell me about Maiden Harlow."

"Mae?" Smith blinked at him, and a smile threatened before he reined it in. "She's nice, really sweet and smart. Everyone likes her, well, guys like her. Women can be a bit hit or miss."

"Why is that?" David suspected he already knew the answer.

"Because she's..." Smith had been in the process of tracing an hourglass shape with his hands when he evidently realized he was being unprofessional. "Um, I couldn't really say for certain. Sir."

"Have you ever heard claims of an unusually sharp memory?" he asked dubiously.

"The Human Camera?" Smith nodded with a smile. "Oh yeah, Mae's got a crazy weird memory…it's kinda hot."

"Are you in love with this woman or what?" David shook his head at him. "You turn into a sixteen-year-old whenever her name comes up."

"Oh, no, sir! I'm sorry, sir!" He sat up straight and tugged at his shirt to straighten it. "I've known her and Vonny since we were kids. We're only friends. Honestly."

"I have no qualms about keeping you out of this case," David warned. "Tread very carefully."

"Yes, sir!" Smith's voice cracked. "Justice comes first. I would never let friendship stop me from doing the right thing."

"Great." He pinched the bridge of his nose. "So, if Miss Harlow sat in front of me and described the victim in minute detail while claiming not to have known him…you wouldn't find that odd?"

"No, sir, not if it's Maiden," he said with a helpless shrug. "She's always been known for the memory thing. She was banned from the annual school spelling bee. The principal claimed that she had an unfair advantage. Mrs. Harlow argued that it was discrimination, but he wouldn't budge."

"I am *not* in the big city anymore," David muttered. "Did a scoop like that make the local paper?"

"Oh yeah." Smith nodded. "Opinion was *very* divided."

David's wry smirk faded, but was soon replaced by a more genuine chuckle. This *was* the kind of life he'd been hoping to find after all.

Chapter Eight

Maiden walked through the front door of Harlow House and was not at all surprised to find the rest of the family at the reception desk waiting for her. She met her father's questioning gaze and shook her head. She knew she must've looked as unimpressed as she felt.

"How'd it go, baby?" Gloria asked cautiously.

"I'm not really sure," she admitted and continued into the quiet and privacy of the office. "The captain didn't give any real indication of what they're looking for."

"They probably have no idea," Vonny scoffed. "Especially if Greg Smith has his stupid, fat fingers in the pie."

"Oh, you and little Gregory, honestly," Gloria said with an exasperated tsk as she followed her daughters inside, while Alfie wisely stayed out behind the desk. "You fight like cats and dogs, only louder."

"He started it!" Vonny exclaimed. "He insulted me in front of everyone and I was just sitting there!"

"And you just sat there smilin' sweet as pie, I presume?" Gloria gave her a knowing look that Vonny quickly glanced away to avoid. "You're gonna have to behave yourself, baby. This is serious business. And speakin' of business, this won't exactly be good for us if it goes on too long."

"I know. I'm sorry," Vonny said quietly. "But they really were rude."

"They have that luxury, sweetie, we don't." Gloria patted her shoulder gently and sat down. "Now, what are we gonna do about this?"

"Damage control," Maiden said firmly. "We have to emphasize to the remaining guests that Mr. Creevey was an unusual sort of guy that most likely brought trouble with him. We don't want to give anyone the impression that this was a random act or that the inn isn't secure."

"All right," Gloria agreed with a nod. "Hopefully the police will wrap this up before it gets spread around too much."

"And," Maiden gave them both a serious look, "it's quite possible that one of the other guests was responsible. So, we need to keep an eye on things."

They looked at each other as the frightening possibilities became clearer. Everyone there was in danger to some extent. Their best chance to stay safe and protect their business was for the killer to be caught as soon as possible. They all nodded in silent agreement.

Any hopes of keeping the matter quiet were blown to pieces when Amelia Ferris stopped by. She, like her son Tony, had been a very close friend of the Harlow family since they moved to Golden Glen years ago. Amelia was a force to be reckoned with in the community and had a personality far bigger than her stout, five-foot-tall frame suggested.

She barely slowed as she pushed through the front door and waddled past the desk. She paused just long enough to beckon Gloria along with a finger crowned with a long blood-red nail.

"Hurry up, Gloria. I think you'll agree that we have things to discuss!" she said, giving a shake of her head as she trundled on into the dining room. "You should've called me yourself!"

"Nice to see you too," Von murmured with a fond smile and a dry tone as she and Maiden were ignored in favor of a juicy story.

"Crap," Gloria muttered the second her friend was out of earshot. "If Amelia knows then so does the rest of the town. That woman has the biggest mouth in the state!"

Maiden smiled as Gloria pranced off after her. The two women made for an interesting pair, somewhere between allies and squabbling sisters; their relationship was occasionally catty but fiercely loyal at the same time.

When they weren't engaged in pointless arguments about soul food versus southern cooking—as far as Maiden could tell, the major differences were spelling and pronunciation—they were discussing the personal affairs of half the town.

She left them to it. Maiden wasn't immune to the allure of gossip, and whenever Gloria and Amelia were together, coffee and donuts always appeared as if by magic. But even those enticements weren't enough to make her listen to more talk about Mr. Creevey's murder. Although knowing Amelia, she probably had more information than they did.

Maiden had long suspected that Amelia got her news from Tony, along with a few dozen friends around town who had retired years ago and had plenty of time to prattle. But wherever she sourced her information, she was usually among the first to know and was rarely mistaken.

A minute later Tony walked in and grinned excitedly at her and Vonny. It was late afternoon, so he was out of uniform. And he still hadn't had a haircut.

"Hey, I didn't know you were here too." Maiden smiled as he hurried to the desk and rested his elbows on it.

"I was parking the car. Mom made me drop her off at the door." He glanced heavenward even as he chuckled. "Evidently she couldn't wait the extra three minutes."

"You must have left the house in a hurry." Vonny said by way of greeting as she reached over and smoothed down his twisted collar.

Not for the first time, Maiden noticed that Von found an excuse to touch him. She smiled to herself and said nothing.

"Who cares how I'm dressed?" Tony asked incredulously. "There's been a murder here!"

"Yeah, you heard about that, eh?" Maiden winced.

"Are you serious?" Tony stared at her. "*Everyone* has heard about it! That's all I've heard all day. Why didn't you guys call me?"

"And say what exactly?" Maiden asked with a sigh. "We don't want to help this spread, Tony."

"Oh, Maiden." He gave her a look of such sympathetic concern that she immediately knew they were doomed. "You can't hush up an actual murder, it's all over town."

"Great." Maiden pulled a face and sank down in her chair. "I wonder how many reservations are going to be canceled."

"Sorry." Tony frowned worriedly and strove for something positive to say. "Well, it'll be okay. Hey! Have you met the new police captain yet? He's supposed to be sharp; he'll probably wrap it up pretty quick."

Vonny gave him a sour look, and even Maiden slid her gaze away with a disheartened sigh. Tony noticed and offered a pathetically weak smile that made them both laugh.

"Besides, you aren't the only news in town," he said with a confidential look. "You've heard about the robbery in Westfield, right?"

"I haven't." Vonny frowned. "What robbery?"

"It happened Monday." Maiden told her, fighting off another internal chill. "It was in the newspaper."

"Yeah, a couple of guys robbed a bank there," Tony murmured ominously. "They split up and got away. Apparently, the cops think it might have been an inside job. The crooks knew *exactly* what they were doing and got there at the most vulnerable time."

"How do you know that?" Maiden stared at him.

"I deliver mail to the police station, Maiden," he reminded her with a pleased smile. "I see Greg almost every day."

"Lucky you," Von grumbled. "Did he tell you about my interview?"

"A little. Yes." Tony slid his gaze away and quickly changed the subject. "He said he doesn't know of any clear suspects for the robbery, but they've been advised to be on the lookout for anyone suspicious."

"They think the robbers would hide out in Golden Glen?" Maiden felt her heart beat a little harder. She had already considered that, but it made it worse to know that others had too. It made it feel more likely.

"It's possible." Tony nodded.

"So is murder," Maiden whispered to herself as she started to think over the implications. Mr. Creevey had barged in and demanded a room not long after the robbery. He had also paid in cash and refused to show any ID. And now he was dead.

CHAPTER NINE

I t was almost 7 pm when David arrived at Harlow House. He'd had a few hours to consult colleagues, receive some preliminary reports and re-examine the existing evidence. All of which led him back to the scene of the crime.

His immediate quarry was Maiden Harlow, and he was determined to get more accomplished with this discussion. She'd surprised him the first time they met, in more ways than one, but he was better prepared now.

He walked inside the warmly lit foyer and suppressed a groan when he saw Vonny at the desk. She stilled when she spotted him and glanced around as if looking for help. She was alone, however, and therefore made herself almost sort of smile at him.

"Is this a raid, Captain?" she asked lightly enough to betray her discomfort. "Should I stash the hooch?"

"You're free to imbibe all you want, Miss Harlow." He smiled a fraction. "I'm here to speak with your sister."

"Oh?" A concerned frown darkened her expression.

He was neither obliged nor inclined to explain himself, so he just waited. She took the hint and slid out from behind the desk and headed for the staircase.

"I'll take you to her then," she murmured and led him up the stairs to the second floor without another word.

David followed her, studying the hallway carefully as they went. It was empty except for the officer he had stationed outside room 6. He noticed, but didn't mention, that someone had brought him dinner and a flask of coffee.

Vonny went to the door of the Harlows' apartment and pulled out a key. He wondered if they had been so cautious prior to the murder. She threw him a cool look as she opened the door and stepped inside, leaving him waiting in the hall.

"Mae!" Vonny called out. She leaned against the doorjamb and smirked at David as she folded her arms across her chest. "That cute guy is here and wants to talk to you again."

"Which one?" was the cautious reply.

Vonny snorted in amusement and straightened, digging her elbow into David's arm.

"That would sound like a boast if it was anyone but Maiden," she sniggered. "She's not the smoothest person you'll ever meet."

David didn't find her antics amusing and was confident that his expression made that clear. Vonny wasn't easily dissuaded, however, and clearly disliked him enough to prod him further.

"Uh, it's that guy...the new cop." She squinted as if struggling to remember. "I think his name is...Nickel Stirred...My Alice Turd, no wait, it's Mick A-lister, he must be famous!"

"You're a real sweetheart, aren't you?" he said coolly and walked inside.

The interior of the large, open area was warmly lit and inviting. He looked past a rectangular table to a kitchen that was remarkably big considering the proportions of the apartment. There was a long counter that snaked across the entire length of the kitchen, separating it from the rest of the space. The edge facing into the room had an overhang that provided more seating. Half a dozen cushioned barstools sat in front of it.

He spotted Maiden perched on one of them while a slightly older woman who must have been Gloria Harlow was standing across from her, pouring them both a glass of wine.

Maiden knew she appeared startled by McAlister's unexpected presence. She braced herself to speak to him without letting him get to her this time. But then Gloria glanced over and saw the very attractive man striding towards them. A smile lit up her face as she set the bottle down and looked him over.

"Ooh! Well, hello there." She patted her blonde curls into place and smiled brightly. "Come on in, handsome! How can we help you?"

"Mom, don't," Maiden pleaded under her breath. "That's Captain McAlister. He's probably here to arrest us."

"Nonsense!" she tittered and gave her a light swat on the shoulder. "Now sit up straight and look pretty."

Maiden cringed and forced herself to turn and face McAlister. He was watching her with a smile; she lost all hope that he hadn't heard her mother's embarrassingly loud whisper.

"Well, it's the spelling bee champ, eh?" he threw her a teasing look. "Officer Smith mentioned your brush with the higher academic circles."

"Then he exaggerated," she sniffed. "I was only allowed to compete once."

"That was totally unfair!" Vonny grumbled as she walked over to stand loyally beside her. "Who gets penalized for winning fair and square? The principle was a crazy old crank."

"That little cow Tanisha Cauldwell won three years in a row without the old windbag callin' *her* a freak," Gloria muttered, her southern accent growing heavier with her irritation.

"Mr. Sanders called me a freak?" Maiden blinked widened eyes at her.

"Oh crumbs." Gloria gave her youngest daughter a quietly aghast look. "I swore I'd never tell you that."

Maiden grinned and tried not to laugh, but the captain stepped a bit closer and spoke up before she could reply.

"Ladies, please, let's not get bogged down by past injustice. There's no changing it now." He held up his hands in a soothing manner and then nodded to Gloria. "Mrs. Harlow, we haven't met yet. I'm Captain McAlister, I'm heading up the investigation into Jim Creevey's murder."

"You can call me Gloria, sugar." She flashed him a winning smile.

"Very kind." McAlister's expression gave very little away as he gestured towards Maiden. "I had a few more questions about today's incident, if Miss Harlow could spare me a minute."

"Hmm? Oh!" Gloria's face brightened again. "Of course, Captain. You two have a nice little chat, Vonny and I have plenty of other things to do. Move it, Vonny!"

This last command was issued with a speaking look when her oldest daughter made no move to leave. Maiden felt herself blush when her mother sashayed to the door, gently nudging Vonny ahead of her. Gloria stopped and gave them a dainty waggle of her pudgy fingers before shutting them inside together.

McAlister cleared his throat and turned back to Maiden. She met his gaze and exhaled through her nose. Her mom hadn't embarrassed her since she was a teenager, and she had not missed the experience.

"She seems…" he began slowly.

"Peculiar?" Maiden offered when adjectives failed him.

"Friendly," he said instead. "I haven't met many people that are too happy to see a cop in their house."

"Better than a burglar." She forced an anemic smile. "What can I do for you, Captain?"

"When you stormed out in the middle of our previous discussion—" He paused when she gave him a look. "What?"

"*That's* how you're starting?" she asked patiently.

"Right. We'll move on." He smiled and took the seat beside her when she pointed towards it. "I had a few more questions about this morning. Firstly, did you see anyone else when you came downstairs?"

"No." She had already thought about that; she'd been thinking about the case all afternoon. "I left the apartment and everything was quiet. I walked downstairs and started setting up for the day. Then Billie came in. I didn't see anybody."

"And Billie let herself into room 6 and found him?" McAlister prompted.

"Yes. Oh…" Maiden's eyes widened, but she quickly recovered. "Yes. She did; she must have."

"You don't sound convincing, Miss Harlow," he informed her.

"Yeah, you mentioned that the last time we spoke too," she replied, but then chewed at her lip as she drifted into thought. "I just remembered something odd."

"Feel free to share." He leaned forward, resting an elbow on the counter.

"The key to room 6 was on the hook this morning," she said pensively. "That's why I asked Billie to go make up the room so early. Check out usually isn't until 10 am, but the key had been returned so I assumed Mr. Creevey had left already."

"Was his room locked?" McAlister asked as he pulled out his notepad and started writing.

"I don't know," she admitted. "I didn't ask Billie. But I didn't think anything of it until now."

"All right, I'll look into it," he said, looking down at the page before glancing back at her. "What happened when she found the body?"

"She thought he was drunk and came to get me," Maiden said as she replayed the events in her mind. "When we realized he was dead she screamed, a couple of times, and Mr. Gilford came to see what had happened."

"Did Ms. Randall come out at all?" McAlister checked an earlier note. "She's in room 9, I believe?"

"She is." Maiden nodded. "But she didn't come to her door. I think she got drunk last night...Billie mentioned quite a mess that needed cleaning up."

"Poor Billie." McAlister shook his head wryly. "Not a good morning for her, was it?"

"Not especially." She decided not to be petty and mention that *she* was the one who stood by the body for ages waiting for his officers to turn up.

"Where's your bedroom?" he asked abruptly.

"What?" She felt her eyes widen in surprise.

"Oh, sorry." He had the decency to look uncomfortable. "I mean, in proximity to the scene of the murder. Of course."

"Because *that's* a less offensive suggestion," Maiden muttered under her breath before clearing her expression and meeting his expectant gaze. She pointed to the open doorway on the back wall of the kitchen. "Down that little hallway, my room is in the far corner, to the front of the house."

"And you heard nothing strange through the night?" he asked.

"Nothing that woke me, no." She shook her head. "But it was quite windy last night."

"And none of the rest of the family mentioned anything at breakfast either?" he pressed.

"I didn't see them. I wake up long before anyone else," Maiden explained. "Von will sleep in for ages if she's not scheduled to work."

"But you don't?" A dark brow quirked.

"Why waste hours in bed?" she replied lightly. "Once you're awake there's nothing interesting to do there."

The second brow rose to join the first. Maiden felt heat touch her cheeks and slid her gaze away.

That's right, Maiden, cool and collected, she thought dryly. *You don't sound like an idiot at all.*

McAlister was amused again, but whether it was from her remark or her obvious embarrassment was harder to tell. It wasn't his fault if she kept saying stupid things, but it was still annoying to be laughed at.

"That sounds very logical, Miss Harlow," he said nicely. She felt her irritation intensify.

"Where's *your* bedroom, Captain?" She decided a brazen reply might cure her embarrassment; see how *he* liked awkward and unexpected questions. "In proximity to the scene of the murder? Of course."

"Um...in my house, across town." He looked back at his notes to hide his grin.

"Are you a heavy sleeper?" she inquired.

"No, not really." He still wasn't looking at her.

"And it's too far for you to have heard anything, I suppose?" she continued relentlessly.

"I'm afraid so." He nodded. "It was quite windy last night."

Maiden held in her laughter at his well-aimed retort, but she had to look away from him to manage it. She quickly settled when he shifted beside her.

"Getting back to the murder," he said calmly. "Did you get the impression that any of the other guests knew Mr. Creevey? Any sign of familiarity at all?"

"No, not that I noticed." She crossed her legs and saw him glance at them and then very quickly away again.

"Are you familiar with many of the guests staying here?" he pressed on, looking determinedly at his notes.

"What does 'familiar' mean in this instance?" she asked quite genuinely.

"Do you know them personally?" He glanced at her again for the sake of giving her a watchful look.

"You've never worked in a hotel, have you?" She almost smiled at him. "Captain...no. We typically get a name and address when someone books in; that's pretty much it as far as personal knowledge goes. I don't have a lot of meaningful interactions with the guests. Well, except for Mrs. Varney, I guess...Oh, and Ms. Randall. I talked to her more than I wanted to, to be honest. That's not really typical though...I may need you to be more specific."

"Are you being deliberately difficult, Miss Harlow?" He shook his head a little.

"No, I'm just awkward under pressure." She shifted uncomfortably.

"Let's try something easier." McAlister rubbed his eyes. "Have you met anyone here that strikes you as being capable of murder?"

"Yes. The dead guy," she replied sardonically. "Needless to say, that's my best theory out the window."

McAlister's expression was complicated. He was somehow annoyed, confused, and laughing at her all at once. Maiden suppressed an urge to fidget as he glanced over at her wineglass.

"Have you had a few of those already?" he asked.

"No, I have not." She arched a brow, not appreciating the insulting implication.

"Do you want a few? Will it make you more lucid if you're relaxed?" he murmured, but immediately looked as if he wished he'd kept his mouth shut.

"I doubt it." She glared at him. "Did *you* want a few? Will it make you any easier to deal with?"

"I doubt it." His expression hardened. "And I'm really not supposed to drink while I'm working."

"You're probably not supposed to encourage women to get drunk either," she pointed out.

"I'm starting to question the wisdom of coming here alone," he said candidly.

"I'm starting to question the wisdom of telling you where my bedroom is," she replied similarly.

The look of shock on his face was priceless and only a little mortifying; his mouth fell open, and he quickly looked away. Maiden released a silent sigh and resisted the urge to sip her wine while he was there to see her do it.

I met you six hours ago; I could probably stand to be a bit more demure, she thought ruefully. *Oh, look at your face. Poor thing, I think I've frightened you...that's a new one.*

McAlister rallied and turned back to her with a begrudging smile. Maiden shifted her gaze away briefly, hoping that he'd just say goodnight and leave. She honestly didn't know what she'd say if the optimistic fool tried to continue the conversation.

"Awkward under pressure." He nodded at her earlier assertion. "Yeah, you are a tiny bit."

"And you're insulting," she replied before she could stop herself. "That must be why this is going so well."

McAlister shut his eyes and took a deep breath. He risked looking back at her, for an indiscreet moment his gaze slipped south before he dragged it back up to maintain eye contact.

"Well, thank you for your…assistance," he ventured carefully. "I'll be on my way. Unless you had anything else to add?"

"I think I've said plenty." She sat straighter and clasped her hands together on the countertop.

"Right, have a nice evening, Miss Harlow," he said as he pushed to his feet. He pulled a card from his pocket and handed it to her. "That's my number if you want to call me."

Maiden wasn't sure of her exact expression as she accepted the card, but she didn't know how to take that remark and knew it showed.

McAlister cleared his throat and slowly put his notepad back in his pocket.

"If you *need* me…to talk to me." He scowled at himself and backed toward the door. "About anything to do with the investigation. Come to me…right."

"Enjoy your evening, Captain McAlister." She kept her tone mild, hoping he'd finally leave rather than cram his foot any further into his mouth. She'd done enough of that for both of them.

He nodded again, turned, and left rather quickly. When the door shut behind him, Maiden let her shoulders droop and buried her face in her hands.

It could've gone better. So far, all the police seemed to have established was that she was the only one in the house up and around before the body was found and no one else stood out as a strong suspect.

Captain McAlister had said nothing directly, but with no other leads, there was a real danger that he might suspect her or her family of being involved in Mr. Creevey's death. And her inadvertent flirting probably wasn't helping.

Speculation and docile cooperation weren't getting her anywhere; it was time to take a more active part in figuring out what had actually happened to Mr. Creevey.

"Did you flirt with him?" Gloria asked smarmily the second Maiden entered the office.

She had given McAlister a few minutes to be well and truly on his way before heading downstairs herself. She was still embarrassed and uneasy; she was in no mood to be prodded.

"Not on purpose," she muttered under her breath as she stalked over to the small table and plunked down into a chair beside Alfie. "Don't be silly, Mom."

"Okay, fine." Gloria shrugged a shoulder. "Do as you like, honey. But, under the circumstances, it might not be a bad thing if that dishy captain is well-disposed towards us. Just a little food for thought."

"Thank you, Mother," Maiden sighed dryly.

"What's this?" Alfie scowled at his wife and youngest daughter. "What are you telling her to do? And with whom?"

"Relax, Alfie," Gloria soothed. "Everything's fine, little Maiden is a good girl. She knows what she's doin'."

"I will not have my daughters cozying up to corrupt policemen," he said grimly and fisted his hand on the tabletop. "I know the mayor! I'll get this man sorted out!"

"Dad stop it!" Maiden blushed again. "I haven't done anything to anyone. Please keep in mind that someone was murdered in our hotel! Carrying on like flirts or angry loons isn't going to help us!"

"Yes, yes the murder," Alfie sighed and pinched the bridge of his nose. "That poor man, what a thing to happen on a vacation. So, who do the police suspect?"

"I don't know, it only happened this morning." She shrugged. "But it could have been almost anyone here."

"None of us would have hurt that guy." Alfie shook his head.

"But the doors and windows are all locked at night," she reminded him.

"I suppose someone could've snuck in before that." Gloria patted her bouncy curls absently.

"And hid somewhere until everyone went to bed." Maiden considered it. "Maybe, or another guest could have accidentally left the door open a crack...it's feasible, but we can't ignore the most obvious possibility."

"You think one of the guests killed him?" Alfie whispered, his eyes darting watchfully towards the empty doorway.

"Well, I don't think any of *us* did it," she replied.

"Of course not!" Gloria's eyes widened, but then narrowed irately. "Except maybe the cook. That Kylie girl is sour enough for anything."

"She's fine, Mom!" Maiden gave her an exasperated look. "Where's your patience?"

"She's spent it all," Gloria sniffed. "I don't like unfriendly people here; this is a family inn with a *warm and friendly* atmosphere."

"Except for the murder, of course," Alfie pointed out.

"Yes, Alfie." Gloria slid him a wry but fond smile. "Except for the murder, Harlow House is a happy place to be."

David lay in bed that night, thinking about the case. He was still waiting for a bit more information on Creevey to come through, but the initial findings were promising. The guy had a record stretching back to his high school days; nothing major, but a lot of minor offenses. They all added up to a casually dishonest person who might be inclined to more ambitious schemes. As ambitious as bank robbery, perhaps.

Their counterparts in Westfield contacted his department and gave them what information they had about the robbery. The timing and circumstances of the heist suggested greater than average knowledge of the running of the bank. The robbers knew when the vault would be most accessible and which employees had the means to open it. He had his suspicions about Creevey, but it got more complicated since the guy was dead.

It didn't sit well with him; violent murders shouldn't happen in little towns like Golden Glen. It was a quiet place; it was nice.

David glanced at the window and tried to remember the last time he had lived somewhere that didn't have security bars on every access point. Judging by the other houses on his street, locks were enough to make people feel safe there. It reminded him of when he was a kid; long before he'd followed his father's footsteps and become a cop.

He dragged his mind back to the present and Creevey's suspicious death. Maiden Harlow had been right about at least one thing: amongst the guests, Creevey seemed the most likely person to have committed murder. It was ironic that he was the victim.

David smiled at the thought of her; he couldn't help it. She was a total fox, that was obvious, but his second interview had blown away his initial impression of her. She came across as confident and witty, but then out of nowhere she was quite funny, and it wasn't always intentional.

She seemed to just say things without thinking, and other times she was so brutally on target that it caught him off guard. She was definitely observant, definitely clever, and kind of silly. It was a distracting combination.

She's still a suspect, David, he reminded himself. *And the murder happened down the hall from where she lives. She found the body and examined the room, possibly before calling the station; you don't know for certain. You can't afford to like this woman; she could be anything.*

Appropriately chastened, he turned off the bedside lamp and shut his eyes. He'd get more answers tomorrow; this wasn't Stanton, where everyone could be anonymous if they wanted to be. This was Golden Glen. Someone knew or saw something to do with Creevey's murder.

David was sitting at his desk, typing away at his computer. He had no idea what time it was; he didn't even remember getting there. It distantly occurred to him that the room looked different; it still felt like his office, but the window was missing and the furniture was wrong.

He was distracted when the door opened. He glanced up and stilled when Maiden Harlow slipped inside wearing a snug little black dress. It was silky and strappy and cut low enough to get his attention and hold it.

Her big green eyes never shifted from him as she shut the door and leaned back against it with a breathless sigh. He frowned uncertainly and pushed to his feet. Her gaze never shifted as she reached behind her and locked the door with a stark and resounding click.

He shook his head and opened his mouth to speak, but before he could force any words out, she walked straight up to him. An instant later she nestled in close and slid her hands up over his shoulders. She let her eyes drift gently shut and kissed him.

He could have pulled away and asked a dozen different questions in that moment, but he didn't. Instead, he grabbed her by the waist and started kissing her back, a lot. She felt warm and soft and perfect; he caught a hint of her perfume and held her tighter. About the time she pressed herself against him and started unbuttoning his shirt, he woke up.

David sat bolt upright and looked around his darkened bedroom. His breathing was loud and unsteady; his heart was pounding, and he was covered in sweat. The fleeting images of that beautiful face vanished cruelly into the surrounding darkness. He let out a shaky breath as he ran his hands over his face and back through his hair.

"Thanks a lot," he muttered to whatever part of his subconscious had churned out that little slap in the face, "that was helpful."

He threw back the blankets and got to his feet. Without letting himself relive what he'd seen and felt, he staggered down the hall to the bathroom. He stepped into the shower without bothering to undress and turned on the cold water.

CHAPTER TEN

The next morning Maiden slipped outside through the door between reception and the staircase. She stepped onto the stone path and looked around.

Off to the left was the start of the gardens; her mother's pride and joy. Apart from peonies and several varieties of roses, Gloria also dabbled in pumpkins and squash. She talked about entering one of the 'biggest veggie' or 'best pie' categories at Summerfest every year, but so far she'd always come up with some excuse not to.

Typically, she would hurry to turn her best pumpkin into pies and serve them to the family before she could be cajoled into entering the annual fair.

Maiden wasn't interested in pie at the moment; she wanted a look at the back of the house. The thought came to her in the night, and she was eager to check for anything of note outside.

The inn had verandas that wrapped around the second and third floors, providing generous balcony space for each room. They were separated by partition walls and offered beautiful views of the orchards and wineries in the distance. But the ground floor was another matter; those rooms enjoyed small patios that were lined with shrubs for privacy.

She walked towards the far end of the house, taking care to keep quiet and not risk alerting any of the first-floor guests as she passed by. She had every right to be there, but she really didn't want to be observed just now.

It was early, and no one was around, which was exactly what she'd hoped for. She made her way to the furthest corner and looked up at the balcony outside Mr. Creevey's room. Everything appeared tidy from the little she could see. But she was more interested in the ground underneath.

Maiden lowered her gaze to the surrounding shrubs, and again, everything seemed normal. She crept closer. As she peered over the top of the handsomely pruned bush, she noticed some broken branches on the opposite side.

She held her breath and edged around to get a better look. Several branches had been snapped and trampled. Her gaze went first up to the railing of the balcony and then slowly lowered to the nearest ground-floor door. It was the door to the Varney's room.

The damaged side of the bush was on the inside edge of their patio. Maiden hesitated to actually enter their private space, but she needed to take a closer look. She glanced around surreptitiously before dropping to her knees.

She crawled forward, ducking her head into the bush and studied it carefully. The ends of the broken branches were green, and the trampled leaves weren't dried out. This hadn't happened all that long ago...maybe only yesterday.

Her gaze again strayed to the Varney's door. Their room was directly below Mr. Creevey's.

"Good morning, Miss Harlow."

Maiden gasped; her head struck the leafy canopy above her as the placidly voiced greeting made her jump. She tried to crawl back out of the bush, but her hair had gotten tangled. She reached up to tug it free, trying not to panic about who might've caught her.

"Oh, I'm sorry! I didn't mean to scare you; are you okay?" Officer Briggs knelt beside her and pushed the branches out of her way.

"Yeah, I guess," she said uncomfortably as she pulled the last of her hair free and looked at him warily. "How did you know it was me?"

His gaze dropped over her indiscreetly. Maiden immediately regretted the question.

"Deductive reasoning," his voice trailed off.

Maiden quickly sat back a little so he couldn't see down her shirt. Briggs didn't look irate or even curious about finding her prowling around. He still knelt beside her and smiled as he pointed towards her hair.

"You've got some leaves there," he told her.

"Oh, thanks." She reached up and ran her fingers through her hair a few times. "I guess this looks weird, huh?"

"A little bit," Briggs admitted and cleared his throat. "Is everything okay? I mean, did you lose something?"

"No." She looked confused by the question. "I noticed these shrubs are a bit damaged, so I was just looking them over. Have you guys checked out here already?"

"Yes. Well not personally, but someone did," he said as he shied away from her direct gaze.

"Okay, and did they notice the damage on the other side?" she asked as she pointed to the bush she'd been trapped in.

"I don't know." He was looking at her again and sounded distracted.

"You might...want to ask somebody, then." Maiden pushed to her feet and eased back a step. "Just in case."

"Yeah, I will. Thank you, Miss Harlow." He stood up as well and brushed his hands clean.

Maiden wasn't sure what to do at that point. Briggs hadn't said anything about it, but he had caught her crawling through potential evidence. She really didn't want to ask if she was under arrest, but she needed to know.

"Is it okay if I go back to work?" She rubbed her arms.

"Of course." He nodded once. "You're fine, Miss Harlow, you haven't done anything wrong."

Maiden bit the inside of her cheek to stop from pointing out that she'd been acting quite suspiciously. She wasn't sure if Officer Briggs believed that she just happened to notice the damaged branches or if he just didn't want to get her into any trouble. Either way, both their actions bordered on questionable. It was time to leave.

She smiled as neutrally as she could at Briggs and headed for the back door. She could feel his eyes on her and walked a little faster.

By the time Maiden was back inside, it occurred to her that Briggs wouldn't be the only cop on site. Her eyes widened when she heard Captain McAlister's deep voice heading up the stairs. Without hesitating, she scampered to the office and shut the door as softly as she could.

I am not a coward, she assured herself, *but he's incredibly good-looking and I babbled like an idiot last night. It'll be fine, I'm sure I can run the desk from in here.*

She sat at the small table and considered what she had learned before getting caught. It looked as though someone had stood in the shrubs below Mr. Creevey's window. Was it possible that they had climbed down from the balcony? Maybe the killer wasn't a guest after all.

She'd assumed that Mr. Creevey was trying to see the guest register because he was looking for someone; that's what he'd claimed. But if he was one of the robbers, and she was convinced that he was, maybe he had been trying to ensure that his partner hadn't found *him*.

Maiden stiffened and looked over sharply when the doorknob rattled. Relief poured through her when Vonny slipped inside a moment later.

"You're up early," Maiden said as her sister came and sat beside her.

"There are killers and cops in the house." She shrugged. "Even I can't sleep through that."

Maiden nodded in agreement, but then gave her a curious look. "Hey, did Mr. Creevey have much luggage when he checked in?" she asked in a low voice since Von hadn't shut the door behind her.

"Um," Vonny frowned in thought, "no, he didn't have much. Just a grubby old backpack."

"That was it?" Maiden stared at her. "And he paid in cash?"

"Yeah," Von said. "It was all really weird. Why do you ask?"

"I'm considering some possibilities," Maiden demurred. "The sooner this is figured out the better, for *everyone*."

Saturday morning rolled around, and more guests would be arriving in a few hours. They'd heard nothing definite from the police, and room 6 was still off limits. Maiden was sitting at the desk reading her library book when her mother slid in beside her.

"Maiden, baby." Gloria gave her a smiling look. "Do Mama a favor and go ask that nice captain if we can use room 6 yet."

"What?" She felt her cheeks turn pink. "Why me? Shouldn't you or Dad go?"

"No, I'm too busy and your father will call him a turkey," Gloria said in a perfectly reasonable tone. "And your sister don't like him so she'll be cranky. That leaves you, angel. Hurry up now, we're runnin' out of time."

"Um...okay." She suspected her mother had ulterior motives in sending her, but none of her reasons were a stretch of the imagination either.

"I knew I could count on you, baby." Gloria pinched her cheek and then gave her a quick, serious look. "Wear somethin' nice."

Maiden frowned but didn't argue, though she also didn't intend to change her clothes.

Gloria meandered off to deal with whatever kept her too busy to do her own dirty work. Maiden stared down at the cover of her obnoxious book. The picture of the burly, shirtless hero with the busty heroine clinging to his leg didn't lessen her uneasiness at all.

She'd spent the last day or so alternating between being embarrassed over her last discussion with McAlister and laughing at herself for being such a brazen goofball. She really, really didn't want to face him again.

They needed that room back, though. She thought about calling him; she had his card tucked in her phone case. But it was easier to say no over the phone. There was a better chance of getting the room released if she asked in person. Maiden closed her eyes and summoned her courage.

Come on, then, she gently goaded herself. *Go and be gutsy. It's a straightforward inquiry. What's the worst that could happen?*

She slipped out through the office door, climbed into her green sedan, and tried to steady her nerves as she drove to the police station. It wasn't easy, and she was feeling quite foolish by the time she got there. She knew she was only asking a reasonable question, but she was struggling to get past the awkwardness of their last discussion. Not to mention that she was also a suspect.

As she walked into the dull, yellowed foyer, she found it almost empty. Now that she was directly facing the prospect of seeing McAlister again, she quickly decided to be a coward and talk to Greg instead. He could at least ask on her behalf, and then she wouldn't have to deal with the captain.

Her footsteps sounded quite loud on the faded beige linoleum. Towards the far end of the room was a huge wooden reception desk; it was sturdy and ugly and had probably been there since the 1970s.

There were about a dozen chairs pushed against every unoc-cupied bit of wall. She glanced from the water cooler sweating away in the far-left corner to the large bulletin board behind the desk, covered in public service notices, a faded map of Golden Glen, and a handful of wanted posters.

Maiden walked up and smiled at the lady on duty. She was a tall, middle-aged woman with her pale hair pulled back in a simple twist. She didn't return the smile but appeared pleasant enough. Maiden had seen her very briefly the first time she'd come to the station, but she had merely directed her to the captain's office and continued on with her work. Her name was Nancy, if the plaque on the desk was anything to go by.

"Good morning," she said simply.

"Yes, hello." Maiden kept smiling and wished she weren't so nervous. "Um…Is Officer Smith here at the moment?"

"No, he's out," Nancy replied and had begun to offer to take a message when she glanced down the hall and fell silent.

Maiden turned and held her breath when she saw Captain McAlister walking towards them. For a wild moment she con-sidered pretending to faint, or maybe throwing a shoe at him and running for the door. He stopped and rested a hand on the desk as he studied her with an air of watchfulness.

"What's this about Smith?" he asked warily.

"I was just asking if he's in." She shrugged, feeling even more nervous now.

"Has something happened at the inn?" His dark brows drew together. "Because you should be coming to *me* with any information, not your friend."

Nancy lowered her eyes awkwardly, but still stayed close enough to hear every word. A little flutter of annoyance bubbled up inside Maiden, easing her nerves a bit.

"If I had any information I *would* come to you, Captain," she said steadily. "I only wanted to know when we'll be able to use our room again."

David felt himself tense but tried to tamp down his irritation. He reminded himself that this was not worth getting angry about. It didn't matter who Miss Harlow asked about the room, this was not a reflection on his role in the case. And it wasn't her fault that he'd dreamed about her again last night. He told himself all those things as he stood there looking at her; none of it helped.

"That's also a question that should be coming to me," he said, a touch coolly. "Smith has no authority in this case, Miss Harlow, trying to make use of a personal connection isn't going to help you any."

"Excuse me?!" she demanded, her eyes wide and flinty now. "I just happen to know Greg. I'm only here to ask a legitimate question, not to beg special favors!"

"Irrelevant." He folded his arms across his chest. "I gave you my number, you call *me* if you have an issue."

It occurred to him too late that he could've phrased that better. He saw Nancy's eyes snap to him and then slide curiously to Maiden. He could see the woman's burgeoning interest in the exchange and knew he needed to rein it in before either of them got any more upset.

"I was only asking a question." Maiden took a deep breath that did little to hide her annoyance. "Does it matter who brings it to you?"

"Miss Harlow," he said with forced calm, "it's more appropriate for all questions to be put to me directly since I'm the one heading up the investigation."

She released the breath she'd drawn in a low hiss and glanced at Nancy, who then looked at David. If the lady thought her captain was overreacting, she wisely kept it to herself and raised a coffee mug to her lips.

"Fine," Maiden said tightly, and after a long pause. "I didn't realize it was such a touchy subject. I'll ask you directly then; are we able to use room 6 yet?"

David watched her grimly for a moment. He wasn't an unreasonable man, but she was pushing his buttons. He hadn't forgotten that the Harlows were waiting for the room, but he wouldn't be rushed. The investigation had to take precedence.

I specifically told you to contact me if you wanted to discuss the case, he muttered internally as he held her vibrant green gaze. *I couldn't have been much clearer.*

He'd already planned to inform the Harlows that they could have the room back, but then Maiden turned up to ask Smith. That wasn't okay, and he couldn't let her get that impression.

"No," he said simply. "I'm not ready to release it today."

"Really?" She was fuming, but trying not to show it. "Still?"

"I'm a thorough man, Miss Harlow," he said with a shrug.

"*Efficient* would be more helpful in this instance, Captain McAlister," she said crisply. "But we'll have to be understanding of your pace, I suppose you are still settling in."

Nancy choked on her coffee and finally had to step away. David watched her go with quiet annoyance before turning back to Maiden.

"You can get on with your business, Miss Harlow," he informed her gruffly. "The longer you waylay me with complaints the longer the investigation will take."

"If only I'd thought of that before coming in here asking to speak to someone else entirely," she retorted.

"Or just made a phone call and saved yourself a trip." He was getting angrier, and she obviously was too.

"You'll do great in a small town with those manners," Maiden muttered as she turned and stalked out.

David watched her slip through the front door.

"Is everything all right, Captain?" Nancy had resumed her place behind the desk and gave him a concerned look.

He glanced at her and felt himself smile a little. He liked Nancy; she was always respectful but had made a real effort to make him feel welcome. It was appreciated too; he had walked into an established station where everyone knew everyone else, except him.

"Yes, thank you, Nancy," he said mildly and turned back to the long hallway that led to his office. "Tell Officer Smith to report to me as soon as he gets in."

Maiden stormed back into the foyer of Harlow House and straight into the office. She threw her purse into the corner and started pacing. Gloria was sitting at the small table and stared at her; Maiden never got that angry.

"What happened, angel?" she asked warily. "You weren't gone very long."

"He accused me of trying to use Greg! Can you believe that? I'd been there two minutes and just asked if Greg was in, that's it!" she grated. "Then he told me that I should only go to him because he's heading up the investigation! Excuse me, your highness! I didn't realize you were the only person in the entire station that I'm allowed to speak to!"

"Why'd you ask for Greg?" Gloria shook her head slightly, making her long silver earrings dance. "I told you to speak to the captain."

"That's not helpful, Mother!" Maiden resisted the urge to shout at her. "The point is, no, we can't use the room simply because King McAlister is displeased with the insolence of the peasants!"

Gloria seemed to wade through her daughter's rant to pick out what she considered the most pertinent information. She looked intrigued despite the inconvenience.

"He's jealous! Already!" Her eyes were wide and delighted. "That's fantastic!"

"He's not jealous, he's a tool!" Maiden fired back.

"Oh, sweetheart, don't use that word, it's so tacky." Gloria shut her eyes and laid a hand across her generous bosom. "Now, we'll work around this. The Kaminsky's were meant to stay in room 6, we'll upgrade them to room 3. It's bigger, they won't mind."

"It isn't bigger, it's the same size," Maiden grumbled.

"Which means it's just as good!" Gloria gave her a look that typically ended any argument; this was no exception. Having claimed victory, her southern charm sprang up again like a freshly watered daisy. "It'll work out perfect. It might even discourage their kids from playin' on the stairs."

"Fine. Great. Whatever," she muttered, not remotely mollified by the solution. "I'm not talking to that man again."

"Never say never, baby," Gloria tittered and scampered, actually scampered, off to the dining room where she would doubtless regale Vonny with the tale.

Maiden pulled a face and stalked behind the reception desk. If Greg had only been there, she wouldn't have had to deal with McAlister, and they'd have been free to get their room back.

She didn't believe for a second that it still needed to be closed off; he'd said no out of pure spite. McAlister was obviously so petty and insecure in his new role that he felt it necessary to defend every crumb of authority. She forced herself to stop and take a deep breath.

"Don't sulk," she ordered herself in a whisper. "This is exactly the reaction he wanted, don't let him win."

David had calmed down in the hour or so since his tiff with Maiden Harlow. He sat in his office reviewing a few background checks on the guests at Harlow House. Everyone seemed to be normal, law-abiding citizens. No one had much of a criminal record. The closest was Vera Randall, who'd been arrested for public indecency, along with the guy she'd been publicly indecent with, about fifteen years ago.

Despite Officer Smith's complete and unquestioning confidence in them, he'd ordered background checks on every member of the Harlow family as well. They were all squeaky clean, and he was quite pleased about that.

He didn't want to have to tear apart one of the more respected local families less than a month after hitting town. He would do it if he needed to, but he'd prefer that it wasn't necessary.

His thoughts strayed to Maiden Harlow; he wondered if she was actually angry with him. It was possible that she was nervous and trying to keep him at a distance. Just because she had no record of criminal conduct didn't mean she had done nothing, only that she'd never been caught. She was still a suspect; they all were.

He glanced at the slightly open door when a soft knock preceded the sight of Smith peering in at him. David sat up straight and beckoned him to enter.

"You wanted to see me, sir?" Smith asked as he approached the desk.

"Sit down," he murmured with little inflection.

He watched Smith sink down into the chair in front of him. Smith looked uncertain and possibly scared; that was good. David had no idea how much the man was in contact with Maiden Harlow regarding the case or anything else, but he would not let it go on.

Smith was waiting to find out what he'd done; the anxious worry was obvious in his innocent, corn-fed expression. David let the silence stretch for another minute and then put him out of his misery.

"Have you been talking to Maiden Harlow?" he asked seriously.

"Sir?" Smith frowned in confusion.

"Has she contacted you, or have you contacted her about anything to do with this case?" he clarified.

"No, sir." He shook his head. "I haven't talked to her at all since she came to see you the other day."

He appeared almost too guileless to lie, although looks meant nothing. But there was enough genuine fear in the younger man's eyes to suggest that he was telling the truth.

"Did she say something about me?" Smith asked cautiously.

"She came here asking to see you about a question to do with the investigation," David informed him. "Despite the fact that I'm in charge of it. And despite having had a very candid discussion with me previously."

"'Candid'?" he asked.

"Candid. Frank. Open. Almost informal," David expounded, not sure that he should have added the last part.

"You mean...friendly?" Smith was watching him intently now.

"No. That would be taking it a little out of context." He frowned as Smith's eyes rounded.

"Wait a minute," Smith said seriously and raised a hand to stop him, "are you saying that Maiden flirted with you?"

"I absolutely did *not* say that! Where did you get that from?" David's dark brows furrowed at the personal question. "I'm saying that she came here to see *you* about the case. Now, let me be clear that anything to do with the case comes directly to me."

"Why'd she ask for me?" Smith frowned uncertainly. "You said she was flirting with *you*."

"I never said that! I said candid. And I don't know why she was here looking for you, but I'm not putting up with it, do you understand?" David asked tightly.

"Do you think she's avoiding you because she likes you?" Smith's eyes were wide, and his voice was low and intent.

"Are you twelve years old, Smith?" He shook his head slowly.

"Mae doesn't flirt without meaning it, sir." Smith was staring at him in quiet awe. "She's way too nice for that…How'd you do it? I've known her since we were both five; you just met her."

"I didn't say she flirted," David reminded him seriously. "And she's probably not speaking to me after our last discussion."

"You already blew it?!" Smith blurted out before he could stop himself. He clamped a hand over his mouth and squeezed his eyes shut.

David wasn't sure whether to yell or laugh at the man. Smith dropped his hands to his lap and glanced away as he tried to absorb what was evidently the most outrageously incredible thing he'd ever heard.

"You all right?" David asked, a tad sarcastically.

"Sir…I can't even explain to you…" Smith took a deep breath and then turned to him and held up his hands like he was holding the other man's stupidity. "*Maiden Harlow*! How do you—I couldn't even—the hottest girl in the whole stupid school!"

"Are you aware that you've graduated?" The anger was gone, and David was purely amused now, but kept it in check.

"Oh, Captain," he sighed and shook his head wearily. "Can I please go, sir?"

"Yeah, you absolutely can," David murmured dryly. "But you remember what I said. I'm not joking, Smith."

"I understand, sir." He pushed to his feet, still shaking his head in disappointed wonder. "Don't worry. Believe me, I know where I stand with Maiden."

CHAPTER ELEVEN

That afternoon Maiden was sitting behind the desk, flicking through some posters advertising Summerfest. Someone from the event coordinator's office had dropped them off yesterday, along with some promotional pamphlets. The city council was in full swing, and preparing for the tourists to come flooding in.

She was looking forward to it. While it meant more work and maybe longer hours, it was always fun to see the decorations spring up around town and then walk through the sprawling carnival that would set up in a few weeks.

She heard footsteps on the stairs and saw Billie descending. She was carrying a wadded-up bundle of fabric. She glanced at Maiden, gave an unimpressed look that was clearly aimed at whatever she was holding, and walked out through the side door that led to the backyard.

Maiden wondered if Ms. Randall had been sick in her room again. She hadn't seen much of her since the murder, but none of the guests had been excessively sociable of late. In any case, she decided to leave Billie to it.

She turned her attention to the computer and the booking schedule. They had managed to adapt their arrangements around Captain McAlister's capricious whims, but she still thought it was petty. She tried not to dwell on him and get angry again.

The important thing was that they had found solutions and everything was running smoothly. She gave a satisfied nod and picked up the newspaper, only to groan loudly when she looked at the front page.

Crazed Murderer Still At Large!

A local landmark, the Harlow House Inn, has played host to an unwelcome guest: murder!

The cold-blooded killer of Jim Creevey continues to roam free. Police have revealed very little about the case; it's only known that Mr. Creevey died in the early hours last Thursday from a blow to the head. The new head of the Golden Glen police department, Captain David McAlister, stated that the investigation is well underway and the staff of Harlow House has been cooperative so far. He declined to give an interview.

Maiden felt like blowing a raspberry at the sight of McAlister's name but just smiled at herself and read on. It was mostly unhelpful drivel, a sensationalized account of cold-blooded murder by person or persons unknown. There was nothing new or suggestive, just a bit of filler to keep the hysteria going.

She turned the page to find another mention of the bank robbery in Westfield.

Westfield Robbers Vanish

The CEO of the National Bank in Westfield, which was robbed at gunpoint early Monday morning, has issued a $5,000 reward for infor-

mation leading to the arrest of the people responsi-
ble for the crime.

The article went on to detail the getaway cars as described by onlookers. Maiden doubted either of the men would still be driving them, but she supposed finding the abandoned vehicles could yield some clues.

Her thoughts shifted to Mr. Creevey and the bushes outside the Varney's room. She wished she'd had more time to examine the area before Officer Briggs found her. There might have been footprints in the dirt. Not that she had any idea what to do about it if there were. Ultimately, she'd discovered something strange and alerted the police; she had done her duty.

That silent acknowledgment did nothing to stop the wheels from turning in her mind. She glanced at the edge of the hallway and willed Reg or Emily Varney to appear. Like most of the guests, they'd kept quiet since the murder.

Her eyes slid to the front door when she heard it open. Robert Gilford walked in and smiled when he saw her. He approached the desk and gave her a kind and enquiring look.

"Hey, Maiden," he said. "How's it going?"

"About the same." She shrugged. She didn't know what else to say. Nothing seemed to be progressing in the case, and she'd managed to get into a fight with the highest-ranking officer in town. She decided to shift the focus from herself. "Is your wife still coming? I thought she was supposed to be here by now."

"Oh. Yes, she was. But in view of...everything that happened, I called and asked her to wait." He cleared his throat and winced at her. "Please don't get the impression that I feel unsafe here. I mean, I could've done without seeing a dead body, if I'm honest. I promise I'm okay, but I can't stomach risking my little Anna."

"I understand, Mr. Gilford," Maiden said politely. "Believe me, I truly regret this disruption to *everyone's* plans."

"You poor thing. I'll bet this has been awful for your whole family," he said with a sympathetic smile. "Don't let it get to you though, these things always get cleared up. The police will figure it all out, you'll see."

He gave her a wink and headed for the stairs. As he turned away, she noticed a dark pink smudge on his collar. It looked like lipstick. Maiden blinked at the sight and then frowned pensively.

Robert had been incredibly easygoing about the disruption to his plans. He talked as though he were devoted to his wife, and Maiden could certainly understand not wanting to drag her into a situation that involved murder. But as she thought about that lipstick stain and listened to his cheerful whistle as he bounded up the stairs, she couldn't help wondering if he'd told Anna to stay away because he had found another means of enjoying his vacation.

It was Sunday morning when David turned up at the inn. He walked in alone and knew he didn't look especially happy to be there. The lobby was empty except for the two Harlow sisters stationed behind the desk. Vonny looked up and gave him a polite smile of greeting. Maiden did not.

He came and stood directly in front of the darker-haired woman, who sat reading a catalog. He craned his neck to see a page covered in pictures of linens and fake plants. David pulled a face before nodding to Vonny, who was standing off to the side eyeing him curiously, and then turned his attention to the top of Maiden's head.

She still hadn't moved and was obviously ignoring him. It was immature, and he knew he should pretend not to notice, but it annoyed him.

He cleared his throat, but she refused to budge. He rested his hands on the desktop and drummed his fingers loudly. No response. Finally, the tension became too much for Vonny to bear.

"Good morning, Captain McAlister," she said cheerfully. "What brings you here today?"

"I'm here to release your room, *potentially*," David qualified and kept his gaze fixed on Maiden until she finally looked up at him. "I'd like you to join me for the final inspection."

"You have a key," she said, and went back to her catalog.

"I want you to join me," he repeated.

Maiden sighed ungenerously before glancing at her sister. "Von, go with him."

"I asked for *you*," David reminded her steadily.

Vonny was observing the exchange with quiet amusement, her eyes darting between them as if she were watching a tennis match. Maiden shifted and glanced around for some sort of inspiration.

"I need to use the bathroom," she blurted the instant the excuse occurred to her.

"I'll wait." His voice was flat and unperturbed.

Maiden muttered under her breath as she slapped the catalog shut. She stood and stalked around the desk, ignoring her smirking sister, and went straight to the stairs. Without a word, she started briskly up them, only assuming that Captain McAlister was following her.

She reached the second floor and headed for room 6, all the way at the far end of the hall. It wasn't until she stopped in front of the door that she remembered McAlister had her key; she hadn't bothered to grab a spare. She was forced to wait as he approached with a slowness that she assumed was deliberate.

Maiden draped her hands on her hips and stared at the opposite wall; she kept her expression blank. She saw him look at her from the corner of her eye as he unlocked the door and pushed it open. She exhaled slowly through her nose and glanced inside, finding exactly what she'd expected.

The room was spotless thanks to a very thorough forensic unit. The floor was bare; the unfortunate rug having been removed and doubtless tagged and bagged in an evidence drawer somewhere. She was idly wondering if the police actually stored evidence in drawers when Captain McAlister leaned casually against the doorjamb.

"All right, I think we're done here, Miss Harlow." He smiled mildly. "Thank you for your cooperation."

Maiden exhaled very slowly and was sure she'd felt her eye twitch a little. He had delayed opening the room, forcing them to scramble to make alternate arrangements, and insisted that she escort him upstairs personally only to take a cursory look over the threshold and open the stupid thing up as he could have done in the first place with a word.

Her icy expression held all the colorful retorts she was too ladylike to utter.

"You're welcome," he murmured when she continued silent.

"Kindly go away immediately," she said in an emotionless monotone.

"Despite your subtlety, Miss Harlow, I can tell you're still angry," he said. "Please bear in mind that I have to put the interests of the investigation, and by extension the entire community, ahead of anyone's personal wishes."

"You're saying the community is safer for keeping a perfectly usable room closed off out of spite?" she asked dryly. "The risk to our business has contributed to the greater good? I'm thrilled we could help."

"It's not worth getting that upset over." He attempted to keep his tone patient.

"Sure, it's nothing to you if we lose money and reputation." She gave a dismissing wave. "You have your job to do, so why bother thinking of anyone else's?"

"It was one day," he pointed out.

"It was a day that could have cost a small business a lot of money, and ruined an innocent family's vacation. We made it work, but what were we supposed to do if we couldn't? Do you even care?" she replied with a slight shake of her head. "And for what? Because I accidentally stepped on your toes? Do you honestly think I was trying to go behind your back?"

"You did go behind my back," he said implacably.

"I did not! I did nothing!" she protested. "Mom insisted that I go and ask you to pretty please release the room, I had no intention of asking you for something that you would *never* agree to, so I was going to ask Greg if he knew when you'd be done."

"That isn't the impression you gave at the time." He hooked his thumbs in his belt loops.

"What impression did I give then?" She arched a black brow.

"You were standing there looking guilty and anxious because you knew you were asking to see your friend despite knowing perfectly well that *I'm* the one who makes decisions about this case." He pointed at her and took a step closer. "You were trying to use his clumsy infatuation with you to get special favors, and you knew *exactly* what you were doing."

"Ew! I would never encourage Greg, I used to watch him eat paste at school!" She pulled a face at the suggestion and ignored his quickly hidden amusement. "I don't use anyone, Captain McAlister, and I'd like to know how asking if he was on duty is tantamount to seduction. You're letting your personal dislike of me lead you to assume bad motive and that isn't fair. I haven't done anything wrong."

"I don't dislike you, Miss Harlow." He looked surprised at the suggestion. "Not at all, in fact."

"Oh, come on." She folded her arms. "I dared to set foot in the station without reporting immediately to you and you practically threw me out. Please rest assured that I won't go anywhere near the place again if I can avoid it."

He said nothing for a moment, and an awkward silence stretched between them. Maiden felt as unsettled as McAlister looked; there was a hint of regret in his eyes when he finally spoke.

"Well...that certainly isn't the impression I intended to give, Miss Harlow. I hope you aren't really that uncomfortable around me now, but I won't press you on it. Here," he said quietly and dropped the key in her hand. "The room's free for you to do as you like. I apologize for any inconvenience."

Maiden felt her anger bleed away as he turned and walked back down the hall. His steps were slow and thoughtful. She watched him go, wondering what he was thinking.

Did I overreact? she asked herself as he disappeared down the stairs. *I know I'm not good at being angry, but I didn't say anything that wasn't true. He looked disappointed, though, and now my stomach hurts. This sucks.*

A tiny part of her questioned whether her mother might have been right, had Captain McAlister reacted as he had to her asking for Greg because he was jealous? No, that was silly.

She shook her head at the notion, refusing to believe that anyone would be jealous of Greg. They were friends, and that was how she'd always treated him. He was nice enough, but...no, just absolutely no, never.

Besides, she and Captain McAlister knew nothing about each other; there was no way he was interested in her. He couldn't be.

That afternoon Maiden spent a bit of time in her room cleaning and sorting out her closet. She was in a strange and unsettled mood still, and she didn't feel like being around people.

She was trying not to dwell on her argument with Captain McAlister, and it wasn't easy. Vonny had asked her about it, but she'd just told her to stop being nosy.

Far from being offended, Von had been intrigued by her refusal to discuss it. The direct prying stopped, but the knowing looks didn't. That was when Maiden escaped upstairs.

She looked at her much tidier closet and decided she had wasted enough of her day hiding. She kicked aside the small pile of clothes she'd discarded and headed towards the kitchen.

By the time she'd grabbed her phone and was ready to leave, she was stopped by voices outside the apartment door. She crept closer and used the peephole, distantly wondering why Vonny hadn't been that sensible for *her* eavesdropping, and saw Vera Randall and Robert Gilford standing in front of the door to his room.

Vera stepped quite close to him and put on her usual sneer of a smile while Robert looked uncharacteristically annoyed. Maiden thought back to yesterday and the lipstick stains she'd spied on Robert's collar. Judging by his evident irritation with her, it seemed a safe bet that it hadn't been Vera's.

Knowing it was impolite to snoop but letting the circumstances of a suspicious death justify it, Maiden pressed her ear to the door and listened carefully.

"It's something worth thinking about, Robert. I can be a very generous woman, very sympathetic," Vera said coyly. "And your wife *still* hasn't joined you?"

"Obviously not," he said with a loud sigh. He eased away, looking a little flustered by her overt manner. "If she was here, I'd be right beside her. You know how it is when you're in love."

"Oh, I sure do," she purred. "But I hate to think of you all on your own. It's been days, you must be so lonely by now."

"I'm fine, Ms. Randall," he said firmly. "But I'm beginning to wonder if you're hard of hearing."

"Careful." A hint of frost entered her voice. "You don't want to be on my bad side, that can be *very* dangerous."

"I don't want to be on any side of yours, bad or otherwise. I really have to go." He sounded harassed.

Maiden went back to the peephole in time to see Vera shutting herself loudly in her room. Robert shook his head in irritated disgust and glanced briefly at his door before turning and walking off down the hall towards the stairs.

Maiden rested her shoulder against the door as she took a moment to digest what she'd heard. Vera's words had come across as flirtation, but there was a definite threat behind them too.

She said it was dangerous to be on her bad side, she thought. *Mr. Creevey was on her bad side...Don't jump to conclusions, Maiden.*

Chapter Twelve

Maiden felt a little more like herself by the following morning. Von had volunteered to do the early shift for the first time in months, and Maiden was happy enough to let her have it.

She had actually been offered the whole day off, but said she'd think about it. She knew her mother was moved either by pity or a hope that she'd use her free time to throw herself into the path of Captain McAlister. Neither possibility appealed to her, so she stayed hidden away in her room until Gloria left.

Maiden crept out of the apartment and headed downstairs. Before she'd even reached the foyer, she heard the phone ring. Vonny answered politely enough, but with a weariness in her voice that suggested she'd said her welcoming spiel more than a few times. Maiden rounded the corner in time to hear Von explaining that they were fully booked for the next six weeks.

"Yes...I understand that, yes." Vonny's tone was courteous, but her expression certainly wasn't. "The murder did take place in one of our rooms, yes. I'm afraid that specific room is booked out for the next *eight* weeks, sir. Yes, I can put you on a cancellation list. Thank you, goodbye."

Before Vonny could set the phone down and complain to her, it rang again. She muttered crankily before putting on her polite voice as she answered it. Maiden smiled in bemused wonder as a very similar conversation to the last one unfolded.

She slid in beside her sister, and they took turns answering calls for the rest of the morning. Time flew as people kept calling and asking about the murder.

Amazingly, rumors of Mr. Creevey's death hadn't put most people off staying at the inn. Only two reservations had been canceled, and without charge under the circumstances. But three times as many people had called and booked in, most of them having heard of Harlow House for the first time in the news reports of the case.

Several callers had requested the room where the murder had taken place. It was all a bit grisly, but as Gloria pointed out on her way to hide in the peace and quiet of the office, business was business and money was money.

For a few hours at least, Maiden kept her focus on the running of the inn. They even started talking about hiring some seasonal staff to help in the kitchen besides the girls they already employed to wait tables. The increased food prep was looking like too much for Kylie to keep up with alone.

Most of the guests had been dining at the inn lately, particularly once they'd sampled Kylie's delicious creations and correctly surmised that they wouldn't do better elsewhere in town. More guests meant more meals, which meant more revenue. Maiden hoped the extra business would finally soften her mother's dismal view of the shy cook.

She also hoped the increased workload would keep her own mind off a tall, handsome police captain who hadn't spoken to her since he'd released room 6. Maiden kept telling herself she was blowing it out of proportion. She'd only met the guy a few times, and she didn't need to develop a deeper liking for anyone that petty.

Not that he thought he was causing any actual harm, she betrayed herself by admitting. *And it didn't impact the business. Not really. You overreacted; it's not that big of a deal.*

It wasn't the point; she reminded herself stubbornly. Besides, he had other things to occupy his time. She felt torn and therefore rather sulky, but didn't want it to show. So, when Vonny sailed into the room after her coffee break, she was eager to get away before the inevitable remarks.

Vonny's knowing about her run-in with Captain McAlister was almost as uncomfortable as the argument itself had been.

"All quiet on the front lines?" Vonny asked cheerfully.

"Yes, the phone hasn't rung since you left." Maiden stood and vacated the seat. "Hopefully it'll stay quiet for a while, we don't have too many vacancies until November anyway."

"The good old seasonal festivals." Vonny smiled as she perched on the empty chair.

"And the violent murder of a guest." She pulled a face and shook her head. "Room 6 is now officially the most requested of all time."

"Yeah, it's pretty icky." Vonny wrinkled her nose but got over it quickly; she slid her little sister a sly look. "Sooo, nothing of *interest*?"

"Not that I'm aware of." She gave her a warning look.

"Oh, that's disappointing." Vonny pouted. "I was hoping he'd make some kind of effort before things cool off too much."

"You're as bad as Mom," Maiden sighed. "Captain McAlister is not interested in me, Von. Please drop it."

"Mae, honestly." She rolled her eyes. "You can be so clueless sometimes. You didn't see his face when he left yesterday, he was like a kicked puppy, it was awful."

"Then why hasn't he called? Or stopped by again? Or *any-thing*?" she challenged, more than tired of the insinuations and outright nosiness.

"Because you tore his heart out and wore it like a hat," Von said dramatically as she leaned closer and gave her a deadly serious look.

Maiden couldn't help laughing at her. "You're an idiot."

"I'll never agree to that." Vonny held up a chiding finger and then started perusing the papers on the desk. "But it's only been a day and Captain McCutie-pants does have the hots for you. So, take comfort in that if nothing else."

"I'm endlessly comforted, thank you," Maiden said sarcastically and hurried away before Von could say anything more.

Being teased and cajoled about an imaginary romance was bad enough, but it was extra embarrassing because there was no romance there. Yes, she knew Captain McAlister had taken more than one opportunity to enjoy the view when they were together, but that had been it.

Was she supposed to pin hopes and desperately read meaning into every man that gave her a second look? She'd end up like—

"Oh, hello, Ms. Randall." Maiden flushed when the woman she had been cautioning herself against suddenly appeared beside her in the doorway of the dining room.

"Hmm?" Vera glanced at her as though she'd been too busy to notice her. She was clutching her phone; her bright orange nails a glaring contrast to the pale purple case. She had been smiling at the screen until Maiden dared to speak to her. "Oh, it's *you* again."

"Yeah, I guess it is." Maiden suppressed a sigh at her rudeness. "You seem to be feeling better today, that's nice."

"I'm feeling fantastic," Vera said smugly. "Life is full of op-portunity and my fortunes are definitely on the up. Something a receptionist that works for her parents couldn't even fathom. Goodbye."

With that, she swept past with a disdainful sniff.

Maiden watched her go straight to the furthest table and sit down; she took a deep breath and shook her head at the unkind woman.

A moment later, Reg and Emily Varney appeared in the doorway. As soon as they looked inside and spotted Vera, they abruptly turned and murmured something to each other about having lunch in town.

Maiden nodded in acknowledgment of Emily's smile and watched them hurry to the front door and out into the bright sunshine.

She considered their retreat a wise one; she then entered the dining room herself and started fixing a cup of coffee. She glanced over and saw Billie watering the plants.

"Hey, Billie." She smiled and waved her over. "Join me for coffee."

Billie returned the smile and walked over, setting her watering can on the table. It was a whimsical creation in the shape of a flower basket; using it made for a rather bizarre sight as one blossom regurgitated water onto another. Billie poured herself a cup and headed back over.

"How's your day been, Maiden?" She gave her a quietly hopeful look as she sat across from her. "Anything exciting happening?"

"Have you been talking to Mom?" she asked suspiciously.

"Only a little." Billie shrugged sheepishly. "Sorry, I didn't mean to be nosy."

"Speaking of nosy," she hurried to change the subject. "Did Captain McAlister question you again?"

"Not a lot." Billie tapped her short nails on the side of her mug. "He asked me if the door to room 6 was locked when I found that Creevey guy's body."

"And was it?" Maiden leaned towards her.

"Yeah, I had to use my key." She nodded and patted the heavily loaded keyring on her hip. "Does it matter?"

"Yes, it does." Maiden chewed at her lip. "Whoever killed Mr. Creevey locked the door behind them and then went downstairs and put the key on the hook."

"Why would they do that?" Billie asked uncertainly.

"I don't know," she said and sipped her coffee. "Maybe so that not just anyone could walk in and find him? No, that doesn't make sense, who else would go looking for him?"

"Maybe that Vera chick?" Billie whispered and slid a glance to the table where the woman in question was sitting and smirking down at her phone. "She's been trying to reel in any man she can since she got here."

"I don't think so." Maiden shook her head. "He made a pass at her the other day and it fell very flat. She was furious with him."

"Do you think she killed him?" Billie's eyes were wide as she leaned in a bit more.

"I...don't really know," she admitted. "Anything is possible, but I don't think she's strong enough."

"How strong do you have to be to clock someone on the head?" Billie asked.

"I couldn't tell you." Maiden smiled wryly at that, but her expression grew serious again. "But I doubt Mr. Creevey's death is as straightforward as it seems. I've been thinking about how he was laying in the room...I don't believe that's where he actually died."

"What?" Billie gasped loudly, but lowered her voice when a few of the guests glanced at them. "What do you mean?"

"It didn't look right," she said pensively. "He was too close to the door and was positioned at a weird angle…I think he was dragged in and left there."

"That's so creepy." Billie grimaced. "Have you told the police that?"

"No, they've probably thought of it too," she replied a little too quickly. "The last thing they'd want is someone like me butting in."

"Maybe if you apologized to Captain McAlister?"

"Apologize?" Maiden glared at her. "For what exactly?"

Billie looked startled by her sudden anger and shrank back.

"I'm not really sure," she admitted in a small voice. "Vonny said you were mean to him…but she may have exaggerated."

"She may also have volunteered an opinion without knowing half of what actually happened," Maiden grumbled irritably. "It's not like he walked in acting sweet and I started yelling at him!"

"I never thought that," Billie assured her.

"You just thought I was mean?" She sat back and folded her arms. "Thanks a lot."

"You *are* being a bit crabby, Maiden." She cleared her throat and sipped her coffee. "Don't get mad at me. I only wanted to let you know since it's really unlike you. I thought maybe he'd caught you on a bad day."

Maiden stared down into her cup and fell silent. Billie wasn't entirely mistaken, but the bad day was McAlister's fault. She didn't want to feel guilty about reacting naturally to an aggravating situation.

But if you'd stayed calm, it wouldn't have gotten that heated. You could've told him he was being a turkey and laughed it off.

She told the unwelcome thought to get lost and decided she was done talking for a while. She pushed to her feet and collected her coffee.

"Well, the police don't need my help, regardless." She managed a smile. "I'll go and lavish my crabbiness on Von, she deserves it more than you do."

Billie chuckled and turned her attention back to her coffee.

Maiden entered the foyer and scowled at her obnoxious sister. Vonny had the gall to look confused by it.

"I didn't say anything," Von said quickly, as discreet as ever.

"Stop gossiping about me and mind your own business, please," she said firmly, but left it at that. Getting angry with Vonny rarely improved a situation.

Von looked away self-consciously and pretended to browse through a catalog. Maiden walked into the office and shut the door behind her in hopes of finishing her coffee in peace.

A couple of hours later, she retreated to her room and slipped out onto her balcony with her silly library book. The peacefully sheltered space outside her bedroom was one of Maiden's favorite spots to go when she wanted to see without being seen. And the balcony that adorned the lavish attic suites above her provided not only privacy but also shaded relief from the hot afternoon sunshine.

She was curled up in one of a pair of wicker peacock chairs. They were an old-fashioned design with soft cushions and matching footrests; they would have looked at home on the veranda of a Georgia mansion.

Maiden's book lay forgotten on her lap as she studied the bustling street below. From her vantage point, she watched some guests as they went out and others as they came back to the inn to stash their purchases, have coffee, and take naps before dinner.

Most of them chatted, or at least smiled and said hello, to whoever they happened to walk past, with the notable exception of Vera Randall. She sauntered down the street with her nose in the air, swinging a few bags from *Sweet-n-Chic*, the most expensive clothing boutique in town. Vera cheerfully ignored the looks and occasional smirk, as she wiggled past in her neon orange mini-dress and dashed inside with her new treasures.

Maiden wondered what she'd meant when she was boasting about the future. Considering how miserable she had looked after Mr. Creevey tried to buy her services, she acted like a different woman now. Something must have worked out quite well for her.

Apart from Vera, Robert Gilford went out once more, and the Kaminsky family headed noisily towards the playground on the next street. The Varneys stayed out for most of the day and returned carrying a lot of bags from various stores and a couple of wineries. They looked much happier than they had earlier.

Maiden closed her eyes as weariness washed over her. The past week had been strange, frightening, and uncertain. She wondered what evidence the police had actually found and if they had any strong suspects.

To her, it felt like nothing was moving forward. The cops had come in, taken statements, and generally poked and prodded their way through the entire inn, but it didn't seem to have yielded much. She hoped Officer Briggs had reported that damaged bush...and kept her name right out of it.

She'd been keeping a discreet eye on all the guests since the murder. Most had gone very quiet for a day or two, but everything seemed to be returning to business as usual. She supposed that was because Mr. Creevey had been there alone and was far from friendly with anyone. As sad as it might be, no one missed him.

She considered what she'd said to Billie about the body. It was a suspicion that had been floating around in the back of her mind for a little while, but that was the first time she had actually mentioned it out loud. Surely the police would have reached the same conclusion; it was pretty clear to her, and she wasn't a trained investigator.

So, if Mr. Creevey really had died somewhere else, that raised new questions and opened some different possibilities.

To her mind, it made it less likely that the killer was a woman. Not impossible, but unlikely, at least for the particular women who were on hand and had the opportunity to have done it. That potentially narrowed down the suspects, at least.

What worried her was that the more time that passed, the colder the trail would get. What if it ended up as another unsolved crime? Would their inn always have a tarnished reputation?

She knew she couldn't let that happen.

That evening Maiden was back downstairs helping in the dining room. The inn was full, and everyone had booked in for dinner that night. Her role was to keep everything running smoothly.

Loud conversations and the clatter of dishes and cutlery filled the air. Almost every table was occupied by the time Vera Randall walked in.

She wore a skin-tight black cocktail dress dripping with sequins and a pair of blood-red high heels. Her hair was curled and quaffed and sprayed, and her makeup was heavy but immaculate.

Maiden noticed her stroll in with a pleased smile on her face and then head towards one of the few vacant tables. Number 5, right in the center of the crowded room. That suited Vera perfectly.

She strutted in, cradling a bottle of wine in the crook of her arm as though it were a trophy. When the woman glanced around and turned her brazenly triumphant smirk on the Varneys, Maiden wondered if that was exactly what it was.

Emily gave Vera a look of disgust while Reg's mustache twitched with irritation. Vera enjoyed their ill temper and laughed merrily as she sat down and crossed her long legs. Maiden edged closer to Vonny as she walked past, carrying a coffee pot.

"Is that what you'd call a 'vamp'?" Maiden whispered to her.

Von followed her gaze and looked Vera over with an unimpressed expression.

"I'd call that a cheerleader that's been made into jerky," she replied dryly.

Maiden spluttered in an attempt to hide her amusement. She sobered instantly, however, when she heard fingers snapping behind her. She stiffened and glanced back with an arched brow to see Vera beckoning her over.

"You!" she demanded loudly. "Bring me a corkscrew and a glass."

Maiden set her teeth and waged an internal struggle to be polite. Vera's smug look wasn't helping, but then she heard a voice whisper near her ear.

"I'm surprised she didn't just ask for a straw. Save the time and trouble of pouring it all out." Robert met her eyes with an impish grin when she glanced at him. "I do hope she doesn't get drunk; she's determined enough to claim my chastity as it is."

Maiden pressed her lips together and bowed her head to keep from laughing. He winked at her and gave her a bolstering nudge with his elbow before walking over to a table for one near the back of the room. Maiden was grateful for the sorely needed levity; she made herself go to the kitchen.

The theme for the evening, much to Alfie's annoyance, was Mexican food and margaritas. It was popular with the guests and therefore regularly scheduled. But the preference for the featured cocktails meant Maiden had to dig around for a corkscrew.

They had a bar of sorts, a cabinet in the kitchen, but Maiden had never had much to do with it. She pawed through a few drawers until she finally found a corkscrew. She grabbed it and a wineglass and headed back to the dining room, eager to get the thankless task over with.

By the time she walked in, Vera was hacking at the bottle's wax seal with a butter knife.

"You got that?" Maiden asked mildly as she set the accoutrements on the table.

"Yes, I'm quite capable of getting into a bottle of fine wine," she replied with a petulant sneer.

"I'll bet you are," Maiden murmured and walked away before the unpleasant woman could hiss a reply.

She went back to her duties but kept glancing at her out of morbid curiosity. Vera was a little too smug tonight; something was up. Something she was incredibly pleased about.

Vera finally, and with very little grace or decorum, wrenched the cork free of the bottle. She simpered and smiled victoriously as she tipped out a very full glass and raised it with relish. Stopping only long enough to take an appreciative whiff, she knocked back a third of the glass in one swallow.

Maiden shook her head in wonder, but then got about her business. She floated around the room, greeting the guests she hadn't met yet and exchanging pleasantries with a few regulars who came every season. As she neared the Varney's table, she could hear Emily grumbling.

"Can you believe that awful woman?" She sounded appalled. "Sitting there in that tacky little half of a dress and drinking like a fish! Have you ever seen anything more ridiculous?"

"I certainly haven't, dear, that's for sure." Reg nodded dutifully.

He seemed more agreeable than usual. This was the same man she'd once overheard telling his wife to stop griping when she mentioned that her bacon was a little on the crisp side for her liking. Maiden considered his placid demeanor and noticed that he flitted a few surreptitious looks in Vera's direction.

Maiden followed his gaze and saw Vera smile saucily and wink at him; he quickly glanced away and cleared his throat. Maiden stepped closer to Vera's table to reclaim the corkscrew and walk away before she could demand anything else. She returned to the kitchen long enough to dump the corkscrew straight into a drawer and then hurried back out to help.

After another ten minutes, everyone had had their fill of chips and salsa; it was time to serve dinner. The seasonal helpers they'd called in to assist with the evening meals were hard at work.

Ambitious college girls with smiles, pigtails, and doubtless enough student loans to keep them eager to please, started arranging platters full of food on the long serving tables. Maiden watched them, ready to step in if needed, but was pleased by the care they put into their task.

She glanced over at the nearest table, which was number 5, Vera's table, and frowned. Vera was struggling to sit upright and looked around as though she were lost. She blinked several times and then stared down into her empty glass. Maiden shifted her gaze from the glass to the bottle. Strange, it was still mostly full, but Vera was acting as though she'd finished it and then some.

Maiden watched the woman push her glass away and then fumble as she picked up the bottle. Vera squinted at the label in vain before setting it down and shaking her head as if to clear it.

Frowning now, and more than a little concerned, Maiden walked towards her to see if she needed help. Before she could reach her, however, Vera pushed unsteadily to her feet and turned towards the buffet.

"I think I need to—" she said in an unsteady voice before collapsing on the floor.

Maiden ran to her as loud gasps and startled exclamations rose from the other guests. She dropped to her knees beside Vera and rolled her onto her back.

"Ms. Randall?" she said loudly as she patted her cheek. "Vera! Can you hear me?"

Nothing. Maiden put a hand in front of her nose but couldn't feel any breath hitting it. Struck with a sickening feeling of dread; she looked around and spotted her sister.

"Vonny! Call an ambulance!" she shouted and then added, after another glance at Vera's ashen face, "And the police!"

Chapter Thirteen

Maiden was cradling a glass of white wine between her palms. She sat alone in one of the plush chairs that sat outside the dismally quiet dining room, staring up at the clock that was ticking away on the wall. It was a little past midnight, and she was exhausted. The paramedics had confirmed her fears and pronounced Vera Randall dead at the scene.

The police arrived soon after, and everyone else was ushered out. The forensics team had done a painstaking sweep of the area, taken countless photos, and removed Vera's body.

Alfie and Gloria had again come to the rescue and calmed the guests as best they could. They arranged for meals to be delivered to the rooms as no one could use the dining room for the foreseeable future. Maiden was grateful that Vera hadn't touched the food before she died; the last thing they needed was rumors of poisonings at the inn.

"If I had to guess, I'd say it was poisoning," a slender man dressed in a hazmat suit informed Captain McAlister as they both walked out of the dining room.

Maiden blinked owlishly at them, shocked that he had so casually squashed her one source of meager consolation. McAlister glanced over and spotted her; he stopped and cleared his throat discreetly. The man in the plastic suit followed his gaze and smiled instantly.

"Oh, I'm sorry."

He was mostly bald but had a wreath of short gray hair that ran from one ear across the back of his head to the other, and he wore small round spectacles that perched on the end of his nose. Despite his fading hairline, she guessed him to be no older than fifty. He also seemed quite upbeat, considering the situation.

"Good evening, Miss Harlow. This is the coroner." McAlister nodded to the man. "Doctor Ben Jenkins."

"It's nice to meet you, Dr. Jenkins." She stood and shook his hand. "I apologize for the circumstances."

"It's hardly your fault, my dear." The doctor smiled again as he subtly looked her over. "And how dreadful to have people keep dying in your charming hotel."

Maiden wasn't sure how best to respond to that. "It is. Thank you."

"Send me your report as soon as possible, will you, doc?" McAlister stepped in, giving him a wry look and a nod towards the door.

"Yes, of course. I'd better get to work." Jenkins took the hint and looked as though he'd have tipped his hat to her if he'd been wearing one. "Lovely to meet you, Miss Harlow. Goodnight."

Maiden watched him go and then turned back to McAlister. He smiled until their eyes met, then he instantly sobered.

She hadn't forgotten how curt she'd been during their last discussion, or that her family and their business were at his mercy once again. She needed to make an effort.

"Well, despite the circumstances, welcome back, Captain McAlister." She nodded at her glass before taking a sip. "Sorry, if you weren't on duty I'd offer you one."

"If I weren't on duty I'd accept," he replied.

That's a promising start, Maiden thought. *He's working, though. Be careful and don't read too much into anything.*

"So, you were the one to find the body? Again?" he asked in an unrevealing tone.

"That's not exactly fair," she protested and took another drink. "She dropped dead in front of almost everyone in the hotel. I only checked to see if she was still breathing."

"I phrased that badly," he admitted and motioned for her to sit down before taking up the seat beside her. "You gave a statement already?"

"I did, yes." She rubbed her weary eyes. "It's all such a muddle, though. Do you really think she was poisoned?"

"I'm not inclined to make my mind up about that until I see the official report. They have to do the autopsy and so forth." He winced apologetically when she shuddered at the mention of it. "Sorry, it goes along with these situations. What are your initial impressions? Are you aware of anyone that hated Ms. Randall?"

"There's no polite way to answer that question." She pulled a face.

"Politeness is a luxury that the police can rarely afford." He smiled faintly. "As you may have already noticed."

Maiden almost choked on her wine as she tried not to laugh. She was too shocked, tired, and surprised that this incredibly good-looking man was being nice to her, even after their last encounter. She ran a hand over her face and finally rested her chin in it as she considered his question.

"I think she was widely disliked because she was kind of mean," she said at last. "But I can't immediately think of anyone that had a reason to really *hate* her."

"That's not helpful," he murmured dryly.

"But excruciatingly honest." She shrugged and emptied her glass. "Are you sure you don't want one? I won't tell anybody."

"I thought you were honest," he said with a hint of teasing challenge.

"I am," she assured him as she stood. "I'm just being hospitable, it's another hazard of the trade."

"I see. Well, I'd better not, Miss Harlow," he chuckled as he smiled up at her. "I might get myself into mischief. Good night."

The following day, the dining room was still closed, so Gloria turned the library into a makeshift breakfast nook. They pushed a few coffee tables together and piled them high with pastries and fruit platters. The weather was quite pleasant, so most of the guests flitted in and out to fill their plates before dispersing to the sitting areas outside.

They had to take the food out through the back door of the kitchen and around to the main entrance. It was a minor inconvenience, but at least they could still provide meals for their guests.

Maiden had taken advantage of the warmer temperatures and slipped into a snug little mauve dress and a pair of patent leather kitten heels. It was one of her more flattering garments, but when she chose it that morning, she promised herself that she wasn't trying to look extra nice for any particular reason.

The police had arrived very early and were interviewing the guests, some of whom were shaking with nerves while others lapped up the excitement. Maiden sat behind the reception desk and sipped her coffee, her cherry pastry forgotten at her elbow. It had been a long night, and she was still on edge.

A second murder had taken place, and in a room full of witnesses; it was bizarre and frightening. She couldn't imagine why this was all happening, and why it was happening at their inn. Harlow House had been a pillar of whimsical respectability in the community for years; now suddenly guests were dropping like flies.

Maiden watched as Captain McAlister walked out from the long hallway that separated the lobby from the ground floor guestrooms, with Greg Smith following close behind.

The captain looked masculine and authoritative without even trying. He wore dark trousers and an off-white shirt, but he'd left his collar open and pulled his tie loose. Well-polished shoes and a suit coat completed the look; she distantly wondered if he had a fedora tossed casually on a hat rack in his office.

On the other hand, Greg was buttoned snugly into his crisply ironed uniform. His steps were carefully measured to never outpace his captain, and he leaned as close as he politely could to hear every word the man uttered. His admiration for McAlister was almost tangible.

Maiden didn't wonder at it; Greg had graduated from the police academy a couple of years ago and was still finding his niche. They caught up occasionally, but she got most of her updates from Tony. As far as gossip went, postal workers had ample opportunity to pick up as much as they delivered.

Quite a few rumors were floating around about the new police captain, and they'd picked up noticeably after the first murder, which called a lot more attention to him. A hot-shot detective from Stanton—a place about as different from Golden Glen as you could get—who settled in their sleepy old town for some unknown reason. Theories behind that choice were varied and colorful. Some whispered that he was hiding out from gangsters, while others swore he was there hunting spies.

Maiden assumed the stories were complete nonsense, but she wasn't game to ask him about it, or about anything too personal. She held her breath as he looked up at her. He said nothing but veered towards her as she took another bracing sip of her cappuccino.

"Good morning, Miss Harlow." McAlister smiled cordially and then glanced at Greg. "I'll see you back at the station, Officer Smith."

"Yes sir." Greg took the hint and shot her a quick, careful smile before trundling past and on out the door.

McAlister waited until he was gone and then met her inquiring look.

"I wanted to let you know that the dining room is now available." He smiled so briefly that she almost missed it. "I don't want to inconvenience you needlessly."

"How considerate, Captain McAlister," she replied with a good-natured smirk. "What about Ms. Randall's room?"

"Don't get greedy, Miss Harlow." He smiled again. "I can't work miracles, give me a full day at least."

She shrugged and smoothed her hands down over her knees. His eyes followed the movement of her fingers, and he took a subtle step closer. Before he could speak, they heard rapid footsteps and looked over in time to see a red-faced Emily Varney round the same corner McAlister had come from.

When she saw them, she pressed her lips together and searched desperately for somewhere else to be. She nearly ran into the dining room and out of sight.

"What was that about?" Maiden whispered, mostly to herself, but McAlister answered anyway.

"I'm afraid I had to interview Mr. and Mrs. Varney this morning," he murmured.

"You have a way with people, don't you?" she said, only half-joking.

"Depending on what I'm trying to achieve…" He let the thought dissipate into the atmosphere before changing the subject. "I read through your statement. There are one or two things I'd like you to clarify."

"Oh, okay." She sat up straighter. "Like what?"

"Nothing I want to discuss in the middle of a hotel lobby. Come to my office this afternoon if you can, please. Say around 2 o'clock?" He inclined his head a fraction and left before she could agree or object.

Maiden sat there for a moment, wondering what she might have said that needed explaining. She then remembered Emily and felt her curiosity grow.

Kylie was standing behind her workstation, trying to figure out a way to serve lunch. She was considering sandwiches again, as these would be easy to deliver to the rooms, when she heard the door swing open. She looked up, expecting another policeman asking more horrible questions, but stilled when she recognized one of the guests.

Kylie wondered how she got through the dining room to reach that door; as far as she knew, everything was still closed off.

A guest had never wandered into the kitchen before, and she wasn't sure what to do about it. It would probably be rude to ask her to leave, and the lady already looked like she'd been crying. Kylie held her breath as she stepped closer.

"I'm sorry to barge in like this," the woman mumbled, twisting a handkerchief in her hands. "I needed a few minutes to pull myself together...Do you have any spare desserts by any chance? Something sweet would be very welcome right now."

Kylie looked around helplessly for a moment before processing what she'd said. She nodded and hurried to one of the large stainless-steel fridges. A beautiful chocolate cake that had been meant for dessert last night was sitting there waiting to be eaten.

She pulled it out and served up a generous piece. Setting the plate of cake down in front of the stranger, Kylie even managed a smile, but it faded abruptly when the woman burst into tears.

Kylie held her breath and took a tiny step back. She knew she hadn't said anything wrong; she hadn't even spoken, but she'd have to now. They were alone, and she was inexperienced with comforting people; her stomach tightened as she searched for something to say.

"Um...are you all right?" she tried lamely. "Can I help at all?"

"No!" the woman sobbed into her hands. "My life is unraveling right in front of me and there's nothing anyone can do about it!"

"Oh no." Kylie felt herself grow flushed and lightheaded. She groped desperately for an appropriate response and blurted, "Do you want some ice cream? I have lots!"

The woman glanced up at her as though she were crazy, but then she smiled.

"No, the cake is perfect, thanks," she laughed weakly and sank onto one of the stools in front of the counter that no one ever sat on. "Just let me calm myself down a bit; I can't go back out there looking like this. He might see me."

"Who might?" Kylie asked carefully, not forgetting that two people had already been killed.

"Reg, my so-called husband." She rolled her tearful eyes in disgust and then glanced back at her. "I'm Emily, by the way."

"Kylie. I'm the chef." She managed a tiny smile and gestured towards her uniform. "I guess that's obvious."

"Just a bit." Emily sniffled into her handkerchief. "The food's been excellent."

"Thanks." She wasn't great at accepting compliments, so she didn't linger over it; instead, she pulled a fork from a drawer and handed it to her. "Did you...want to talk about whatever happened?"

"I don't know," Emily sighed and poked at her cake. "It's so humiliating...we've been married for five years, we're here to celebrate our stupid anniversary. I would never do something like this to him, never. And it isn't as though he looks like a movie star either thank you very much!"

"Oh." Kylie glanced away glumly. "He's cheating on you, I'm so sorry."

"And with that withered old bit of trash!" She speared her fork into the thickest end of the cake, scooped up a large bite and shoved it angrily into her mouth. "That's the worst part. He was running around after some alley cat that liked to gobble up other women's husbands."

"I'm sorry, but I don't leave the kitchen very often, who are we talking about?" Kylie shook her head.

"That Randall woman!" she muttered. "The one that died last night."

"Oh!" Kylie paled. She had no idea what to say now. "Well...at least you don't have to worry about her now—oh, that's an awful thing to say! I'm terrible at talking to people, I'm so sorry!"

"You're fine," Emily chuckled and took another bite of her cake. "What can you even say in the circumstances?"

Kylie gave a conceding nod and absently wiped down the gleaming countertop with a cloth. She was curious now; particularly because Vera Randall was dead. Her gaze slid to Emily. The woman must have felt the stare; she looked up and gave her a lopsided smile.

"I didn't kill her, if that's what's worrying you," she said candidly. "I didn't find out about them until this morning."

"I wasn't suggesting that!" Kylie hurried to assure her. "You seem way too nice to hurt anyone."

"I don't know about that. I could strangle Reg." She set her fork aside as she started to cry again. "I can't believe it; our whole life together is a lie! What if she wasn't the only one? What if he's been running around behind my back all this time?"

"You'll leave him then?" Kylie asked.

"Probably. It depends." She sniffled as she calmed a little and took another bite. "I don't know many of the details yet...not that I want to, but I *have* to know."

"Yeah." Kylie nodded. "I understand that."

Emily gave her another faint smile. "You're nice to talk to. Thanks, Kylie."

She blushed but smiled as she looked away shyly.

The door opened, and they both turned sharply toward it. Maiden stepped inside and took in the scene; a kind smile curved her lips when she saw Emily and walked over to join them.

Kylie felt a wave of relief. Maiden was very nice, and while she sometimes wished she wouldn't try so hard to talk with her, she appreciated her efforts. She'd certainly be helpful in this situation.

"You've wandered into the inner reaches." Maiden intoned playfully and sat beside Emily.

"I suppose guests aren't allowed in here." Emily lowered her gaze to her plate.

"*You* are." Maiden rested a hand briefly on her shoulder and glanced at Kylie. "That cake looks beautiful, let's both join in, shall we?"

Kylie started to refuse, but a sharp look from Maiden made her swallow the reflexive reaction. She nodded and served up two more pieces. Emily slid her now-empty plate over and tapped on the edge.

"Keep it coming, bartender," she said dryly.

Kylie smiled as she put another slice on her plate. Emily whispered her thanks and pulled it back towards her. Maiden took a dainty bite of her cake before speaking again.

"Are you all right, Mrs. Varney?" she asked.

"Please, call me Emily." She rubbed her forehead wearily. "I can't be called by his name right now, maybe never again."

"Okay, are you all right, Emily?" she amended.

"Not really," Emily muttered. "I'm here on my wedding anniversary and thanks to Reg and that tramp, everything's ruined."

"Oh!" Maiden barely suppressed a gasp. "You mean Reg and Vera..."

Emily buried her face in her hands. "I'm a complete joke!"

"You're *not*, I promise. But I don't blame you for feeling that way," Maiden said gently and looked at Kylie for support. Kylie stared back vacantly, but then realized that she still had a role to play.

"Yeah," she chimed in, "no one thinks less of you."

"The police might." Emily took a shuddering breath as she raised her head and dabbed at her swollen eyes. "Unless they arrest Reg instead."

"They suspect him?" Kylie's eyes were wide.

"Why not?" Emily shrugged. "Who knows how long they've been carrying on? Who knows if they'd fought and turned against each other?"

"I'm sorry to ask this, but how do you know he was involved with her?" Maiden leaned her elbow on the bench and rested her chin in her hand.

"The police found a gift tag in her room that said '*Love, Reg*'," she grumbled. "And then proceeded to tell him that they knew she worked in his office. She worked with him! He's known her for months, but in front of *me* he treated her like a stranger! He's been lying to me all along."

"They worked together?" Maiden stared at her.

"Yup." Emily stabbed her cake. "And he was disgusting enough to meet up with her during our anniversary trip. Five years of my life blown apart by one crappy week and two dead bodies. Nicely done, Reggie-boy."

Maiden's mind was reeling. A few things made more sense. For one thing, she could understand now why Vera came to stay at Harlow House despite hating small towns. But as she thought back over what she had seen of their interactions, Reg Varney had seemed annoyed by Vera. She wondered if they really had agreed to meet up there or if Vera had made an audacious play for his attention.

"Have the police said they suspect him?" Maiden asked.

"Not in so many words." Emily shrugged. "But they did tell him not to leave the inn without permission. Not just the town this time, the *inn*. What does that tell you?"

"They may just be following procedure," Maiden suggested, and then gave her a searching look. "Did they say how Vera died?"

"Apparently she had enough barbiturates in her system to drop a cow," Emily said with little sympathy. "One of the bovine variety, of course."

"Barbiturates?" Kylie blinked. "Does anyone still take those?"

"Vera Randall certainly did," Emily replied coolly.

Maiden and Kylie exchanged a quietly stunned look. Maiden cleared her throat discreetly and touched Emily's arm.

"What did Reg have to say about that?" she asked.

"He looked genuinely shocked," Emily admitted. "He's obviously a convincing liar, but his eyes nearly dropped out of his head when the police mentioned barbiturates...she mustn't have told him about them."

"Well, he could have been lying." Maiden gave her a searching look. "Do you think he's capable of murder?"

"I don't know." Emily rubbed her temples as though they were throbbing. "I never thought he would cheat, I guess I don't know him at all. It looks like my father was right..."

Maiden wondered about that remark, but felt she had pried enough for the moment, about Vera at least.

"Emily," she said tentatively, "what about Mr. Creevey? Did you or Reg know him before you came here?"

"Creevey?" Emily frowned. "No, definitely not. Frankly, he's not the sort of person I like to get to know."

"So, Reg didn't know him either?" she pressed gently.

"Not that he said." Emily's eyes filled with tears again. "But he didn't say he knew Vera Randall either."

"Yeah, that's a worry." Maiden slid her gaze away uncomfortably but took another stab at learning something. "The night of

Mr. Creevey's murder, did you hear anything strange? His room was right above yours."

"I know, that was creepy to find out." Emily shuddered and wiped at her eyes. "I didn't hear anything from upstairs…but Reg snores like a freight train so that doesn't mean much."

"Oh, that must be challenging." She was running out of polite responses.

She stayed a few minutes longer, though, and did her best to comfort Emily. Kylie was stilted and awkward in her attempts to help, but it was oddly endearing.

Emily finished her second slice of cake and asked for the most discreet way to get out for a breath of fresh air. Maiden directed her through the door that led to the small kitchen garden. She then informed Kylie that the dining room was available again and left her to get on with preparing lunch.

Maiden stepped out into the dining room and immediately spotted Reg. He was slumped at a corner table, a flask sitting open in front of him. She wondered how many people actually traveled with a flask anymore, but it was hard to debate its usefulness at the moment.

While it was a bit early for liquor, she could understand him wanting to numb himself after the revelations of the morning. She hoped he'd gotten himself into a mellow and talkative mood.

"Hello, Mr. Varney." She smiled nicely as she stood beside his table. He looked up at her with little interest.

"Hi," he mumbled.

"A pretty rough start to the day, huh?" she tried again. "Can I get you anything?"

"No."

She resisted the urge to scowl at him as he stared down at his flask. Maybe a more direct approach would get him talking.

"Listen," she said, shifting her weight from one foot to the other, "I'm really sorry about all this trouble with Vera."

"She's got nothing to do with me, all right?" He glared at her. "I'm sorry she's dead, but I don't know anything about her."

"That's not what the police said," she murmured candidly, hoping he was more bark than bite. "Lying about it is the worst thing you can do now, Mr. Varney."

His shoulders sagged, and he took a large swallow of his drink. She could see his defenses weakening, but she needed to get him talking before he got too drunk to be useful. She sat down next to him and gave him an understanding look.

"Listen, I know how things can get out of hand with co-workers." It was a bluff, but his expression softened.

"It all got so complicated so quickly. I didn't know what I was getting into," he insisted. "Vera was an absolute hussy; I didn't realize that in time."

"In time for what?"

"To stop her feeling...encouraged, I suppose." He turned his flask in his hands. "She was an attractive woman, but lonely. Never had any pictures on her desk, never went out to lunch with the others in the office. No one liked her very much."

"Why was that?" Maiden had no trouble imagining a myriad of reasons but was curious to hear his explanation.

"The other women thought she was, well, not a trustworthy friend." He pulled a face. "And there were rumors that she'd made her way through most of the men. She had burned a lot of bridges in the eight months she'd been there. But I felt sorry for her, and she could be very charming when she wanted to be. One thing led to another."

"So, you started an affair." She kept her irritation out of her voice even as she thought of how heartbroken Emily was. She was startled when Reg looked up with a ferocious scowl.

"Never!" he barked, but then caught himself and glanced around. He lowered his tone discreetly, even though no one else was in the room. "I never touched her, never planned to either, but...I spent a lot of time talking with her. We'd started staying behind at lunchtime and eating together and we just, well, just talked."

"But you never mentioned her to your wife?" Maiden asked carefully; he lowered his eyes and shook his head. "What about Vera? Did you tell her you were married?"

"I did. She never seemed terribly fussed about that." He looked uncomfortable. "I hate myself for it, but I got into a habit of complaining about Emily. We've been going through a bad time in our marriage and I kind of unloaded about our problems."

"And Vera was a sympathetic listener, I assume?" Maiden's tone was only slightly dry.

"She was at first. But as a few weeks went by she started getting more and more critical of Emily. That bothered me." He frowned. "They'd never met, but she kept talking about her as though I were a henpecked husband. I began to realize that she may have built up some false hopes. I know it was my fault for letting it happen."

"You also told her you were coming here," she prompted.

"Unfortunately." He shook his head incredulously. "I couldn't believe it when she walked in! The nerve to follow us! I only mentioned our wedding anniversary to give her the brush off."

"You think she followed you?" Maiden kept her expression appropriately shocked. "Why? To ruin things for you and Emily?"

"No." He leaned closer and lowered his voice even more. "The minx was trying to entice me away! She cornered me the first chance she got and said some nonsense about missing me too much to go a whole week without seeing me."

"Wow." Maiden eased away from him, noting the pleased look in his eye as he described Vera's overtures. "What a terrible position to be in. What did you say to her?"

"I told her to leave us alone." His eyes narrowed. "*Permanently.*"

Maiden stared, and he seemed to realize how ominous he sounded. He sat up straight and raised his hands as if surrendering.

"I never threatened her, of course," he insisted, and even shuddered a little. "I could never hurt anyone, but I did tell her to get lost."

"I'm not sure how you'll convince your wife of that," she said more plainly than she'd intended.

"Oh, my sweet Emily!" He put a hand to his face. "This is a disaster! We spent weeks planning this trip. I thought this would be such a nice little hotel."

Maiden felt anger flare up. He'd been appallingly selfish and now had the nerve to speak disparagingly of her family's beautiful inn, as though it were responsible for his problems.

"I would point out, Mr. Varney, that you could've booked a holiday in Buckingham Palace, it wouldn't have made any difference since you brought all your issues with you!" she said a tad frostily. "Ms. Randall wasn't the nicest person for any of us to deal with."

"Touché," he said begrudgingly and let out a weary exhalation. "Look, I know. I was stupid and I was flattered by the attention. By the time I realized how serious she was it was too late to stop it. And now I don't even know where my wife is."

"Yeah, well, she probably needs some time to think," Maiden replied evasively; she wasn't about to tell him that Emily had been crying into her dessert in the very next room.

"I don't want her off on her own stewing away and jumping to wrong conclusions!" His harshness returned as he gripped his flask tightly in his sweaty, fleshy hand.

"Mr. Varney, perhaps you'd be better off figuring out how you're going to explain yourself rather than trying to stop her from comprehending the obvious," she suggested dryly. "It's your choice, but bullying a woman you've lied to and humiliated isn't the best way to get her to forgive you. Assuming that you even want her to."

"Of course I do!" he grumbled. "I love my wife. I never had any interest in that floozy. The way she flitted from me to Gilford and even that thug Creevey. From one man to the next without a moment's pause! It's sickening."

"Oh, that's right." Maiden tapped her chin thoughtfully as though he'd only just reminded her. "She and Mr. Creevey did have words...did you know him at all?"

"Who?" Reg squinted at her. "Creevey? Of course not. He looked like some kind of hoodlum; why would I know him?"

"I don't know," she said ingenuously. "Oh, and your room was right underneath his, wasn't it? Did you hear anything the night he died?"

"No, I certainly didn't," Reg huffed. "The police already asked me about that, it was the middle of the night and I was asleep. They'd have been better off asking Vera when they had the chance; she was the sort that would've been in the room with him!"

"Do you really believe that?" Maiden gasped.

"It wouldn't surprise me," he grumbled and sank deeper into his drink, clearly done with the discussion.

"Mm. Well, I have a lot to do." She stood. "Goodbye, Mr. Varney."

Chapter Fourteen

"So, when she's chasing *him*, she's tragic and misunderstood." Vonny sounded as impressed as Maiden had felt during the discussion with Reg. "But when she starts sharing it around, then she turns into a conniving old tramp. Is that it?"

"Pretty much," Maiden sighed.

She had gone to the office to confer with Vonny as soon as she'd left the dining room.

She hadn't been able to hide her disgust at the man's hypocrisy either. He was happy enough with Vera's flirting and fawning when it was directed at him and kept safely out of his wife's sight, but when she turned her efforts to other men, it was suddenly different. Without question, Vera Randall had been selfish and scheming, but Reg was no better.

"Yeah, a classy pair, ironically they deserved each other." Von rolled her eyes. "Do you think he was telling the truth about not sleeping with her?"

"I don't know." She shook her head. "I guess it's possible. But I do think he at least knew that he was leading her on; no one's stupid enough to cultivate a relationship behind their wife's back and not even realize it."

"Self-deception maybe?" Von mused. "People can make themselves believe all sorts of things if they really want to."

"That'd be cold comfort for his wife." She shrugged.

"Yeah, poor Mrs. Varney." Vonny looked thoughtful as she sipped her coffee. "Do you think she might have killed Vera?"

"I guess she could have," Maiden acknowledged. "I'd be pretty suspicious if she took barbiturates herself."

"Honestly, barbiturates? As in *Valley of the Dolls* barbiturates?" Von snorted. "How big do your shoulder pads need to be to get a prescription for those?"

"You might be mixing up your decades a bit there." Maiden gave her a wry smile.

"Oh, right," she conceded. "What about this, how tall is your beehive? Or how wide are your bell-bottoms?"

"Better. Which means you can stop now." Maiden ran a hand through her dark hair. "What a mess this is turning into."

"But the police said we can use the dining room again, right?" Von smiled when her sister nodded. "Thank goodness! I'm already tired of hearing Mom complain about Kylie."

"How is it Kylie's fault?" she asked.

"It isn't, but Mom's convinced she's not coping." Von rested her chin in her hands. "I think she just hates her."

"Great, because we have nothing else to worry about right now," Maiden sighed. "I'll think of something."

Before she could even try, they heard someone ringing the bell on the desk repeatedly. Maiden frowned at the obnoxious racket and followed Vonny out into the reception area. They were both surprised to see Robert tapping away at the bell with a boyish grin while a red-headed woman stood beside him with a rueful smile.

"Mr. Gilford," Maiden said as she approached. "If you wanted our attention, you have it."

"Sorry, I couldn't resist," he chuckled and then turned to the lady at his side and waved a hand towards her with a flourish. "Behold! My gorgeous wife Anna! She does exist."

"Mrs. Gilford, how lovely." Maiden smiled to hide her surprise; she had started to wonder if she'd ever turn up. "You're reunited at last."

"Yes, I'm afraid Robert is a bit of a worrier." Anna Gilford had a light, pleasant voice and blue eyes that sparkled with her open smile. "He finally relented and let me join him."

"Yes, right after she turned up without telling me," he said with a matter-of-fact nod.

"Sometimes you have to take hold of the reins," Anna laughed and swatted his shoulder playfully.

"Did you just arrive?" Maiden folded her hands on the desk.

"Yes, I breezed into town and came straight here." She nodded. "I have to say, this is an adorable little place! The whole town looks like something from a storybook."

"Thank you." Maiden smiled a little more genuinely; she loved hearing people's first impressions of Golden Glen. "I hope that the latest *incidents* won't impact your vacation any more than they already have."

"Not at all, I'm very stubborn when it comes to enjoying myself, I insist on doing so whenever possible." Robert waved her concerns away.

"And we still have the rest of the week," Anna said brightly. "Lots of time to relax and see the town."

"Thank you both for your understanding," Vonny murmured in her politest receptionist voice.

"None of this is your fault." Robert shrugged and then chortled. "But I do hope the police sort it out soon. If they don't arrest someone by the time we're meant to leave, I'll need a note for work. I doubt my boss will believe me otherwise."

Maiden found the notion of an extended investigation depressing, but smiled anyway.

"But we won't keep you ladies from your more important endeavors." Robert slapped his hands on the desk a few times as if he were beating a drum. "I'm going to take my beloved out to see the sights. We'll catch you later."

Maiden and Vonny waved as they left.

"Well," Von mused, "at least they don't look terrified by the prospect of staying here."

"Yeah, I wouldn't blame anyone for being uncomfortable at this point," she admitted.

"Do you think the rest of us are really in danger?" Von whispered.

"Yes." Maiden nodded.

Maiden arrived at the police station, as requested, at five minutes to 2. The same woman was behind the desk again.

"Good afternoon, Nancy." She smiled serenely at her. "I'd like to see Captain McAlister and absolutely no one else, please."

"Certainly, Miss Harlow." Nancy hid her amusement admirably and gestured towards the hallway that led to the offices. "You can go straight in, he's expecting you."

Maiden nodded her thanks and headed down the sparse corridor. Light filtered through a few open doorways, but the entire station seemed quiet. She wasn't sure if that were normal or not, but she was very aware of her steps ringing out as she walked across the faded linoleum.

She recalled which office was his, even without seeing *Captain David H. McAlister* neatly painted on the frosted glass. She still had no idea why he wanted to see her; she took a deep breath to compose herself and rapped lightly on the door. It opened a moment later, and a familiar face smiled out at her.

"Miss Harlow!" he said happily. "How nice to see you again."

She didn't immediately recognize Doctor Jenkins without his hazmat suit, but she smiled back and walked in when he held the door open for her. McAlister was seated at his desk and gave her a nod of greeting as he pointed her to the chairs positioned in front of it. But she wanted this chance to talk to the coroner, so she pretended not to notice.

"Hello, Doctor Jenkins." She nodded to him with a friendly smile and then glanced back at the handsome man sitting at the desk. "Captain McAlister."

"Thank you for coming in, Miss Harlow," the captain said placidly. "The doctor and I were just finishing up."

"Oh, of course, the autopsy." She gave Jenkins her most charming smile. "What a difficult job you do, doctor, I can't even imagine. And I was so surprised to learn that Vera Randall died from barbiturates."

"How did you know that?" McAlister asked with obvious consternation.

"You now live in a very small town, Captain. Word gets around fast," she said mildly.

"That's certainly true; we can't blame Miss Harlow." Jenkins smiled benignly and turned his attention back to her. "And you're right to be surprised, my dear. Barbiturates are quite rare these days, but that's what we found."

"I was amazed they're even still prescribed." She shook her head.

"They aren't often. I think one or two varieties can be used for epilepsy, but it's not the ideal choice in most cases," he said with a casual wave of his hand. "The risk of dependence and overdose is extremely high; it doesn't take much."

"I heard the amount in poor Vera's system would've killed a horse," she tutted, opting not to use Emily's comparison.

"That's plenty, doctor. Thank you," McAlister grated. "We aren't at a point where we can freely discuss the details of the case with the public. Now if you'll excuse us, I need to speak with Miss Harlow."

Jenkins was clearly not impressed at the terse dismissal but decided not to complain about it.

"Of course, I'll get out of your way. Have a lovely afternoon, Miss Harlow," he said kindly as he smiled at Maiden. He then barely even looked at McAlister, and his tone grew noticeably cooler. "See you later, Captain."

Maiden felt the full awkwardness of the men's exchange; it wasn't an ideal start. She knew she probably shouldn't have mentioned the murder weapon in front of McAlister, but she'd been hopeful of getting some information while the opportunity was there. She let out a soundless sigh and reluctantly turned to face the captain.

"Did Smith tell you about the barbiturates?" he demanded.

"No, I was very busy today. I didn't have time to seduce Greg," she retorted facetiously, but noting his unamused expression, quickly relented. "Emily Varney told me. Do you honestly think I'm that shameless?"

"Please stop making every question a personal attack," he said wearily.

"Then please think about your questions before you ask them," she replied politely, knowing that arguing wouldn't help. "Anyway, you said you wanted me to clarify some things?"

"Yes, I did." He took a calming breath and again pointed her towards the chairs before the desk. "Shut the door and have a seat."

Maiden pushed the door closed and sat in the same chair as last time. She watched him as he shuffled through some notes, apparently looking for something specific. She wondered why he wasn't more prepared; he'd been expecting her after all. Although a more reasonable part of her had to allow that he would be very busy.

She whiled away the moments by admiring the bit of dark chest hair she could see peeking out from behind his loosened tie.

"About last night's dinner." He pulled out a page that turned out to be her statement. "You said Vera Randall was acting strangely, what did you mean by that?"

"She was incredibly happy," Maiden explained. "She walked in grinning and strutting around as if she'd just won a beauty pageant."

"That doesn't sound like the same woman *I* met," he said a tad dubiously.

Maiden shrugged. "That's what I saw."

"Any idea what she was so happy about?" he asked.

"Herself probably." She knew it sounded catty, but it was true.

"How would you describe her mental state before she died?" he pressed. "Could the prior display of happiness have been for show?"

"No." Maiden dismissed that theory without hesitation. "She'd been genuinely and smugly delighted. She looked confused before she collapsed but not depressed or anything like that."

He appeared displeased by that summation, but quickly recovered. He handed her a few photos of the dining room taken after Vera died; her body was still lying on the floor.

"Does anything look out of place to you?" He watched her closely.

Maiden looked the pictures over carefully, comparing them with what she remembered seeing on the night, and frowned.

"The wine bottle is gone," she said.

"Wine bottle?" he asked.

"Yes, the one Vera brought in with her. I mentioned it in my statement." She pointed to the table and tried to ignore the image of the woman's prone form. "It was sitting right there when she collapsed."

McAlister picked up her statement and skimmed his eyes over it. He gave a tiny, conceding nod and set it aside again.

"That's strange, isn't it?" she asked.

"Yes," he said in an unrevealing tone, prompting a sharp look from Maiden.

"You don't believe me." It wasn't a question.

"I'm not saying that." His tone was more placating now.

"Okay." She frowned and waited for him to explain what he *was* saying.

"Did you serve Ms. Randall the wine?" he asked instead.

"No." She felt a scowl crease her forehead and hoped he wasn't thinking what she was afraid he was thinking. "I brought her a glass and a corkscrew, after she demanded them. She served herself...from the wine bottle."

"Did anyone else handle the wine or the glass?" he asked.

"Not that I'm aware of." She shook her head.

"How rude was Ms. Randall to you during her stay at your establishment?" His eyes were trained on hers.

"Pretty rude." She scowled at him. "Why do you ask?"

"Just collecting information."

David watched her as she took that in. She didn't look pleased, but she didn't look too upset either. He knew she was clever, and he was convinced now that she had few qualms about pushing the boundaries a bit to get what she wanted. He steeled himself when she leaned a little closer.

"Well, information is vitally important," she allowed. "Out of curiosity, did you find anything of note in Mr. Creevey's backpack?"

David stilled and felt a twinge of annoyance flicker to life inside him. They hadn't found a scrap of luggage in Creevey's room, and he wasn't pleased to only be hearing about any now.

"I was not aware he checked in with a backpack," he said flatly. "Your sister never mentioned it."

She didn't appear one bit worried. She was studying him with watchfully narrowed eyes, very much the way he studied someone he'd caught lying...or admitting to something stupid.

"Did you..." the barest trace of a smile curved her lips, "*ask* her if Mr. Creevey checked in with any luggage?"

He wasn't about to admit that he hadn't. It was obvious as his silence stretched on, but he wasn't going to admit it. Her smile grew.

"She clearly volunteered the information to you." He tried to sound stern, but his heart wasn't in it.

"No. I asked her." She grinned briefly before biting her lower lip to try and hide it. He felt his eyes narrow grimly.

You are staggeringly hot, Harlow, he thought as he fought not to glare at her. *Even with your sexy little smirk that you're only wearing because you're laughing at me. Don't break eye contact, McAlister, don't let her win.*

She finally glanced away. He relished his pointless victory until he saw her gaze lower without leaving him.

You're actually checking me out, David took a deep breath. *You're that smug and brazen that you've essentially just slapped me in the face and now you're messing with my head by checking me out…Stop staring at me like that you evil little monster…pretty sure I'll be having another cold shower tonight.*

"Ah well." She finally looked him in the eye again and continued with a hint of a sigh. "Maybe it doesn't matter anyway. The killer must've taken it…for some reason that we may never know. It probably had the murder weapon in it, or something like that."

David pinned her with a steely look and started drumming his fingers on the desk. She was pushing his buttons again, deliberately and successfully.

"You realize that you were one of the only people that potentially handled anything that Ms. Randall consumed?" he pointed out coolly.

"What?" Her big green eyes widened incredulously. "Are you serious?"

He shrugged, pleased that she looked so startled. "It's a fact, Miss Harlow."

"You actually suspect me?" Her left eyebrow rose impressively high.

"I'm not saying that I do or that I don't," he murmured. "I have to look at the situation from all angles."

"Well, what about the missing wine bottle?" She watched him closely. "Are you going to look for it?"

"We've already searched the dining room, kitchen and the dumpsters outside. There weren't any wine bottles discarded last night," he informed her. "We have removed the open bottles and sent them to be tested for traces of the drug."

"Fair enough," she conceded, but stuck to her guns. "But it still seems suspicious that Vera's wine bottle is gone."

"Is it actually gone?" He tapped the paper on his desk. "You said in here that she only had a glass or two, if there was still wine in it, it may have been stashed in the kitchen."

"Possibly." She looked doubtful. "But the room wasn't touched until after these pictures were taken, nothing was cleared away. Certainly not Vera's table. Who would have removed potential evidence?"

"You've raised some valid points." He used his most diplomatic tone. "We'll find out when the tests come back. But I don't think there's reason to get too worked up about it."

Miss Harlow's expression revealed her misgivings in breathtaking clarity. She might as well have spoken the question aloud: *Are you an idiot?*

David shifted in his chair and engaged in an internal debate over how to proceed.

"I'm not completely convinced that she was poisoned," he finally admitted.

"Pardon?" Miss Harlow shook her head.

"I suppose I can tell you; it'll be officially released soon enough anyway." He rubbed the stiff muscles at the back of his neck. "It's very possible that Vera Randall died of a deliberate overdose."

She looked at him through half-lowered lids. "How is that not poisoning?"

"The circumstances surrounding an overdose are not necessarily suggestive of foul play." He managed not to roll his eyes.

"True," she allowed as she sank into thought.

It was obvious that she didn't accept the idea, but experience had taught him not to dismiss a plausible option until there was a valid reason to.

Vera Randall, by all accounts, was moody and unstable. Drug abuse wasn't a far-fetched notion; she had exhibited other self-destructive behaviors.

He could see that Miss Harlow was drifting further into whatever went on in her rather interesting head. He tried to pull her back to the present before she wandered too far.

"Barbiturates are notoriously dangerous, particularly when combined with alcohol," he informed her, quietly pleased when she looked at him again. "So even a small amount of wine could have interacted with what she'd taken."

Miss Harlow shifted her large green eyes to his and studied him for a moment. He braced himself for whatever was coming.

"Do you think Vera's death is connected to Creevey's?" she asked as she laid the pictures back on his desk.

I knew you'd ask that. He hid a pleased smile.

"I can't go into that, sorry," he said.

"Fine," she sighed tolerantly. "Why ask me about Vera's drink then?"

"I'm thorough," he said without apology.

"I see." She smirked at him. "And what about Creevey? Do you think I knocked him on the head and dragged him to his room too?"

David stilled and locked his gaze on her. She had no reason or right to have that information. He'd already told her more than he probably should have, but that was his prerogative; this was different. His heart started pounding, and he had to tamp down a sudden urge to shout at her.

"What makes you think Creevey was dragged into his room after he was killed?" he asked a little too softly.

"He kind of had to be." She gave him a watchful look. "He was laying a couple feet inside the door facing into the room."

"It's not impossible that he fell that way after being struck." David's thoughts immediately went to Smith; he realized his knuckles were turning white and forced his hands to unclench.

Miss Harlow was watching him, and she looked far too calm considering how irritated he was getting. He tried to shift his attention to something that wasn't infuriating, but he found it almost impossible not to look at her when she was in the room. That realization did not help at all.

"Greg didn't tell me," she said simply.

"I never said he did!" he snapped.

"You were going to," she said with absolute certainty. "At the risk of leaning on a sore point, I saw Creevey the way he fell, you didn't."

You have got balls, lady. David's mouth curved upwards ruefully, but his eyes betrayed his growing anger.

She finally seemed to realize that she was antagonizing the head of the investigation and attempted a pleasant smile. David drummed his fingers a little louder on the desk.

"Are you saying that you remember the position of the body accurately enough to guess that he didn't die there," he paused for emphasis, "but you had to roll him onto his back to realize he was dead?"

"It sounds dumber when you say it." She pulled a face.

"It sounds as dumb as it is," he retorted.

"Thanks a lot." She frowned at him. "Incidentally, are you angry with me now because I guessed correctly or because you didn't know he was moved until I mentioned it?"

"Listen, sweetheart," David said as he propped his forearms on the desk and looked her in the eye, "I was working on my first murder case while you were still in high school, I don't need you to tell me anything about investigating a homicide. You got that?"

"Yeah, I got it, honeybunch," she replied without missing a beat. "Could you answer my question, please?"

"Do not waste my time with sarcasm, Miss Harlow," he warned, but then noticed her confused expression. He shut his eyes and ran a hand through his hair. "You were serious, weren't you?"

"Kind of." She rubbed her arms self-consciously. "I'm not entirely sure why you're mad at me this time."

He realized she was actually waiting for an explanation; he said nothing. After a moment, she released an uncomfortable breath and shifted.

"Okay, awesome." She slid to the edge of the seat. "I'll be on my way then."

"I know exactly how he died, Harlow!" David muttered tightly before she could run away.

"Do you?" She looked politely interested, but perhaps unconvinced. "Exactly?"

"Apart from what you ruined by moving the body," he grumbled.

"I wasn't trying to ruin anything! Look, I'm sorry. I can describe it in detail if you want," she offered earnestly.

"Not the same as seeing it for myself," he countered and gestured towards the floor. "Unless you want to—"

He stopped himself in the middle of the grumpy suggestion, but he'd already said too much. He shut his eyes when Miss Harlow folded her arms across her impressive chest.

"Unless I want to come into your nice, private office and lay down for you?" she asked sardonically, but it was a momentary victory as the words kept spilling out. "If we're going that far, wouldn't it make more sense for you to come back to the hotel room with me?"

She immediately looked away and visibly kicked herself. David saw the hint of pink that stained her cheeks even as she set her teeth and shook her head at herself. He fought valiantly not to burst out laughing.

He couldn't remember knowing anyone else who could alter his mood so radically and often in the course of one short conversation. He fixed his gaze on the top of his desk while she attempted to salvage her dignity.

"I gotta go." She stood and walked to the door.

"Miss Harlow," he managed to say, somewhat steadily, when she interrupted.

"Nope," was all she said as she slipped out and headed for the foyer.

Maiden stalked down the hallway. She was annoyed at McAlister for getting cranky with her, but she was disgusted with herself for continuing to blunder like a twit whenever she spoke to him. She heard his heavy footsteps behind her even as she neared Nancy's massive desk. She closed her eyes and muttered to herself.

"Miss Harlow." McAlister's smile was in his voice. "I didn't say we were done yet."

"Well, I don't have all day to wait around for you to get on with it." She met his sudden grin with one of her own. "Shut up!"

Nancy glanced between them and cleared her throat delicately. "Is everything all right, sir?"

"Yes." He barely flicked her a glance, but his demeanor sobered.

Before he could say anything more, Greg walked in from down a long hallway on the other side of the foyer. He smiled when he saw Maiden, but then he saw McAlister and his cheerful expression vanished.

Maiden noticed the stark change, and it fed into her annoyed mood. Greg had been her friend for over twenty years, but now some guy that hadn't been in town for a month was making him afraid to even look at her. She draped her hands on her hips and turned to McAlister.

"Did you actually have anything else to say to me or do you just enjoy ordering me around?" she asked with a loud sigh.

Greg slipped further into the room and tucked himself off to the side of the desk and watched them subtly.

"You're getting a little too impatient with this whole process," McAlister pointed out. "Especially considering how you tampered with the evidence."

"I 'tampered' with it now," she turned and muttered to Nancy, who smiled a little but said nothing. She faced McAlister again. "What if he hadn't been dead? Should I have left him lying on his face and not even tried to help because it would've been easier for you?"

"You could've checked for a pulse without moving him," he pointed out, earning himself a scoff from the lady.

"Because that's what your average person would do if they found someone collapsed?" She was almost laughing at this point. "Stand back everyone! Don't worry about anything else until I check for a pulse!"

"It's not that difficult to check. Most people know how to do it," he said after a slight pause.

"Ugh. I hate it when hot men are stupid," she glanced away and muttered under her breath, but not quite as quietly as she thought she had.

Nancy's eyes widened a fraction, and she pressed her lips together to hide her growing smile. McAlister blinked at her in obvious surprise.

"What did you say?" He frowned.

"That I should go now; I need to get back to work." She managed a mellow tone. "Something along those lines, anyway."

"Not what I heard." He braced his hand on the edge of the desk. "Did you just call me stupid?"

"Did you hear me say 'Captain McAlister, you're stupid'?" She was bolstered that he didn't seem to have heard her call him hot.

"Are you deliberately provoking me, Miss Harlow?" He quirked a brow. "You realize I have the authority to arrest you right now?"

"Is being a smart-ass illegal, sir?" she asked ingenuously.

"You'd better hope not," he replied.

"Oh, I do." She nodded once. "Do you realize that I know half the people in this town and could certainly call attention to an unreasonable arrest?"

"Cheap threats now? Cute." He folded his arms across his chest and looked her over from head to toe. "If you really want to spread lies around town and tell people that I'm some kind of overbearing, reactionary idiot, be my guest."

"If that's what you want, Captain." She smiled playfully at him. "And at what point should I start lying?"

David squeezed his eyes shut and pinched the bridge of his nose as he tried not to laugh, but his shoulders shook too much to hide his amusement. He reined himself in quickly, but the damage was done. Nancy was staring at him with obvious interest. He ignored her in favor of facing Miss Harlow again; he refused to lose a battle on home soil.

"If I hadn't walked into that, I'd resent it more," he informed her.

"You're very tolerant," she chuckled.

"I try to be," he said.

She was still smiling at him and was now leaning casually back with her elbows propped behind her on the desk, drawing inadvertent attention to her full bust. Her dress fit her incredibly well and fell just to the knee. He forbade himself to look at her legs right there in front of everyone and loosened his tie a little more.

Nancy and Greg exchanged a look. Nancy cleared her throat again and tried to appear busy scribbling a note on the desk blotter.

"Have you two known each other for a while, then?" she asked.

"No. It's been about a week." David flicked her a look before shifting his eyes back to Miss Harlow.

"Feels like longer," they said in smirking unison.

Their eyes met, and then they both glanced away uncomfortably. She pushed away from the desk and took a step toward the door.

"Um...I should go," she said quietly.

"That's fine, Miss Harlow." David also attempted to salvage some professional distance, but a flicker of mischief passed over his face. "Just stay out of trouble, and stop trying to flirt your way around all my officers."

Maiden stilled at that teasing remark and swept her eyes back to McAlister. Putting her foot in it was one thing, and him being clumsy she could deal with. But that was a little cheekier than she was willing to let slide.

"Yes, you've made your feelings very clear. You gave me your number, and I'm only allowed to come to you." She gave him a wink as she turned to go. "Thanks, Captain."

He stared at her in startled surprise again; she really hoped he was embarrassed, but she had no intention of sticking around to find out.

She stalked away with swift, determined strides and didn't look up until she was almost at the door. It opened abruptly as Briggs walked in without seeing her. Maiden raised her eyes in time to see Briggs' startled expression before walking straight into him.

She wasn't sure whether to feel mortified or giggle like a twit as she felt her breasts press against his chest and his hands rest on her back to steady her. Maiden stiffened and stepped back immediately; Briggs' face turned bright red, and he whipped his arms to his sides.

"Sorry, officer." Maiden met his pale gaze and smiled sweetly.

"It's okay. My fault," he barely managed to reply.

Don't laugh, don't laugh, don't laugh, she chanted to herself as she glanced back at Captain McAlister. He was leaning against the desk and watching her with a faint smile.

"That doesn't count, does it?" she couldn't resist asking, and was proud of herself for keeping a straight face.

"You're hilarious," he said tolerantly.

"So, I've accidentally made contact with another policeman, should I call you at this point?" she asked with a slight shake of her head, holding her hand up to imitate putting a phone to her ear.

"Would you get out of here, please?" he said in an exasperated voice.

She raised both hands in surrender and escaped outside.

David exhaled slowly through his nose as he fought an amused grin, but no one missed it. It occurred to him that following her out into the lobby had been unwise, particularly as he thought back over some of the things he'd said. He'd never openly flirted with a suspect before and was already kicking himself.

He wasn't sure how to classify the success of that interview; it didn't help that he'd been a bit turned on for most of it. His best option at this point was to ignore and, if necessary, deny everything. Well, in all fairness, almost everything.

"I did deserve that last shot," he acknowledged quietly to himself.

"Yes, sir," Nancy whispered. "You really did."

"Thanks, Nancy." He smiled wryly at her.

CHAPTER FIFTEEN

Maiden returned to Harlow House and walked straight past reception and into the office. She was hoping for a few minutes to collect herself after that incredibly strange encounter at the police station.

She laid her purse on the table and stood in front of the back door, staring out the inset window at the trees on the other side of the parking lot. She took a deep breath and tried to sort through what had just happened.

Apart from the flirting, only some of which had been accidental, she had learned a few things. Firstly, she was still a suspect. Secondly, she'd been right about Creevey's body being moved after the murder, and thirdly, the barbiturates that killed Vera had been in her wineglass. Or in the wine.

There was also the matter of Creevey's backpack. The police knew nothing about it, which meant the killer likely took it, or hid it and came back later to collect it. She recalled the damaged bush outside the Varney's patio. Maybe someone had stashed the bag there, but who? And how would they have retrieved it without being seen?

Okay, one problem at a time, she thought to herself. *Where did Creevey die? It would have been hard to drag him up or down stairs without anyone noticing, even in the middle of the night. So, it was most likely on the same floor as his room.*

She wasn't sure how thoroughly the police had searched the other rooms that sat alongside Creevey's. As far as she knew, they hadn't searched her family's apartment; maybe they hadn't checked the other rooms for anything strange either.

Robert, and now Anna, were still occupying room 8. Vera had been in room 9, and the police would certainly have combed through it by now. Room 7 and 10 had been empty that night...but they were full now. What if something subtle yet telling had been there, but nobody had ever looked?

Billie. She'd have to talk to Billie again. She was the only one who might have gotten a look into every room after the first murder.

Maiden turned to find Vonny standing close behind her. She gasped loudly and staggered back a step.

"What are you doing?" she demanded as she pressed her hand to her chest and tried to pull in a full breath.

"Nothing...just checking on you." Von shrugged, but her eyes were curious as she looked her little sister over. "Cute dress, by the way."

"Thanks." Maiden was instantly wary. "Why are you checking on me?"

"You went back to the police station to talk to Captain McAlister, didn't you?" she asked. When Maiden nodded, she smiled knowingly. "So...cute dress."

"I've been wearing this all day, Von. You know that," she said, fully aware of where this was headed. "I didn't change to go and see him."

"You also knew that he'd be here today," she pointed out, her pale blue eyes turned eager. "Did he ask you out?"

"Of course he didn't." Maiden gave her a chiding look. "For the last time, *I hope*, he's a policeman investigating two murders, in which we are *all* suspects. He's not sniffing around here looking for a date!"

"Maybe if you tried harder…" Vonny let the thought trail off.

Maiden arched a brow but didn't really get angry about her persistence. Mainly because she knew what prompted some of it.

"How's Tony today, incidentally?" she asked, earning her a sharp look from Vonny. "I didn't see him this morning, did he come by after I left?"

"No. I don't think we got any mail today." Von was suddenly more circumspect.

The days of resentment were long gone between them, but Maiden had noticed before that Vonny was often happy to nudge her toward a relationship. Even though Maiden had no romantic interest in Tony, they got along very well. But Von liked him a lot, and she worried he preferred her sister's company.

Maiden wasn't casual about men, and she never gave encouragement without being sincere about it; she believed it was mean to get someone's hopes up despite knowing they'd end up disappointed. She loved Tony like a brother, to the point that the thought of any warmer relationship between them grossed her out.

But Von was insecure where Tony was concerned, most likely because he meant a lot to her. Her teasing about McAlister made sense now, and Maiden didn't enjoy seeing her anxious.

"It's always kind of sad when Tony doesn't stop by. He's such a wonderful guy," Maiden said nicely. "It's like missing a visit from a big brother. Isn't it?"

"Um…yeah." She was blushing now and walked over to the coffee pot.

It was switched off and probably stone cold, but she still picked up a mug and filled it. Von took a sip and suppressed a grimace. Maiden took pity on her and headed towards the door.

"I've got a few things to check on, I'll see you later." She swatted her sister's bottom as she walked past. "And dump that out, it's been sitting there festering all day."

Maiden started hunting for Billie. She glanced into the kitchen, dining room and library before finally finding her rummaging in the supply cupboard behind the stairs. After glancing around to ensure they were alone, she walked over and tapped Billie on the shoulder.

"Hey, Maiden, what's up?" She smiled inquiringly.

"I need to ask about the rooms," Maiden whispered and kept looking into the hallway. "Have you cleaned all of them since Mr. Creevey's murder?"

"Oh," Billie mused, bracing a hand on her lean hip as she thought that over. "Um...no. I haven't been in room 7, 8 or 10."

"That's Mr. Gilford's room and the two that were empty that night." Maiden chewed at her lip. "You cleaned room 9 though? Vera Randall's room?"

"Once, sort of." She made a distasteful face. "She got sick all over the floor and flagged me down to clean it up without so much as a thank you."

Maiden gave her a sympathetic look. "Did you see anything out of place while you were in there?"

"Apart from what she ate the night before, you mean?" Billie asked dryly.

"Oh yuck!" Maiden laughed and shook her head. "Yeah, anything else?"

"Only that the room was trashed." She shrugged. "Clothes thrown everywhere, empty wine bottles falling out of the wastebasket. It looked like a whirlwind had hit the place, I wasn't looking forward to cleaning it all up, that's for sure."

"Nothing else that stands out to you?" Maiden chewed at her bottom lip.

"Not at the moment." Billie shook her head. "But if I think of anything I'll let you know."

Maiden had slipped upstairs and changed out of her dress before her mother found out she'd gone to see McAlister in it. She wriggled back into her favorite jeans and a transparent pink blouse over a matching camisole. She headed down to the lobby in time to hear Gloria's voice floating out from behind the computer.

She stepped off the bottom stair and rounded the corner to find Gloria talking in hushed tones with an anxious Emily Varney. Sympathy for the poor woman snaked through Maiden; she approached and plastered on a kind smile as she slid in beside her mother.

"Is everything okay?" It was a ridiculous question under the circumstances, but the standard niceties rolled out on their own sometimes.

"I was just asking Mrs. Harlow for a different room," Emily said miserably. "I can't leave the inn and I *really* can't stay with Reg tonight!"

"And I was trying to explain that we're fully booked," Gloria sighed, but noticing Emily's devastated expression, took another look in the system. "Oh, let's see what we can do."

Maiden studied the screen over her mother's shoulder and pointed out the attic suites. A few years ago, they'd converted the top floor of Harlow House into three luxurious suites. Each had its own theme, a full spa bath, and a large private balcony. They were typically booked out well in advance, and they didn't come cheap.

"Ah, yes." Gloria nodded and flitted her gaze to a hopeful Emily. "The only thing I have, Mrs. Varney, is the Secluded Getaway suite. It's on the top floor and is vacant for the next four nights."

"Perfect!" She bounced happily and clapped her hands softly together. "I'll take it!"

"It's also three times the price of your current room," Maiden pointed out tactfully.

They stared in surprise when Emily waved that away with a laugh.

"Money's no issue," she said wryly. "This may sound crass, but my father's loaded."

Maiden felt the hairs on the back of her neck rise.

"Is he?" she asked quietly.

"Oh yes." Emily nodded confidently. "I can easily afford the best you have, I'm in the mood for a bit of spoiling anyway."

"I see." Maiden tried to think of a tactful way to ask a rather impolite question. "Then, forgive my asking, but why didn't you book one of the nicer suites to begin with? Being your anniversary and all."

"Oh, that's a story and a half." Emily pressed a hand to her chest and looked anxiously over her shoulder. "I don't want to risk seeing Reg, show me to my new room and then we'll chat."

Maiden gave her eager mother a discreet look and grasped the key before Gloria could. The lure of gossip was strong, but she would just have to wait and hear it later. Maiden had a feeling that she was about to learn something significant.

Emily threw a surreptitious look down the hall towards her old room as she hurried to follow Maiden up past the second floor. Maiden could almost feel the other woman's anxious fear of being spotted by her husband; she obligingly quickened her pace. They both chanced a look at the door to Vera's room, with the police tape sealing it off as they continued up the far less used stairway to the attic suites.

The difference in atmosphere was obvious as they stepped onto the third-floor landing. Gloria had spent a lot of time and money transforming the attic space into a haven of luxury.

The walls of the foyer area were painted a rich shade of teal and embellished with gold ornaments and a few pieces of silky mahogany furniture. Emily smiled appreciatively as she looked at the large stained-glass window above the stairs.

Maiden led her along a plush, intricately woven carpet to the first door on the right. She glanced back with a smile as she unlocked the door and pushed it open. Emily's face lit up as she stepped inside and peered around.

The room had a soothing beach theme. The walls were light blue and faded into pale hardwood floors strewn with woven mats. Most of the furniture was wicker, but piled with soft cushions in shades of peach and buttery yellow. Whitewashed tables sat below paintings of waves crashing onto unknown shores. There were several potted plants with broad, glossy leaves and a bank of windows dressed with linen drapes and floating sheers.

"How relaxing!" Emily said with an approving nod. "This is exactly what I need right now. I haven't stayed in such a beautiful place since I got married."

Maiden gave her a curious look but still smiled politely as she pushed back the curtains and opened the French doors that led out to the private balcony. She nodded toward the view.

"You can see the Oakley's vineyards from here." She pointed to the neat rows of grapevines in the distance. "And over there are some of the forests that give Golden Glen its name, in the autumn at least."

"Oh, there's that little lake we drove past on the way here," Emily said as she joined her outside. "Just beautiful."

"It freezes over in the winter and we use it for ice skating." Maiden smiled at the thought but hoped Emily remembered her promise to chat.

"I might come back here sometime, you know." She stared out over the quaint town. "It's been painful, but...it's been liberating too. I sacrificed a lot to be with Reg, and he wasn't the easiest person to live with."

"That's easy to believe, all things considered," Maiden said gently.

"Mm," Emily grunted as her eyes grew distant. "That didn't matter when I thought he loved me. I put up with a lot...I always told myself that it was worth it. That it would all be okay. I hate him now; I hate that he stole five years of my life."

"I'm so sorry." Maiden couldn't think of anything else to say to that; she tried to steer the subject back to Emily's earlier intimations. "Your family didn't approve of the marriage?"

"I'll say." She gave a humorless laugh. "Dad told me I was being an idiot; he was so sure that Reg was after the family's money. Won't he be pleased to learn he was right."

"But if he married you for your money," Maiden struggled to ask the question in a way that didn't sound as nosy as it was, "why..."

"Why don't we live as if we had money?" She slid her a sideways smile. "I'll tell you why, Reg doesn't have my money yet...and he'll never get it now. Let's sit down; it's a bit cool out here."

Maiden watched her walk back inside and then followed her into the large sitting area. Emily went to the cabinet that sat against the side wall and poked around until she found a bottle of wine and two glasses. Maiden nodded at her inquiring look and sat down at one end of the sofa.

Emily perched on the other end and filled their glasses. The woman took a sip and leaned back; she tucked her feet up under her and broodingly studied the lush orchards in the distance.

"My father is very clever," she said softly.

He would be if he's rich, Maiden thought to herself but didn't interrupt.

"He saw through Reg the first time he met him. A middle-aged, former military man turned accountant; he wasn't exactly what Dad expected me to choose for myself." Emily's expression was somber. "He called him a fortune hunter. Looking back on it now, I wish I'd paid more attention to the things he warned me about. Reg came on very strong when we met, and I liked that. I thought it meant he'd be forceful and passionate. Well, he wasn't, not with me...maybe he was with her."

Maiden felt a little awkward listening to such personal musings from someone she barely knew, but poor Emily had no one else at the moment. She sipped her wine and waited for her to continue.

"So, Reg chased me like a lovesick teenager. I was a bit lonely, and very stupid, so I let him catch me," she said with a self-deprecating smile and took a larger drink. "But Dad knew what he was after from the start. He couldn't stop us getting married, and he would never disinherit *me*. So, he put what I had thought was an outrageous stipulation on our prenup. Of course there was a prenup!" Emily laughed at Maiden's wide-eyed look. "Don't be silly. Anyway, Dad said that not only could Reg never touch my money for himself, but he had to completely support us for ten years before he could benefit at all."

Maiden's mouth fell open; she'd never heard of such a thing and couldn't believe that anyone would agree to it. She wondered just how much money Emily had, and some unpleasant suspicions started to surface.

"What did Reg say when he learned about that?" she asked.

"Oh, he was furious." Emily giggled at the memory. "He railed and complained that it was hateful and unfair. When that didn't work, he cried and whined that I didn't really love him and wasn't serious about spending my life with him. I should have seen the truth then. Now, the really clever part of Dad's plan was that we *both* had to be serious to proceed. After all, I'd be living on Reg's salary for a decade and he didn't make anything close to what I was used to."

"But you were willing to do it?" Maiden gave her a pleased and admiring smile.

"Yes." She shrugged modestly. "I loved him."

"You're amazing, Emily," Maiden said with a rueful shake of her head. She hated to think of this self-sacrificing woman scrabbling with anyone for her own husband's affections. "So, if you leave Reg—"

"*When* I leave Reg," she corrected, "he'll get nothing. And the five years he spent pretending to care about me go up in smoke."

"Fair's fair." Maiden nodded with a faint smile. "What will you do now?"

"In the short term, I'm going to hide out in this gorgeous room and wait for the police to wrap this case up." She stretched out her legs and propped her feet on the coffee table. "And after dinner I'll call my father and apologize for not listening to him years ago. Then I'll ask him to contact his lawyer and get things underway."

"You know Reg is still denying the affair," Maiden murmured as she ran a fingertip around the rim of her glass.

"He won't be for much longer." Emily said triumphantly. "I've got him by the scruff of his neck and he doesn't even realize it yet."

She set her glass aside as she stood and hurried over to her purse; it only took a moment to find what she was after. She dug out a phone with a pale purple case that Maiden recognized immediately.

"Is that..." She started to feel uneasy again.

"Yup. It's Vera Randall's phone." Emily smirked as she walked back and sat beside her. "She didn't even have a password on it, can you believe that? What an idiot."

Maiden sucked in a startled breath and set her glass on the table with a louder clatter than she'd intended. She watched Emily smile cunningly as she tapped the screen and started scrolling through something.

The look of ice-cold intent on Emily's face was terrifying. Maiden stared at her as she waited with steadily growing concern. Had she read this charming, decent-sounding woman so wrong? Could she have lied about when she learned of the affair? Had she been planning this all along?

"Here it is!" Emily said. She blinked back tears as she glanced away and handed the phone to Maiden, who accepted it with a trembling hand.

"Oh wow!" she gasped, and her eyes widened as she stared down at the picture.

It was a selfie Vera had taken. She checked the date and found it was from three months ago. Vera wore a skimpy pink lace teddy and was smiling broadly while Reg lay asleep and completely naked behind her. Maiden looked up to find Emily clutching her glass with tears streaming down her cheeks.

"I hate his fat, stupid guts, but it still hurts to see it," she croaked. "Scroll to the next one."

Maiden obliged and gasped even louder. "*Whoa!*"

She made herself look away and tried not to let the appalling image emblazon itself on her memory. Between Vera's bony frame and Reg's middle-aged sag, it wasn't pretty. She forced herself to stay calm; she could understand Emily's pain, but the most pressing question had to be asked.

"How did you get this phone, Emily?" she spoke as gently as her nerves would allow.

"I found it in Reg's shaving kit this morning. Just before the police came and knocked on our door." Emily sniffled into her sleeve. "I thought it was hers so I slipped it into my purse to look at it later."

Maiden stilled and then stared back at the phone.

"Well, how did *he* get it?" she asked slowly.

"I don't know." She shook her head. "He was asleep in those photos, but she must have told him she had them. I guess he got scared and took it?"

Maiden swallowed hard and went to the sent messages. There were several recent ones, and the only recipient she was interested in was there; he was listed in her phone as Reggie. She opened the messages and saw the last one Vera had sent him.

Vera's slyly grinning face stared back at her in that same damning selfie, and underneath she had simply written: *Don't do anything hasty, Reggie.*

Emily was blinking her tears away and staring at Maiden's frown. She sniffed again and brushed her hair out of her face.

"What is it?" She shook her head.

"Emily." Maiden looked up slowly and showed her the screen. "Vera sent him this picture the day she was killed."

Emily paled and clapped a hand over her mouth. For a timeless moment they stared at each other as the implications sank in and the suspicions grew. Maiden took a deep breath and stood, heading resolutely for the door.

"What are you doing?" Emily quickly followed. "I need those pictures as proof!"

"It's all about to become very well known, don't worry," Maiden said dryly. "I have to take this to the police before anything else happens. Stay here and keep the door locked."

"What?" Her eyes somehow widened further. "You think Reg would—"

"I don't know what he'd do if he thought that you had this." She held up the phone. "But it's incredibly incriminating and I doubt he took it from Vera while she was still alive. Whatever you do, stay put and don't open this door unless it's me or the cops!"

Chapter Sixteen

Maiden's heart pounded as she hurried downstairs, fearful of bumping into Reg Varney any second. If he knew Vera's phone had been taken, his most likely suspect would be Emily. He had to know that if the police had found it, he would have heard about it by now.

She needed to get to the police before Reg saw her and guessed where Emily was. It was possible he'd already killed for her money, and if he feared Emily was going to leave him and that money was gone, his freedom was all he had to lose now.

Maiden reached the landing of the second floor and froze when she saw the door to Vera's room ajar and the police tape hanging loose.

Her heart pounded, and she was very aware of Vera's phone clutched in her hand, its bright purple case clear for anyone to see. She quickly shoved it deep into her back pocket.

As she drew closer, she could hear someone shuffling around inside. She debated the wisdom of confronting whoever it might be, but if she did nothing, they'd get away with whatever they were looking for, and they may never know for certain who it was.

Her family's apartment was just down the hall, but she would have to pass next to Vera's room unnoticed to reach it and get help. Assuming anyone was even in there. Before she could decide what to do, a gloved hand curled around Vera's door. She gasped loudly before she could stop herself, and a man in a black knitted ski mask appeared. He started when he saw her.

"*Help!*" Maiden screamed, desperately hoping that someone was nearby. An instant later, the door to their apartment flew open, and Alfie peered out.

"What's going on out here?" he demanded as he looked out into the hallway.

The masked man was clutching something in his fist; he squeezed it tighter and barreled towards Maiden. He slowed long enough to drive his shoulder into her side, shoving her hard into the wall and leaving her to drop to the floor with a grunt as he went.

"Maiden! Are you all right?" Alfie asked anxiously as he ran to her and pulled her to her feet.

"He's getting away!" Maiden winced and hugged her shoulder as she hurried down the hall after the intruder.

She heard her father close behind and ignored his fussing at her not to trip and fall down the stairs. She reached the foyer in time to see the intruder running towards the front door.

"Stop him!" she yelled to no one in particular.

The man was almost at the door when they heard and then saw Billie. Maiden and Alfie could only stare as the short but solid woman let out a yell that sounded like something from a kung fu movie and cracked him across the back of the knees with her mop handle as he reached for the doorknob.

He cried out in shock and crumpled to the floor. Billie stood over him with the mop slung over her shoulder, both hands gripping it tightly, ready to strike again.

"Don't move a muscle, pork chop," she warned in a menacing tone, "or you won't like what happens next."

"Billie, you're magnificent!" Alfie said happily as he drew an umbrella from the coat stand near the door and joined her in her vigil over the stranger. "Maiden, call the police."

"I'm on it." Her phone was already out along with McAlister's card; she quickly dialed and didn't waste a second when he picked up. "Captain, this is Maiden Harlow. Can you get to the inn straight away? I just caught Reg Varney searching Vera Randall's room."

The man on the floor looked back at her sharply; she responded with an angry glare of her own. McAlister muttered some sort of affirmative and hung up. Maiden lowered her phone, ignored the growing ache in her shoulder and hip, and cautiously approached.

Reg pulled the mask off his head and smoothed back his hair. He was still holding whatever he'd taken from Vera's room; his eyes were coldly calculating as he glanced at each of them.

"What the heck are you doing, Varney?!" Alfie shook his head irately. "What's going on?"

"Nothing at all," he muttered with an unimpressed sniff. "I'd like to know why you and your staff have attacked me without reason! You'll be hearing from my lawyer."

"What a load of garbage!" Alfie snorted. "I saw you attack my daughter and then try to run for it!"

"After breaking into a room that was sealed off by the cops," Maiden pointed out.

"I was looking for my wife," Reg said after a slight pause. "She's been acting strangely ever since the police made some unfounded allegations this morning. She's unstable and likely to do anything, I was afraid she was up to something so I went to find her."

"And the ski mask?" Billie's tone dripped with sarcasm. "Was that in case you got cold in there?"

"Sounds like a lot of turkey business," Alfie said with a scowl.

"A fine suggestion coming from you!" Reg blustered. "You're the one running some sleazy murder-hotel! First that Creevey guy and then that Randall tramp! No wonder there's trouble if that's the sort of person you let in!"

"You pig of a man!" Alfie's grizzled brows shot towards his hairline. "Everyone here has your number, pal, so stop trying to play innocent! Running around like a randy teenager at your age! Your poor wife must be humiliated."

"There's no point arguing with him, Dad, just wait for the police," Maiden cautioned. "It's possible that Mr. Varney was involved in Vera Randall's death."

"I was not!" Reg shouted angrily. He pushed to his feet and tried to weave past Billie.

"He's holding something!" She glowered at him and pressed herself against the door.

Alfie caught Reg's arm with the handle of the umbrella, knocking him off balance. Billie took advantage and kicked his hand, sending the object he'd been clutching flying across the room.

Maiden ran over and grabbed what turned out to be a prescription bottle. She checked the label and saw Vera's name printed on it. She frowned as she looked back at Reg; he was red-faced and seething. Billie and Alfie leveled their makeshift weapons at him, holding him at bay.

A few moments later, they heard sirens and then loud footsteps outside the door. When the doorknob rattled, Billie yelped and scrambled to open it. Captain McAlister stalked inside with half a dozen officers close behind him. He took in the scene and turned to Reg, who had gone pale and was passing his ski mask rather awkwardly between his hands.

"Explain," McAlister said.

"I, um, was looking for Emily," Reg said quietly, and then glared at Billie and Alfie. "Then I came downstairs and was attacked!"

"Miss Harlow?" McAlister glanced at her inquiringly.

"He was searching Vera's room," she replied steadily. "I heard him rummaging around inside and saw him come out...wearing that ski mask. He tried to run but Dad and Billie stopped him."

"That's a lie!" Reg grated.

"Do you want to tuck the mask behind your back and deny it again?" she asked dryly.

"It's my word against yours," he hissed with a hint of an unspoken threat.

"And mine, and Billie's," Alfie scoffed and narrowed his eyes. "Stop glaring at my daughter, you creep."

"Right, I've heard enough," McAlister said coolly as he stepped between them all. "You can come to the police station and answer a few questions, Varney. Take him away."

He motioned to a few of the officers who approached and handcuffed Reg. He looked startled at first, but quickly found his tongue and started insisting that he'd been attacked and was now being illegally detained. The officers ignored him and dragged him out the front door.

McAlister turned to survey the rest of those assembled; Maiden did the same.

Alfie and Billie were looking rather pleased with themselves while she was rubbing her arm and trying to absorb the roller-coaster that the last half hour had been. McAlister glanced over her shoulder at something.

Maiden spotted Robert and Anna Gilford standing near the doorway of the dining room, watching the proceedings with wary and confused expressions.

"Looking for someone?" McAlister asked as he approached, but stopped at Maiden's side.

"Uh no, sorry." Robert swallowed hard. "It's, well it's...we heard shouting and we were just coming to check if everyone was okay."

"Yes, so sorry." Anna held up her hands and shook her head apologetically. "We walked in and saw someone being arrested; we honestly didn't know what to do. We weren't expecting to see police here."

"I'm surprised it's not in the brochure by now," McAlister said under his breath and waved them on their way.

The Gilfords retreated into the dining room; Robert gave Maiden a worried look and an uncertain shrug before they disappeared inside. Maiden waited until they were out of sight and turned back to the captain. He was still looking at the empty doorway, but then shifted his warm brown eyes to her.

"So, what happened?" he asked.

"A lot, and I've found something," she whispered and edged towards the library. "Could we talk privately?"

He glanced over at Alfie and Billie; the pair were murmuring to each other as they studied their improvised armaments. She doubted McAlister could even begin to guess why they were comparing a mop with an umbrella, but the thought made her smile faintly.

She knew that time was an issue, however, and quickly turned and slipped into the elegantly masculine room. He followed her inside and quirked a brow when she pressed the door shut and hurried to his side. She reached into her back pocket and pulled out Vera's phone with a hint of triumph.

McAlister's handsome face became darkened with an incredulous scowl when he saw it. He obviously knew exactly who it had belonged to, but he didn't look happy as he took it from her. He gave the case a cursory glance before flipping it open and looking at the handful of credit cards with Vera's name on them tucked into the pockets in the cover.

"We've been searching for this!" he said tightly. "How did *you* find it?"

"I have my ways." She shrugged, trying not to be annoyed at his grim reaction.

"Great. I doubt any fingerprints survived your pocket, not to mention that you've probably searched through it all already," he grumbled as he started tapping at the screen. "You're a pain in the neck sometimes, you know that?"

"You're welcome, by the way!" She scowled at him. "I took a fair bit of personal risk to get that for you and all you do is complain that I didn't wear gloves and carry it with tongs?"

"That's true, sorry," he acknowledged as he went to the call log and started scrolling through it.

"It was a text, not a phone call," she informed him pertly.

McAlister glanced up long enough to give her a look before going back to the phone and opening the messages. He skimmed through them and quickly found what he wanted.

"'Reggie' eh?" he said under his breath as the photo opened up. "Interesting."

"What do you think of it?" Maiden hovered anxiously.

"I prefer black lace personally," he said casually.

"I thought policemen liked blue," she grumbled, not appreciating his evasive manner, considering she'd handed him the evidence.

"I'm willing to keep an open mind." His tone was ridiculously reasonable under the circumstances. He met her gaze very briefly before looking down again. "Now stop hitting on me, I'm on duty."

"You—" Her eyes widened and she felt irritation well up when he interrupted.

"First you press me to have a drink with you and now you're showing me dirty pictures. I can see the obvious, Miss Harlow." He grinned broadly but didn't look up. "I'm a detective."

To her further annoyance, she noticed that he had a dimple in his left cheek when he smiled enough to show it. It was cute and sexy and made her angrier.

"You drive a desk most of the time, hotshot." She glared at him and wished she could think of something more scathing.

"As opposed to what you do, right?" he asked.

"Yeah, right," she muttered and turned toward the door.

"Were you planning to withhold evidence?" he murmured before she could take more than a step.

"What?!" she demanded indignantly. "I gave you the stupid phone!"

His expression was completely placid as he locked his eyes with hers and pointed at her hand. She pulled a face and looked down, finally remembering the bottle of pills she was still holding. She rolled her eyes and handed them to him.

"I like the way you start blathering about lingerie and then blame *me* for getting sidetracked," she said as he accepted the bottle with a slight nod.

"Thanks, I'm glad you enjoy my methods," he said, and then read the label. "Where'd you find this?"

"In Reg Varney's fat, sweaty fist after Billie clocked him with her mop." She folded her arms.

"What would I do without Billie?" he asked with an exaggerated sigh.

"Why don't you go and ask *her*?" she suggested coolly and went to the door.

"Miss Harlow."

Get lost, jerk, Maiden grumbled to herself as she ignored him. She threw the door open and walked briskly back into the foyer. She had no idea how one man could be so obnoxious.

She didn't mind his teasing; she doubted he felt free to do that very often, but he could've thanked her for her trouble. Surely that wasn't asking too much. Maiden shook her head and retreated behind the front desk.

By this time, Gloria had appeared and was listening to Alfie and Billie describe the whole encounter. She looked both appalled and delighted by the drama. Maiden ignored them all, and the pain in her side, and pulled her never-ending library book from the drawer she'd left it in.

David walked out of the library after stashing both the phone and the pill bottle in the depths of his trench coat. He saw Miss Harlow frowning down at a ridiculously thick book and smiled.

She looked sulky, which was rather cute, and he doubted she was actually reading a word. He knew he'd been too familiar, but he was really struggling to keep a professional distance with her.

He wasn't used to this kind of repartee; there had been no friendly or pleasant interactions with suspects or even witnesses at his previous assignment. The station in Stanton had been all business, and it wasn't a very nice business.

But this was Golden Glen; things were different here. And every time he turned around in this case, there was Maiden Harlow. She bantered with him and held her own, which threw the old rules out the window. He knew he needed to be more careful around her.

David had barely entered the foyer when Gloria Harlow spotted him and strutted over like an angry hen. Her flouncy, polka-dotted dress swished around her knees with each step.

"Captain McAlister! Thank goodness you're here!" she exclaimed, planting her fists on her hips. "Did you arrest that awful man?"

"Which one?" he replied. He didn't see the need for the question; he had no doubt that the others would have told her everything they'd seen.

"Don't you play games with me, mister!" Her dark eyes were flinty. She stamped her little foot and pointed over at Maiden. "Did my sweet baby tell you that Varney idiot attacked her?"

"No." He stilled and shifted a displeased gaze to the beautiful woman who was still refusing to look at any of them. "She didn't tell me that."

"She mostly listened, if you recall," Maiden said tersely.

David walked over and stood right in front of her. She didn't budge or even look at him, so he reached out and gently closed her book, leaving his hand over the cover. She muttered to herself and sat up straight, evidently deciding that she would rather face him than cause a scene.

She raised her eyes to his but offered no explanation. David felt his professionalism float back to the surface. The levity that had seemed so easy to get caught up in a few minutes ago was long forgotten. Everything was grim and serious now.

"Are you all right?" he asked calmly, folding his arms across his chest.

"Yes." She managed not to roll her eyes, but the effort it took was obvious.

"What happened, Miss Harlow?" He looked her over for a moment as though he might find an injury she was hiding from him.

"Nothing really." She tried to shrug but flinched at the movement and glanced away again.

I wouldn't have teased you if I'd known you were hurt, he groaned internally. *I wish you'd started the conversation with that, but no, you went straight to the evidence.*

"Well, come on." He nodded toward the front door. "You can tell me more about it at the station."

"So, I'm under arrest for getting bashed into a wall?" she demanded, her eyes flying back to his.

His shoulders tensed, and his jaw tightened at that. David reminded himself that she was sitting in front of him, perfectly fine, and he was impartial anyway. He needed facts, and he needed to put her at ease so she'd cooperate. He banished any visible irritation and smiled politely.

"Of course not, you've been very helpful, Miss Harlow, and the entire department appreciates that," he said and gestured towards the door again. "You have witnessed quite a bit and you need to give a formal statement; you must know the drill by now. Come on, I'll drive you over."

Maiden sighed and nodded. It was to be expected, of course. She threw her book unceremoniously into a drawer and walked around the desk. Trying to ignore the way McAlister kept looking at her as if she was about to explode, she followed him to the door, giving her parents and Billie what she hoped was a confident smile as she went.

In reality, she wasn't feeling confident at all. She was even more aggravated now; the captain had gone all quiet and polite, and her shoulder was aching, but she was too annoyed to tell him that. She wished she'd hidden under the desk when she had the chance.

They stepped outside into fresh air that was unseasonably cool. She regretted not grabbing her jacket; she hadn't even taken her purse. Her jeans offered some protection from the breeze, but she was still only wearing a snug camisole with a thin blouse over top. She reminded herself that she wouldn't be out for long and that she needed to get this over with.

McAlister took her elbow long enough to guide her towards his car. It looked normal until she got close enough to see radios and other devices she couldn't identify carved into the dashboard.

"You aren't going to handcuff me and shove me in the backseat, are you?" she asked as she gave the car a dubious look.

"I asked you to stop flirting," he quipped reflexively, but quickly shut his eyes and cleared his throat. "I'm sorry. As I said before, Miss Harlow, you aren't under arrest. Please don't worry."

"Mm-hmm." She went to the passenger side and opened the heavy door. As she slid inside and settled into the seat, a few more aches and pains sprang to life.

"Are you okay?" He watched her through half-closed lids as he climbed into the driver's seat and shut the door firmly.

"Yes, fine." She wasn't sure why it was becoming a point of pride, but she stubbornly ignored the growing ache in her shoulder and hip.

"You winced," he informed her.

"I'm fine," she replied sedately.

They sat in tense silence for the brief drive to the station. She remembered too late that her earlier visit had deteriorated into brazen public flirtation. She felt mortification wash through her and shook her head. They'd already pulled into the parking lot;

there was no chance of jumping out of the car and running for it now.

McAlister parked and escorted her into the lobby. She spied a quietly interested Nancy and slid her gaze away.

Down the hall to the left of the lobby she could hear Reg Varney shouting about false accusations and conspiracies. From the corner of her eye, she saw McAlister set his teeth as he led her down the opposite hall and on towards his office. He flicked the door open when they reached it.

"Have a seat please," he murmured politely. "I'll be right back."

He then slipped out, leaving the door open a fraction behind him. She wasn't sure where he went at first, but it was only a few moments before Reg Varney's distant shouting abruptly stopped. She shut her eyes and enjoyed the silence.

The room was on the cooler side; she wet her lips and rubbed her arms against the chill in the air. As she ran her hand over her right arm, she had to admit, if only to herself, that she would have bruises by morning.

A moment later, McAlister walked back in with a calm expression. She watched him take off his coat and hang it on one of a row of hooks. He pulled Vera's phone and prescription bottle out of the pockets before walking to his desk and settling behind it. He glanced at her briefly.

"I've asked Doctor Jenkins to come and check on you," he informed her.

"That's really not necessary," she said firmly.

"Nevertheless, it's done." He gave her a serious look that ended the debate. He then pulled his keyboard closer and started clicking away with his mouse. "All right, when you're ready, what were your movements this afternoon and what led up to Varney's actions?"

Maiden quickly organized her thoughts. She told him about walking into the foyer and finding Emily Varney desperate for a room away from her husband. She then detailed their conversation once they'd reached the attic suite, including the unusual conditions of their prenuptial agreement.

"Ten years?" he asked with widened eyes.

"Yeah," she nodded, "it's weird. But justified as it turns out...sadly."

"Okay. So how did she end up with the phone?" McAlister typed a few more words and looked to her expectantly.

"She said she found it in Reg's shaving kit and thought she recognized it," Maiden replied.

"And why did she look in his shaving kit?"

"I don't know, maybe it was open. Maybe the phone made a noise and she heard it." She shrugged. "She didn't say."

"So, she just said that she found it there?" he clarified and typed a bit more when she nodded. "Fine. Tell me about the altercation with 'Reggie'."

"I got the phone from Emily and told her to lock herself in until I turned it over to you." She shifted, but only the slightest narrowing of her eyes betrayed any discomfort. "I was headed downstairs when I saw that the door to room 9 was open and the police tape was broken."

"And what made you decide to investigate it yourself?" he asked with a sigh. "You could've called me then."

"I called you about a minute and a half later, Captain," she said. "I was right by the door and it all happened a bit fast."

They both turned when the door opened, and Jenkins stepped inside and looked immediately at her. He smiled at Maiden as he came and knelt at her side.

"My dear Miss Harlow," he said kindly and patted her hand. "David said you've had a mishap."

"Who?" She blinked at him and then glanced at McAlister. "Oh. I really am okay, there's no need to make an issue of it."

"Part of the charges against Reginald Varney will now include bodily assault," McAlister advised her. "Could we stop wasting time with pride and bravado and get on with an examination, please?"

"Examination?" Maiden arched a brow and folded her arms.

"Nothing invasive, don't worry." Jenkins held up his hands in a reassuring gesture. "Let's start with something simple, tell me what happened."

She gave up arguing and described the brief but violent encounter with Reg. Jenkins pulled a face and muttered something colorful under his breath.

"All right, may I check your shoulder and arm?" He pushed to his feet. "Would you be more comfortable in my office?"

"Are there corpses in it?" Maiden asked with a concerned frown.

The doctor chuckled, and even McAlister smiled again. It might have sounded silly to them, but she meant it and wasn't sorry for asking.

"Not at the moment," Jenkins assured her, and then patted the corner of McAlister's desk. "If you prefer, I can take a quick look right now."

Maiden considered that as she glanced dubiously at the desk. She wasn't sure which option would be more uncomfortable, but the desire to be done was strong enough to prod her into action.

She pushed to her feet and, ignoring the doctor's startled expression, pulled her blouse off over her head. She felt the cold temperature of the room even more so in only her camisole but didn't complain; she tossed her shirt over the back of the nearest chair.

McAlister snapped his gaze back to his computer screen when she came and perched on the edge of his desk. She heard a few keys tap slowly. Dr. Jenkins was studying her pale shoulder with a frown; she joined him in his perusal and was surprised by how red and angry the skin looked.

"Not very nice, that Varney fellow," he said with barely concealed annoyance. "I'm afraid you'll have quite a bruise coming up, Miss Harlow."

McAlister had stood almost silently and was soon standing beside the doctor, eyeing her sore flesh with an unreadable expression.

Maiden knew she could have insisted that he not be in the room, but she didn't honestly feel threatened by the situation. Besides, if her injuries were part of the case, there would probably have to be pictures anyway. As if reading her mind, McAlister spoke up.

"Miss Harlow," he said mildly, "would you consent to some pictures being taken for evidence?"

She shrugged her good shoulder and nodded. McAlister went back to his desk and dug around in the top drawer until he found a camera; she supposed he couldn't take the photos on his phone without crossing some sort of professional line.

"What's funny?" He gave her a wry look before focusing on snapping a clear picture.

"Not a lot at the moment," she replied as he tapped the button a few more times and then stepped out of the doctor's way.

"Okay." Jenkins stood a little closer and blew on his hands. "I apologize for cold fingers. I just need to check a few spots, now tell me if anything hurts."

He carefully pressed one spot after another; she winced once or twice but remained stoic. He got her to move her arm and shoulder through a basic range of motion and was pleased that she was only a bit stiff.

"Well, that's going to be very sore for a week or so," he said. "Any pain anywhere else?"

"In my hip," she admitted and flicked a quick look at McAlister before turning back to Jenkins. "I don't really want to whip it out though."

"Certainly not," he laughed and gave her good shoulder an avuncular pat. "Did you hit your head at all?"

"Not badly..." she allowed after considering what still hurt.

"Stubborn little pixie, aren't you?" Jenkins smiled fondly and pushed aside a lock of dark hair at her temple and gently felt around. "A bit pink...and a minor bump."

McAlister returned to his desk, and Jenkins prattled away about aspirin and Epsom salts while Maiden stood and picked up her shirt.

McAlister watched as she started to raise her arms to slip the garment back on but stopped and winced at the resulting pain. He said nothing but pecked at his keyboard again when she instead unbuttoned the shirt and shrugged into it gingerly.

"Jenkins," McAlister cut in when the affable doctor paused for breath, "we took these off Varney. Well, Miss Harlow and her gang of vigilantes did, can you do me a favor and figure out why he wanted them?"

"Gladly. Anything to put that pig in his place." Jenkins smiled grimly as he took the bottle. "I'll get started. Please take care, Miss Harlow. See you later, David."

"Thank you, doctor," Maiden said politely.

After the door shut behind him, she sat down quietly. McAlister turned to her and looked her over.

"Do you feel up to continuing?" he asked.

"Yeah, I'm all right." She ran her fingers through her hair and frowned as she felt for the bump near her temple.

He watched her for a moment and then pushed his chair back.

"We'll leave it until tomorrow," he said simply.

"No, it's all right." She shook her head. "I really am fine, I swear."

"I promise you, Miss Harlow, it'll keep a little longer." He stood and gestured for her to follow suit. "Come on, I'll drive you home."

Chapter Seventeen

By the next morning Maiden was as sore as she'd been promised. She managed to slip on a button-down shirt and tucked the front into her favorite jeans. She headed downstairs and saw Anna Gilford looking through the pamphlet display.

Anna's red hair was swept into a high ponytail, and her faintly tanned skin boasted a heavy dusting of freckles, particularly on her forehead and cheeks. She wore a blue Capri-length jumpsuit that revealed thick ankles but dainty feet.

"Good morning," Maiden said as she walked past. "Thinking of touring the town a bit more today?"

"We might visit a few of these wineries," Anna replied as she opened one of the brochures. "Robert told me he really liked the Tavis Vineyard."

"They're a local family," Maiden told her. "They've been growing grapes and selling their wines for four generations."

"How cool." She smiled down at the picture inside. "I can't wait. Hey, what happened with that weird guy yesterday?"

"Who?" Maiden feigned ignorance as she slid in behind the desk.

"That man we saw being arrested." She almost whispered the word 'arrested' and edged closer, her ponytail bouncing as she walked. "He looked kind of scary. Is he the one that killed those people here?"

"We don't know yet." Maiden shrugged, but tried to sound reassuring. "I don't think anyone else is in danger now though."

"I hope not." Anna winced. "Robert told me about that woman who dropped dead in the dining room."

"Nothing to do with the food, that's been confirmed." Maiden forced herself to look calm and confident; inside she was nervous and confused and wished the woman would get on with her day and leave her alone.

"Oh, I wasn't thinking that, don't worry!" Anna laughed. Her dark blue eyes twinkled; she seemed to share her husband's good humor. "I was sort of hoping that they'd caught the killer, that's all. Then all this scary business could end and we could just enjoy what's left of our vacation."

"I think it'll be wrapped up soon," was the best she could offer. "I hope you won't get the wrong impression of Golden Glen, or Harlow House. Things like this don't usually happen here."

"Don't be silly," Anna smiled. "You can't help who books a room at your inn, can you? Robert said that both of the people that died had seemed a bit shady. But how were you supposed to know?"

"True." Maiden conceded. "Thanks, Mrs. Gilford. I hope you'll be able to put this out of your mind and enjoy the winery."

Anna gave her a wink and strolled into the dining room in search of breakfast.

The morning progressed quietly, and before long, almost all the guests were downstairs eating. Maiden could hear the cheerful din of dishes clattering and people chatting.

She glanced up when the front door opened and Captain McAlister walked in. He smiled faintly when he saw her, and she felt an unexpected flutter in her stomach.

When the heck did that nonsense start?! she demanded of her treacherous innards as he came closer, looking her over as he approached.

"Good morning. How are you?" he asked and gave her a speaking look. "Honestly?"

"Honestly, I'm sore and slowly turning purple," she admitted wryly. "I'm okay though."

"Progress of some sort," he chuckled and lifted his dark brows a fraction. "Can we speak privately?"

"Oh, yes of course." She glanced around. She knew her sister was in the office and didn't dare let her know the captain was back for a private discussion. "Um, come upstairs. It should be quiet up there."

She led him up to the apartment, fairly certain and desperately hoping that the family were all downstairs somewhere. She unlocked the door and gestured towards the barstools that were tucked along the counter, where they'd sat together before.

"Coffee?" She looked back at him as she walked into the kitchen and found the half-full pot that was always at the ready.

"Sure, thank you." McAlister took up a seat and rested his elbows on the countertop.

"So," she said as she set a cup in front of him and clasped one herself, "what can I do for you, Captain?"

"I spoke to Emily Varney last night and got more details of their situation," he began slowly. "She suspects that Reg, not wanting to lose her and her inheritance, decided to murder Vera. And now that we have the missing phone, we have evidence that she'd been threatening to expose their affair."

"So, the pills that Reg stole from Vera's room were the barbiturates that killed her?" Maiden frowned.

"No. The pills Varney tried to get rid of weren't barbiturates, they were another type of sedative," McAlister admitted after taking a moment to consider how much he wanted to tell her. "But they'd been tampered with."

"How?" Her eyes were locked on his, willing him to keep explaining.

"You can't repeat this," he warned her sternly. "I wouldn't even be telling you if you weren't in this as deep as you are. Jenkins found that, while most of the pills were the prescribed sedatives, one of them was slightly different in appearance. If she weren't paying close attention or if she was drunk, Vera probably wouldn't have noticed."

"What was it?" she whispered.

"Cyanide," he said. "It seems Reg was in the military and still has some contacts."

"Military? You mean, like, suicide pills?" She felt a chill ripple through her.

McAlister looked pleased that she'd followed his reasoning so quickly; he smiled and sipped his coffee.

Maiden clasped her hands a little tighter around her cup as she thought that through.

"Can I ask if you know where the barbiturates came from?" she murmured. "Were those Vera's too?"

McAlister gave her an assessing look as he mulled it over. She wished she knew how to make herself appear more discreet and trustworthy. She considered simply assuring him that she could keep a secret but was pretty sure she'd end up accidentally propositioning him again, so she kept her mouth shut.

Something in his eyes suggested he wanted to tell her, but the grim sigh he released assured her he wasn't going to.

Maiden wasn't surprised that he would keep most of his thoughts to himself. It was annoying but probably evidence of a responsible attitude on his part. She decided to be comforted by that as she had no better alternative. Not wanting to be shot down again, she smiled and shook her head.

"Forget I asked." She held up a hand to dismiss the question. She tilted her head a little and studied him quietly. "Have you handled a lot of murder cases, Captain McAlister?"

He met her gaze and smiled as he absently turned his half-empty coffee mug.

"Yes, I have." He nodded once. "I was hoping to get away from this sort of thing in a small town."

"People are people," she pointed out, "regardless of the space they occupy. For what it's worth, this isn't the first murder we've seen here."

"Is that meant to be a comforting thought?" he asked dryly.

"It was, yes," she laughed softly. "I'd hate for you to feel singled out when you just got here. It's usually a fairly quiet little town, this is all quite weird to be honest, but bad things do happen here too...Do you think you know who the killer is?"

"It's too soon to say." He sounded cagey.

"You can't really think she killed herself?" She held his gaze.

"I never said that I did," he replied, not shying away from her direct look.

"You hinted at it," she reminded him.

"Hinting at a possibility isn't the same as being convinced," he countered. "You think you can read my mind, Harlow?"

She didn't answer that, but the smile that kept slipping into view gave her away. He arched a challenging brow and leaned towards her a little more.

"Really?" He sounded intrigued and possibly miffed. "Go on then, prove it. What am I thinking?"

"I don't want to say." She shrugged coyly. "You'll get angry with me again if I'm right."

"I've never been all that angry with you, Miss Harlow," he said mildly.

"That's a lie." She grinned and shook her head. "It's just as well I can read your mind."

"It's actually a really good thing that you *can't*." He started to smile but quickly caught himself and calmed his expression. "Look, as long as we're talking privately, there's something we need to discuss."

Are you about to ask me out? Her eyes widened a fraction, and her lungs felt like they'd shrunk. He didn't look as if he felt good about whatever he was about to say, though.

You'd better not be about to ask me out; you look like someone just dared you to eat a dog turd. She folded her arms and tried not to scowl.

"I know you've been helpful," he said diplomatically, "and it's appreciated. But you need to stop poking around at this."

"I like vague warnings," she said dryly. "I can insert my own meaning into whatever the heck you're trying to say."

"You are attempting to figure out who the killer is," he obligingly clarified. "That's dangerous and potentially counterproductive. Knock it off."

"Is this about the Reg Varney thing?" she hedged.

"Partly." He nodded. "You also looked around Creevey's room, and collected information and evidence from the guests here. Not to mention detaining a violent suspect. As I said, a lot of that has been helpful, but you've already gotten hurt once. Time to leave it."

"Name one thing I've done that's unreasonable." She kept her tone steady and confident. "Or that anyone else wouldn't have done in the same situation."

"Explain to me why we found black hairs tangled in a bush beneath the first victim's window," he replied just as stoically.

Crap.

"Cat." Maiden effected an innocent shrug.

"A cat with hair that's two feet long?" he exhaled slowly through his nose.

"Long-haired cat. They exist," she responded easily.

McAlister was fighting very hard not to smile at her. He glanced down at his coffee and tried to frown with anemic results.

She hoped he'd change the subject because she had no intention of sitting back and doing nothing at this point. They were both spared the trouble of figuring out what to do next when they heard a loud knocking on the door.

They looked over even as the door opened and Billie let herself inside. The housekeeper's pale eyes widened in mortified horror when she saw them together.

"Oh! I'm so sorry!" she rushed to apologize and turned to leave. "I'll talk to you later Maiden! I need to tell your mom something *right now!*"

"Billie!" Maiden scowled as she called her back. She tried not to look as embarrassed as she felt over the awkward conclusion the woman had jumped to. "Come back here, it's fine."

McAlister sipped his coffee as he eyed Billie curiously, hopefully oblivious to why she was acting like a nut. Billie frowned as she took in the scene more carefully. A look of disappointment flitted over her features when she realized that they weren't up to anything scandalous.

"Oh, okay." She eased a little further into the apartment. "I remembered something weird about the rooms, you know, what we were talking about before. Do you want me to tell you about it later?"

"No, she wants you to tell her about it right now," McAlister answered for her in a dry tone. He gave Maiden a look and then turned back to Billie. "Go on."

"Okay." She shrugged, but looked at Maiden as she continued. "I was thinking about what you asked about anything unusual happening with the rooms. Well, that couple that's staying in room 7 flagged me down the day they checked in and said there was a nasty stain on their rug."

"Was there?" Maiden drew her brows together.

"Yeah, a pretty big one." She braced her fists on her hips. "And I have no idea how it got there, I cleaned that room after the last guests left. I'd have noticed a big dark stain like that. It was odd."

"What sort of stain was it?" McAlister asked seriously as he slid his empty cup away and pushed to his feet.

"I'm not sure." Billie scratched her chin. "All the rugs are a kind of rusty, coppery brown shade. It hides the dirt better than a lighter color."

"Where is it now?" Maiden walked around the counter and towards the door.

"I left it in the sink in Alfie's workshop." Billie nodded in that general direction. "I tried to wash the stain out, but I think the rug is going to be a write off. Sorry."

Maiden's eyes were wide as they flew to McAlister's; he didn't look pleased. She motioned for him to follow her as she headed out the door.

"Thanks Billie," she murmured as she rushed past.

Maiden was aware of McAlister following close behind her on the stairs. Her mind was racing as she led the way to the ground floor and then towards the office. She deliberately avoided eye-contact with Vonny, who was now sitting at the desk, gawking at them as they slipped past her and into the office. Maiden snatched the set of keys that hung on the wall as she passed on her way through the back door.

She stepped onto the concrete pad outside the shed that her father had claimed as his workshop years ago. From the corner of her eye, she saw McAlister look over the large structure while she fished out the right key.

She unlocked and opened one of the double doors, and they both peered inside. It was dark and silent. Maiden looked around tentatively and stepped in far enough to reach over and switch on the lights.

The long fluorescent tubes above them flickered a few times before coming to life with a quiet, constant hum. She blinked when McAlister pulled the door firmly shut behind them.

"The sink's over here," she said quietly and made her way past the shelves filled with her father's woodworking tools.

Alfie liked to spend hours fiddling with projects and had crafted quite a few nice birdhouses and wooden pens that he sold at various fairs and festivals throughout the year. His success provided endless opportunities to tease his wife for being too chicken to risk rejection for her precious pumpkins.

Maiden banished wistful thoughts of pumpkin pie covered in whipped cream and focused on why they were there. It didn't take long to spot the sadly discolored rug Billie had described. It was lying damp and limp over the side of the old, scratched-up sink.

As they drew closer, Maiden could see the results of several attempts to clean it. Even considering the forgiving shade of the material, the off-brown stain was stubbornly set.

McAlister approached and looked it over without touching it, probably more out of habit and training than any hope that many clues had been left intact. Maiden chewed at her lip and studied the rug herself.

She couldn't be certain that the repeated rinsing and application of cleaner hadn't made the stain look larger than it originally was. As she looked closer, however, there was a distinctive line that must've bordered the original spill. It was...really big.

"I'll need to have a look at room 7," McAlister said as he pulled out his phone. "Wait outside while I call this in."

Explaining to the horrified couple in room 7 that the police needed to examine their room for a possible link to a violent killing wasn't the nicest task Maiden had ever been given. She handled it as professionally as she could, however, and was both queasy and grateful for the macabrely interested gleam in the husband's eyes as she told them about the murder.

Hours had passed, and she was sitting alone in the office. She glanced over as a small group of police and forensic experts walked past and on towards the front door. She'd seen McAlister leave a few minutes before; he'd looked grimly pensive and didn't even notice her loitering in the next room.

She hadn't exactly been hiding, but she was happy to avoid him for now. She had a sickening feeling that her family's business was on a knife's edge; it wouldn't take much for him to decide to shut them down completely. The two murders were bad enough, but the clues were still cropping up. It wasn't good.

"What's going on, Maiden?" Vonny walked in from the foyer and gave her a look.

"More evidence turned up." Maiden rubbed her eyes. "Possibly."

"Yeah, I gathered that much." She folded her arms and leaned against the doorjamb. "But what does it mean? Do the cops have any idea who killed anybody?"

"No one's told me that," Maiden pointed out, but thought it over. "I'm sure they suspect something, but...I don't know that I agree."

"Agree with what?" Von scowled and shook her head.

Vonny jumped, and they both glanced behind her when they heard a knock on the door. Greg Smith was standing there watching them; Von obligingly stepped further into the room so he could enter.

"Hey Greg," Maiden said nicely, but remembered that she'd been warned off speaking to him a couple of times already. She didn't need the extra trouble, so she left it to him to explain why he was there.

"Hi Mae," he said and flicked a brief and disinterested look at Vonny. "I just finished my shift and thought I'd stop in before I head home, particularly since the captain isn't looking over my shoulder. I thought you might like a little off-the-record update."

"Ooh!" Vonny's pale eyes lit up happily. "*I* would! If it's good, I'll even make you a coffee!"

"Please, you're spoiling me," Greg sniggered as he came in and settled into the seat Maiden pointed to. "Don't tell *anyone* though. The last thing I need is Captain McAlister on my case again."

"Big Bad McAlister," Vonny intoned dramatically as she went to the coffeepot and filled a mug. "What's that guy's problem anyway?"

"Murder investigations are stressful, Von," Greg informed her in a tone more appropriate for a slow-witted chimp, but still nodded his thanks when she set the coffee in front of him. "Plus, Mae's getting to him big time."

"I am not!" Maiden's eyes widened and her face felt warm again.

"Yeah right," Greg sniggered. "You guys were coming on to each other like crazy right in front of everyone!"

"Oh really?" Vonny grinned mischievously as she turned to her sister.

"No. Not really," Maiden said and tried to change the subject. "You said you had an off-the-record update."

"And so far he's delivered!" Von snorted and turned back to Greg. "What did she do?"

"She just waltzed in looking gorgeous and told him he was a jerk, that's all," he laughed.

"I never said that!" Maiden grumbled. "I have always answered all of his questions, usually politely! He's the one that assumed every conclusion I've drawn is the result of inside information because I dared to try and talk to you once."

"Trust me, I heard about that," he said, and then gave her an imploring look. "Just call me next time, *please*."

"Yeah, yeah. Consider that lesson learned." She raised her hands in surrender.

"Good. Now, between you and me," he glanced over his cup as he sipped, "and Von...I guess, he'll be closing the case soon."

"What!?" Maiden's mouth fell open. "The entire case! Who's he arresting?"

"No one." Greg smirked, enjoying the drama he'd caused. "The murderer is already dead."

"Excuse me?" Vonny narrowed her pale blue eyes at him. "When did that happen?"

"Vera Randall killed Jim Creevey," he said boldly, "and then committed suicide with his pills."

"*His* pills?" Maiden asked.

"That's right. We found a bottle of barbiturates with Creevey's name on them in Vera Randall's room." He tapped his fingertips on the side of his mug. "They were obviously in the midst of an affair; things went sour and she killed him. The guilt got to her so she ended it all. A nice tidy wrap up."

Maiden pulled a face. "No way."

"I'm afraid so." Greg's cheerful smile faltered when she continued to frown. "What? It's good news, I thought you'd be happy about it."

"It's not good news, Greg." Maiden shook her head. "It doesn't make sense. How do you know that Vera was involved with Creevey?"

"I can't tell you that, sorry." He winced. "Let's just say some new evidence has come to light."

"'New evidence'?" Vonny's tone was dubious. "Did you find pictures of them together?"

"No—"

"Love letters? Text messages?" She sounded exasperated when Greg kept shaking his head. "Did you see them shake hands or something? Have you got anything at all?!"

"Settle down, Von," Maiden sighed. "It isn't Greg's fault."

"Thanks, Mae," Greg said sulkily, giving Vonny a dirty look.

"Um...It's interesting though." Maiden kept her tone deliberately light. "Since it's already been confirmed that Vera was having an affair with Reg. Seems odd if she was involved with Creevey too."

"Some people don't worry about things like that." Greg shrugged, but he seemed less cheerful about it all now.

"I guess," Maiden said, noting that he seemed a bit concerned as he shifted his gaze away. "Well...presumably that new evidence is strong enough to explain all those concerns?"

"Hmm?" He woke from his musings and looked at her with a faint frown before forcing his expression to clear. "Oh, yeah. Yeah, of course it is."

Maiden and Vonny exchanged a worried look but fell silent. Maiden sank deep into thought. She had been afraid that McAlister was leaning towards a murder/suicide theory, no matter how unlikely it seemed, in her opinion at least.

She simply couldn't believe that Vera had killed herself. One of the last times she'd spoken to the woman, Vera had been boasting about her bright prospects. She had been happy, not resigned to her fate.

Maiden wasn't sure about Reg either. She was certain that he was willing to kill to further his own interests, but Vera hadn't died from cyanide poisoning. Emily said that Reg was truly startled when he heard that.

Had his reaction been an act? Could he have hedged his bets with two different poisons, or had he realized in that moment that someone else had got to Vera first?

And then there was the stained rug in room 7; it made no sense. What did room 7 have to do with *anything?* She let herself slide into her memories. It wasn't something she did often, but the dubious ability had come in handy occasionally.

"Bloodstains...on two rugs...key on the hook," she whispered to herself as she stared past Greg's uncertain face. "Room 7...room 9?"

Vonny watched her quietly; she'd seen her slip into this kind of deep thought before and knew it was best not to disturb her. She glanced at Greg and put a silencing finger to her lips when he looked as if he was going to speak.

"The wine bottle," Maiden murmured numbly; a moment later she sat up straight and snapped back to the present. "That's right! Have a good night, Greg, bye!"

She stood up and hurried out of the room before either of them could stop her. She ran into the dining room and on into the kitchen, startling Kylie as she burst through the door.

"What's going on?" Kylie gasped and dropped the knife she'd been holding. It clattered loudly on the stainless-steel counter. Maiden turned to her with a triumphant look.

"The corkscrew!" she exclaimed, pointing at her as though she had denied its existence. "He thought I'd forgotten all about it!"

"Who?" Kylie asked nervously.

"Captain McAlister," Maiden said as she ran to the cupboard in the corner that served as the bar station. "An entire bottle of wine goes missing under suspicious circumstances and he looks at me like *I'm* nuts!"

"Did he?" Kylie risked edging closer.

"No, not exactly," Maiden admitted her exaggeration begrudgingly.

She went through the drawers one by one until she reached the bottom left-hand drawer. She pulled it open and peered inside with a small smile.

"Kylie," she glanced over at the pale blonde, "bring me a plastic bag please, and some gloves."

Kylie stared at her for a heartbeat, but then walked over to a drawer on the other side of the room. Maiden waited, staring down at the old corkscrew where it sat glinting dully in the overhead light. Just as she remembered, the cork was still impaled on it.

She'd been too annoyed and eager to finish her task to bother dislodging the cork and throwing it away that night. She was incredibly grateful for that now.

When Kylie held out the requested items, Maiden nodded her thanks and slipped on the thin plastic gloves and shook the bag open. She picked up the corkscrew and examined the cork.

She wasn't sure if barbiturates could be detected in cork, but she had to try. As she looked it over, she paused, and her eyes narrowed. On top of the cork, where the wax had been hacked away, next to the off-center puncture left by the corkscrew, was another, much smaller hole. She turned it over and found a matching exit point; she released a slow breath.

"Ah-ha," Maiden said with soft satisfaction.

"What's going on?" Kylie whispered as she watched Maiden slide the corkscrew into the bag and fold it over. "You're kind of freaking me out, Maiden."

"I know, sorry," she said as she stood and headed for the door. "Everything's going to be okay. Probably."

Chapter Eighteen

Maiden ran past the desk and back into the office. Greg had left, and Vonny was reading a magazine. She ignored her sister's enquiring look and started digging through the recycling bin until she found the old newspaper she was hunting for.

"You okay, Maiden?" Von asked uncertainly as she watched her throw a corkscrew and a newspaper into her purse and sling it over her shoulder.

"Yeah, I gotta go," she said as she hurried through the back door.

Maiden drove to the police station with a new theory taking shape fast. A few nagging questions that had been floating around at the back of her head were pushing to the front. There wasn't much time now; she could only hope that McAlister would listen to her before he closed the case.

She parked rather carelessly across two spots, but it was late enough in the day that the place was fairly empty. She spotted McAlister's car and felt a flicker of relief that he was still there.

Pushing through the front door, she smiled at Nancy and sailed up to the desk, praying that McAlister was in his office and alone. The lady glanced up from whatever she'd been reading; a pale blonde brow rose along with a corner of her mouth when she saw her.

"Hello, Miss Harlow." She sounded a touch nicer than she had the first few times they'd spoken.

"Hi, Nancy. Is Captain McAlister in?" She stared at her hopefully. "It's really important."

Nancy looked intrigued and reached for the phone. She had eyes so pale they were almost a muted gray; her nose was long and straight, and her chin had the faintest hint of a feminine cleft. She had an air of cleverness and good humor that lent a certain appeal to her features.

"I'll just check if he's available." She winked with teasing confidentiality and pushed a button. She waited a moment and then studied her nails as she spoke. "Captain, Miss Harlow is here and quite eager to speak to you...Yes, sir, Maiden...I didn't ask and she didn't say, did you want me to find out? Mm-hmm...very well, sir."

From the tone of Nancy's side of the conversation, Maiden was expecting to be told to push off. She was frowning, certain that she had important evidence, maybe. Nancy hung up the phone and turned to her with a calm and pleasant expression.

"Go ahead, he'll see you now," she said simply. "You know the way."

Maiden tried not to register any reaction to her knowing smile and headed down the hall with nothing more than a quick word of thanks. She made her way to McAlister's office and knocked, refusing to let Nancy's smirk make her feel silly.

"Come in." McAlister's deep voice gave her goosebumps; she ignored them and opened the door.

He was sitting behind his desk, which was covered in neat stacks of paper, tapping away at his keyboard, and didn't even look up as she walked in. He'd rolled his sleeves up and undone his tie completely, leaving it to hang loose around his throat. She studied his serious expression and then his thick brown hair as she waited for him to acknowledge her existence in some way.

He finally flicked her a glance and nodded towards the chairs in front of his desk. She left the door ajar before walking over and sitting in the one closest to him. After erasing a long line of text and scowling at his typing errors, McAlister sat back with a sigh and looked up at her.

"Hello again, Miss Harlow," he said. "How can I help you?"

"I need to talk to you about that wine bottle," she said seriously.

He groaned and rolled his eyes before catching himself and sitting up straighter in his chair. He looked annoyed with himself, but quickly cleared his expression.

"Why?" he asked in a discouraging tone.

Don't say he's wrong; he'll rankle, she told herself sternly. *Be more diplomatic. Suggest that something was simply overlooked; don't say he's wrong.*

"I'm not saying you're wrong," she assured him.

You really suck at talking to this guy.

"Good, because that would be very annoying," he muttered coolly.

"Just hear me out, please." She slid to the edge of the chair and pinned him with an earnest stare. He scowled and looked away.

"What's the problem, Miss Harlow?" he asked at last.

"I don't believe Vera killed herself, Captain," she said firmly, "and I believe her killer is still on the loose."

"Fantastic." He glanced heavenward. "Why couldn't she have killed herself?"

"She wouldn't commit suicide." Maiden shook her head with certainty. "She loved herself too much."

"That's all you've got?" he asked with a sigh. "Do you have any idea how little it takes to push some people over the edge? Vera Randall was a narcissistic ex-prom queen who was fighting a losing battle against time and her own vices. She was a lonely drunk that was two months away from losing the contract for her job. She had no friends that we could find and only one relative, a brother who wasn't at all surprised to hear she'd died of an overdose. Why is that hard for you to accept?"

"She was happy the day she died," Maiden insisted. "She told me her fortunes were on the up, she was looking to the future and she was pleased about it."

"She said that to you?" He sounded skeptical. She nodded. "Why didn't you tell me before?"

"I told you she was happy," Maiden said plainly. "I told you about the wine bottle too, but you didn't believe me."

"I do believe you," he assured her. "But we tested all the bottles and there was no trace of barbiturates in any of them."

"Why would Vera have killed Creevey?" She tried a different approach. "They didn't know each other."

"We have reason to believe that they did," he replied.

"She was involved with Reg Varney, not Jim Creevey," Maiden insisted.

"She was stringing them both along." He folded his arms across his chest. "She and Creevey were overheard arguing in the dining room on the morning of his murder."

"What?" Maiden stared at him. "When did Vonny tell you about that?"

"She didn't," he said slowly, eyeing her more closely now.

"Then who did?" She shook her head. "We were the ones that overheard it. No one else was nearby."

"You're mistaken, Miss Harlow."

"No, I am not, Captain McAlister," she retorted. "Vonny and I were sitting at the table next to the doorway when Creevey walked in. Vera was walking out after being shot down by Reg, she went straight up to Creevey and started flirting."

"So, you're agreeing with me?" He rested his chin in his hand.

"They'd never met before. She nearly threw her coffee in his face because he asked her how much she charged," she said seriously.

McAlister stilled and took in her guileless expression. "Are you absolutely certain of that?"

"Yes, I followed her after she stormed out, she was a mess." Maiden winced at the memory. "She'd just failed at trying to get a rise from Reg and then Creevey mistook her for a prostitute. I actually felt badly for her."

"I'm not really sure who to believe here, Miss Harlow," McAlister admitted. "Why didn't you mention this before now?"

"Because she wasn't involved with Creevey." She shrugged. "The man died that night and she was passed out at the time, I didn't think it was connected."

"I'd have preferred to make that decision." There was a subtle edge to his voice that he quickly banished. "In any case, another witness has come forward and stated that they heard them as well and the discussion was far more familiar. This person was convinced they knew each other intimately."

"Who told you that?" She pulled a face, and he smiled and shook his head. Of course he wouldn't divulge that, but she didn't need him to. "It was Robert Gilford. Wasn't it?"

The look on McAlister's face told her she was right. Her stomach lurched as everything came together in a chilling flash. She hugged her waist and almost doubled over. She was beginning to understand the sort of monster that had been staying at their little family inn, chatting and teasing like a friend, and it wasn't a nice revelation.

"Are you all right?" McAlister started to stand.

"Yeah, I just feel sick," she said weakly. "Give me a second."

"Um, could you not lean forward like that please?" He sounded pained.

She glanced up to find him staring resolutely at the side wall; she looked down to see that she'd pinned her shirt under her crossed arms, revealing a lot of pale cleavage. She immediately straightened and pulled the garment back into place.

Grateful that the resulting embarrassment had distracted her from her nausea, she cleared her throat, and he turned to her again.

"Sorry." She released a slow breath. "Listen, Captain, Mr. Gilford wasn't close enough to overhear them. He was at table 3 and that's at the far end of the room, Vera and Creevey spoke quietly."

"Why would Gilford lie?"

"I'd like to know too, and I think I do," she said seriously. "I'm assuming you checked on him?"

"We did, he's exactly who he claims to be. A senior insurance broker from Ohio." He turned to his computer and clicked away at his keyboard. "He's worked with his firm for seventeen years, no problems and no complaints against him."

"What about before that?" She chewed at her thumbnail. "Could he have known Creevey?"

"Nothing that came to light," he answered slowly, suggesting to her that he had never suspected Robert enough to dig too deep into his past. "He had no motive and was never under particular suspicion."

"I think he did have a motive." Maiden reached into her purse and pulled out the newspaper page. She opened it up and laid the article in front of him on the desk. "You know about the bank robbery in Westfield, obviously."

"Now he's a bank robber too," McAlister said dryly, but edged closer and looked it over. "I read this the other day, Miss Harlow. Why show it to me again?"

"Oh come on!" she exclaimed as she gave the newspaper an exasperated shove in his direction. "I'm not asking you for sworn secrets, but I'm not stupid!"

McAlister cleared his throat and got to his feet. She glared at him, half expecting him to throw her out. He walked past her, however, and quietly pushed the door shut before returning to sit behind his desk again. He folded his hands and gave her a stony look that she met easily.

"I dare you to look me in the eye and tell me you aren't already convinced that Creevey was one of the bank robbers!" she said grimly.

McAlister held her gaze, but he couldn't hide his faint smile. She relaxed minutely.

"Fine. I flagged Creevey straight away," he admitted with a shrug. "What's the connection to Gilford?"

"Robert Gilford turned up at Harlow House, alone, the morning before Creevey. And it was soon after he arrived that I caught Creevey trying to hack into our computer. He claimed to have been looking for the name of someone he thought he recognized, but I suspect he was looking for his co-conspirator's room." She took a steadying breath, hoping the captain would hear her out, as she didn't have much proof. "Creevey had a wad of cash on him, but not $300,000. Robert might have taken the larger portion of the stolen money, and Creevey was looking for him to get it back. I believe Robert killed Creevey and I think he actually did it in *his* room."

"Then why was the bloodstained rug in room 7?" McAlister leaned back in his chair and tented his fingers.

"To get the stained rug out of his room, and to create confusion," she said calmly. "The same reason Creevey's key was put back on the hook. That's probably when he grabbed the key to room 7 and swapped the rugs."

"And then he replaced the key and went back to his room and pretended to be asleep?" McAlister surmised.

"It's more likely than Vera managing to drag Creevey's body down the hall, let alone without anyone noticing," Maiden pointed out.

"She could have had help with that." he suggested.

"Yeah." Maiden gave a conceding nod. "But Emily said that Reg was snoring his head off all night. I highly doubt that she'd lie to protect him now. Do you know if her dad is really as rich as she said?"

"Yes, he is." McAlister lifted his brows and nodded with certainty. "Is that what you think Vera meant by her fortunes being on the up? Because Reg still had to put in another five years."

"That's true, and Reg had rebuffed her publicly a couple of times. I'm wondering if she'd started making alternate plans." Maiden edged a bit closer.

"For instance?" He watched her quietly.

"Blackmail." She resisted the urge to whisper the word. "Mr. Gilford's room was right next to hers, she could've heard or seen something."

"But she was drunk," he said after a thoughtful pause. "That would've made it harder for her to have witnessed anything useful—"

"—Unless she was bluffing," Maiden finished the thought aloud with him.

McAlister locked his eyes with hers and then looked away again. He sat straighter and cleared his throat uncomfortably.

"So, what am I supposed to do with all this?" he asked mildly enough. "You've withheld potentially critical information and there's no proof of anything you've suggested. You claim that no one except you and your sister could have overheard the conversation between Vera and Creevey, but you can't say that definitively. It's your word against his and that's not good enough. You're only muddying the waters, Miss Harlow, so I suggest you stay out of it."

She gaped at him and felt an angry scowl darken her features. She folded her arms and leaned back, crossing her legs and settling in stubbornly.

"No."

"Don't keep pushing me, Harlow," he warned, laying his large hands flat on the top of his desk. "Now listen carefully, I'm not interested in Gilford. I don't think the twit has enough guts to step on an ant, much less bash some rough character like Creevey on the skull. By all accounts Vera Randall was highly strung and desperate, it fits."

"It doesn't." She tapped her foot. "Robert Gilford killed him and dumped his body back in his room. There were bloodstains on his own rug so he switched them. Vera was staying in the room next to Robert. Maybe she started to piece something together and Mr. Gilford got nervous, suddenly she drops dead from a drug overdose."

"You're just speculating," he sighed.

"So are you," she said quickly, but not rudely, then winced as she continued, "and I did actually hear her threatening him in the hallway outside their rooms."

"*Damn it, Harlow!*" he shouted at her. "Are you making this up or have you been concealing evidence the entire time?!"

"No!" She hugged herself and shook her head earnestly. "I promise you this was just bits and pieces of things that didn't mean anything at the time! I'm sorry! I really am, but it sounded like she was hitting on him again. She did it a lot."

He set his teeth and wouldn't look at her. Maiden knew he had a valid reason to be angry, but she needed him to get over it fast and listen to her, or they'd be too late.

"Captain." She leaned closer and spoke in a low, serious tone. "I gave you naked pictures of Reg Varney, you can't really think I'd deliberately keep anything from you."

He shut his eyes, but then cracked them open and slid them back to her. She smiled sweetly and heard him exhale slowly through his nose; she decided to take that as a truce.

"There's also the matter of the missing wine bottle," she said.

"Another piece of 'evidence' that you can't find," he grumbled.

"There was another bottle of wine, Captain," she said adamantly. "She brought it herself, I remember clearly because I had to dig out a corkscrew for her. She started drinking and half an hour later she was dead. No sign of that bottle."

He was quiet now, not happy, but still listening. Maiden uncrossed her legs and sat forward.

"Just tell me this, *please*," she asked with every scrap of earnest deference she could scrounge up, "were there traces of the drug in her wineglass?"

McAlister just looked at her with his golden-brown eyes. She felt her pulse pick up; she was onto something.

"Which suggests that the barbiturates were in the wine, not washed down with it." she said.

"That doesn't mean that she didn't spike the glass," he pointed out.

"True, but it seems unlikely," she asserted in a reasonable tone. "I watched her that evening, Captain, she was acting strangely so it got my attention. She was very confused."

"Confusion is a symptom of barbiturate use, and overdose," he said.

"Yeah, okay. But she was *confused*," Maiden insisted. "Like trying to read the bottle to see what was going on and frowning when she couldn't. And then there's this."

She reached back into her purse and pulled out the bag with the corkscrew. McAlister glanced from it to her and held out his hand. She stood long enough to hand him the bag.

"I brought this to her that night and dropped it in the drawer after. It was Mexican margarita night; no one else had wine. There are two holes," she explained. "One from the corkscrew and one from...well, I think we both know."

McAlister looked at both ends of the cork. He was quiet for a pensive moment and then fixed his dark eyes on her again.

"Tell me exactly what you saw that night," he said in an unreadable tone. "All of it this time."

Maiden was so excited that he was actually listening to her that she had to take a deep breath to calm herself down. She nodded to him and then stared at the wall past his shoulder without really seeing it.

She felt herself shift back to the night of Vera's death; she heard the clatter of silverware and the steady hum of the guests chatting, punctuated here and there by laughter.

"We were preparing for the dinner service, there were more guests that had checked in that morning so it was pretty busy." In her mind's eye, she saw the different guests gathered at the tables. "The Langfords at table 1, the Kaminsky family at table 7, the Ashbys at 2, the Varneys at 4. About ten minutes later Vera walked in cradling a bottle of wine in her arms like a newborn baby. She sat down at table 5, right in the middle of the room."

McAlister watched her in silence as she stared straight ahead and almost never blinked. He turned to his keyboard and started typing out notes as she continued.

"Vera sort of saluted the Varney's, they pretended to ignore her, but they were both angry. Then she beckoned to me and told me to bring her a corkscrew and a glass. That's about the time Robert Gilford came in and sat in the back corner," she murmured.

"What did the bottle look like?" he risked breaking her focus to ask.

"It was a red wine with a burgundy and gold label. It looked like one of Tavis Vineyard's bottles. They're in town," she replied. "It had a wax seal; I saw her carving it away with a butter knife. Then she opened it and started drinking."

"Did anyone join her?"

"No. No one went near the table that I saw. After a bit I collected the corkscrew with the cork still on it." Maiden shook her head. "I took it to the kitchen and put it back in the drawer where I'd found it. After that I stayed in the dining room. I turned away a few times to help serve and direct people to the restrooms. But I kept checking on Vera because she was acting odd, she was kind of woozy and swaying in her seat."

"How much had she had at that point?" He knew from her earlier statement, but she supposed he wanted to be sure she stuck to the same story.

"I looked at the bottle and it was still at least two thirds full. That's what was strange, she acted disoriented and out of breath, but she hadn't had that much." Maiden chewed at her lower lip as she tried to recall every detail. "We had just finished putting the food out; I saw Vera trying to read the label on the wine bottle, but she kept blinking her eyes like they were blurry. She stood up and took a step towards the buffet and then she collapsed. We all ran to her, but she was gone. I didn't see the bottle again after that."

"So, your theory is that Gilford swiped the bottle when everyone was crowded around Vera's body," he said as he mulled it over. "Possible, I suppose, but a bit risky."

"Maybe he wasn't expecting her to bring the bottle downstairs with her. He would've had no choice but to get it back somehow. You'd have tested it for sure and then the suicide cover would be out the window, so would any hope that you would blame her for Creevey's murder," Maiden said as she shook free of the memory and faced him again. "And if he was the one that tried to convince you that he'd overheard a lover's spat between her and Creevey, although he couldn't have, it seems pretty suspicious."

"So, where's the bottle now?" he murmured.

"Long gone." She shrugged. "I think that his wife, Anna, has actually been in town for a while. He could have passed it to her and she got rid of it. Same with Creevey's missing backpack. She was probably the one who trampled that bush below Creevey's balcony. She could've been hiding there and Robert dropped it down to her."

"What makes you think she was in town?" McAlister asked. "He told us that he'd asked her to stay away after the first murder."

"Yeah, he told me that too." She nodded. "But he went out a lot and one day he came in with her shade of lipstick on his collar."

"You *know* that it was her shade?" He almost smiled, but then it vanished.

"I'd be genuinely amazed if it wasn't," she said candidly.

"Look, it's possible..." He shook his head. "I don't know. None of that would be easy to prove."

Maiden held her breath; this would be the biggest hurdle yet.

"I do have a suggestion," she said carefully.

Chapter Nineteen

Late that night, Maiden waited in the dimly lit library. She had already pushed an anonymous note under the Gilfords' door. The trap had been baited and set; she just had to wait and see if she got a nibble.

The note had been brief but bold. In it, she told Robert to come to the library at midnight. She claimed to be someone who saw him drag Creevey's body to his room and, although it was a gamble, added that she had also seen him take the wine bottle from Vera's table.

She waited anxiously; she had already placed her phone on a bookcase to record the conversation. The whole house was quiet; the only sound was the ticking of the large grandfather clock in the corner.

A few more minutes passed; she was worrying what she would do if no one came, but then she heard soft footsteps in the foyer. She took a steadying breath and forced herself to at least look calm.

It was two minutes past midnight when the door eased open and Robert Gilford stepped inside. He feigned a look of disappointment when he saw Maiden.

"Aww, it's you, darn it. I was expecting Billie," he said, and then smiled pleasantly. "But maybe she wasn't clever enough to figure things out. So...what do you want from me, my dear?"

"Nothing at all," Maiden said as steadily as she could. Her heart was pounding, and she still didn't know where Anna was. "But I must tell you that I don't appreciate you choosing our hotel to stage your dramatics. I'm asking you to leave, immediately."

"I'm deeply hurt." He pressed a hand to his chest but smirked at her. "What makes you suspect *me*? I thought we got along so well."

"A lot of little things. You were always hovering in the background when things happened, but you also managed to dodge Creevey." She gave him a look. "And you were the only one staying on the second floor that had the strength to dump him inside his room."

"I suppose." He tilted his head in a conceding nod.

"Then there were the swapped rugs." She arched a brow. "That was a bit careless."

"He'd bled onto his own rug before I got back and saw the blood on mine. Improvisation was never my strong suit." He shrugged; his eyes were frighteningly calm. "You can't prove that, of course."

"True. But I'm sure it wouldn't be too hard to check with the other hotels around and find out where Anna was really staying before she finally turned up here," Maiden pointed out.

"You're a cutie-pie, Maiden." Robert grinned at her. "I knew you were nosing around, but I'll admit that I never thought you'd actually figure anything out. So, why confront me about it now? What are you after?"

"I just want you to leave," she said. "I know you killed Creevey and Vera Randall, it's quite enough, you and your wife need to go."

"That's a terrible thing to accuse me of." His eyes turned cold and calculating; he drew a pair of gloves from his pocket. "And you still can't prove any of it. I could always claim that Anna stayed nearby because I was afraid this place was a death-trap."

"You can try." She shrugged as she watched him draw on first one glove and then the other. "But you won't get too far. You were quite sloppy with Creevey, I don't think that went according to plan."

He smiled after considering her for a moment. "You're quite right. He was an idiot; always had been."

"The barbiturates that killed Vera were supposed to be for him, weren't they?" she asked. "But he came to your room and you got into an argument that night. You didn't get the chance to use them."

"He always went straight to the fight." Robert sighed. "He had a knife on him. It was self-defense really."

"Then why drag him back to his room and pretend otherwise?" she challenged. When he remained silent, she rested her hands on her hips. "You couldn't risk them connecting you two, could you? The bank robbery in Westfield, that was you, wasn't it?"

"Aren't you clever to figure that out too." He patted his hands together in mocking applause. "Yes, me and old Creepy Creevey go way back, unfortunately."

"Mm. He didn't seem smart enough to plan a bank heist on his own," Maiden said candidly. "Not a successful one anyway. So, you double-crossed him and kept most of the money, that's why he was after you. You killed him and then called Anna. She waited outside, under his balcony while you dropped Creevey's backpack down to her, after hiding the money from the robbery in it."

"Oh, I do like you, Maiden," Robert said with a shade of regret as he smiled fondly at her. "I wish you'd kept your pretty little nose out of this."

"Unlike Vera Randall?" Maiden's eyes narrowed. "How'd she get on your bad side? There's no chance she was actually mixed up with Creevey."

"You're a nice girl, and you haven't got long to live, so I'll humor you." He smiled again. "The *charming* Ms. Randall, when she wasn't trying to claw her way into some unsuspecting man's bed, decided to set up a little side business. At my expense."

"Of course." Maiden eased back a step, not forgetting his threat. "Her room was right next to yours. Did she actually see anything?"

"I didn't bother to find out." He shrugged helplessly. "She *claimed* she heard us arguing and saw me grab my gun from its hidey hole on my balcony."

"A gun?" Maiden shook her head.

"Yes, I didn't have my silencer with me, I'm afraid, so I had to improvise." He laughed at himself. "A bit like using a screwdriver as a hammer, but it did work."

"Crude but effective." She gave a humorless smile. "Out of curiosity, why did you put his room key back on the hook?"

"Bit of panic, bit of fun." He held his hand out and shook it indecisively. "It never hurts to create a little confusion."

"Panic? Yeah, that was obvious. You were a lot more careful the second time." She tried to keep him talking and eased closer to the bookcase. "Using the barbiturates on Vera and planting the bottle in her room, which already had Creevey's name on it. The police believed the little fiction you and Anna cooked up. Did *you* lace the wine or leave that honor to your wife?"

"It was my idea. Barbiturates are old-fashioned, but I'm a sucker for the classics," Anna said from the doorway. She was dressed all in black, and her hair was pulled back in a tight braid; she was also holding a gun and had it pointed right at Maiden's chest. "I was rather proud of how well it worked out. So, how did *you* guess it?"

"The pieces came close but didn't quite fit into place," Maiden explained as she dragged her gaze from the gun to Anna's coldly focused eyes. "And, to be honest, once I knew he hadn't made you up, I started to suspect that you were the brains behind it all. No offense, but Mr. Gilford didn't seem the type."

"No offense taken," Robert chuckled and smiled affectionately at his wife. "Anna's always been my sweet little sociopath, and I'm happy to indulge her."

"Charming." Maiden managed not to shudder at the horrible pair. "I wonder that you ever worked with Creevey."

"He's the one who suggested the robbery in the first place. He called me up one day with this inane plot to rob the bank that had been stupid enough to hire him. Hmm, no windows," Robert observed as he glanced around the room. "The door is the only viable entry point, sweetheart."

"Agreed," Anna said simply. "But the angle isn't right for an interrupted burglary. Could you step this way please, Miss Harlow?"

"Where did you get the barbiturates?" Maiden ignored her disturbingly polite request.

"I'm a pharmaceutical sales rep." Anna shrugged modestly. "I visit pharmacies and labs every day of the week. It's easy to swipe all sorts of interesting things. I'm surprised you weren't smart enough to look me up online."

"That is surprising, isn't it?" Maiden smiled a little. "You can't just kill me, you know."

"Sure we can!" Robert said brightly. "What's a third? It's just one more on the pile. And as you see, my sweet Anna has her silencer."

"Always prepared, darling." Anna murmured and aimed her gun with a steady hand. "We'll make a nice story for you, you'll be a hero, Miss Harlow."

"She certainly will be," a gruff voice muttered.

Anna's head whipped to her right as McAlister stepped out from the shadow of the grandfather clock.

He seized her wrist, forcing her gun down and away from Maiden; she cried out in shock and struggled to pull free. Robert turned to see the captain wrench the gun from his wife's hand before twisting her arms behind her. He looked around frantically but froze when Greg Smith stood up from behind the massive desk.

Robert raised trembling hands as Greg trained his gun on him. Maiden grabbed her phone from the bookshelf and tapped the button to stop the recording. She turned to Anna with a smile.

"I did look you up, incidentally. But thank you for admitting to everything so freely." She inclined her head in thanks; Anna glared at her. "We're rarely as clever as we like to think we are."

The Gilfords were summarily handcuffed and dragged out towards a waiting police car.

Greg and Officer Briggs, who had been tucked in the office in case one of the suspects made a break for it, led the grim-faced couple out through the foyer. Gloria, Alfie and Vonny came downstairs and watched them go. Gloria hurried over to Maiden and hugged her tightly.

"My brave little baby girl!" she squeaked. "I knew you could do it! Bright as a button!"

"Thanks, Mom." Maiden smiled as she tried not to be completely engulfed by Gloria's bosom. "You're hurting me."

"Oops, sorry angel." Gloria released her and gave her bruised shoulder a gentle pat.

"You should've let me deal with them," Alfie grumbled as he tightened the belt of his bathrobe angrily. "I don't like heartless killers skulking around my girls!"

"I didn't do it on my own." Maiden nodded to McAlister, who was standing near the front door removing the memory card he'd put in Maiden's phone earlier.

"Oh! Yes, of course! Thank you so much for keepin' my baby safe, Captain." Gloria's eyes widened and a pleased smile curved her lips. She started urging Alfie and Vonny towards the staircase. "All right you two, let's head upstairs. Maiden will be along soon and can tell us all about it. Don't you rush, darlin', I'll start a pot of decaf."

Maiden tried not to look as embarrassed as she felt by her mother's lack of subtlety. She brushed her dark hair away from her face as she turned and approached the door where McAlister stood. He handed her the phone when she reached him.

"Thanks," she said softly and slid it into her back pocket.

She looked up at him and lifted her brows a little. He didn't exactly look upset, but he wasn't smiling either. She wondered if he was annoyed that her theory had been proven right. She would've thought a conscientious policeman would be happy simply to see justice done.

"So," she said when he continued silent, "that went pretty well. Don't you think?"

"Yeah. Basically." He finally dragged his gaze away when the squad car drove off with the Gilfords securely tucked inside. "It...worked out."

"Is there a problem?" She shook her head uncertainly and hugged herself as the cool night air drifted in through the open doorway.

He folded his arms and looked down at the floor. She pulled a face as she tried to figure out what was bothering him; he spoke up soon enough, though.

"I shouldn't have ever agreed to this stunt," he said, looking down at his shoes. "It's *irregular* to say the least."

"Yeah, but it worked." She knew she sounded confused, but she was. "What's the problem? You caught two murderers, who were also bank robbers. How can that not be a good thing?"

"Miss Harlow, do you realize that you could've been shot?" He finally met her gaze again, though his voice lowered grimly. "And I'd have been responsible because I agreed to your ridiculous plan."

"'Ridiculous'?" she demanded incredulously. "Is that what you think?"

"It could have gone wrong a hundred different ways," he said seriously. "It was incredibly risky."

"Had you been expecting anything different?" she asked. "*I* certainly wasn't."

"It's not your job to take those kinds of risks," he reminded her. "You're not a cop, you should have left it to me."

"If I'd done that the Gilfords would be long gone," she said and gave him a watchful look. "Are you sure you're really feeling guilty?"

"What's that supposed to mean?" He hooked his thumbs in his belt.

"Well, you're new to town and still trying to establish yourself," she pointed out, stinging a bit from his criticism. "Do you maybe resent me for solving your case for you?"

"'Solving it for me'?" His dark eyes widened angrily.

"Mm-hmm." She lifted her chin a fraction and held his gaze boldly. "You didn't believe me and weren't interested when I told you about Robert Gilford."

"That's not true," he held up a cautioning finger, "I considered it along with the rest of the evidence. You then took it upon yourself to dream up an incredibly risky—"

"*You said,*" she stepped closer until she was standing right in front of him and staring him straight in the eye, her tone was tight, loud and angry, "'I'm not interested in Gilford. I don't think the twit has enough guts to step on an ant, much less bash some rough character like Creevey on the skull. By all accounts Vera Randall was highly strung and desperate, it fits.' *Word for word!*"

"Stop doing that, it's creepy and unfair," he grumbled, but then smiled faintly. "I didn't mean to sound ungrateful for your assistance."

"Well, you did." She knew she sounded sulky, but she was too irritated to care.

"You blush when you're angry." His smile widened slightly.

"You change the subject when you don't want to apologize," she countered, but in a calmer tone.

"Sheesh, you're brutal," he whispered, but then edged closer and rested his large hand on her good shoulder. "I'm very sorry, Miss Harlow. You've been a tremendous help, thank you."

"Oh, you did it, and you survived it." She grinned up at him, trying to ignore the warm tingle that traveled through her at his touch. "You're forgiven, Captain McAlister. And thank *you* for finally stepping in before that lunatic shot me."

"All in a day's work." The dimple flashed in his left cheek. "How's your shoulder?"

"Well on its way to matching my eyes," she said wryly.

"At least it's a pretty color then," he laughed softly. He let his hand drift back to his side and took a step outside into the cool evening air.

Maiden smiled shyly and leaned against the doorjamb. McAlister looked like he wanted to say something more, but shook his head at himself almost imperceptibly.

"Good night, Miss Harlow," he said as he turned to go. "Please try to stay out of trouble."

"Oh, come on, what else could go wrong?" she chuckled and waved away the warning.

McAlister stilled for a moment and started to look back before thinking the better of it and walking on to his car. Maiden was still smiling as she watched him climb in, start the engine and drive off. As she shut the door behind her and set the lock, she thought about the evening and all that had happened.

Captain McAlister wasn't wrong about the danger of her plan, but she could never just stand by while two criminals escaped. It was a risk, but a calculated one. And it had worked; she couldn't help feeling pleased with her efforts.

It was incredible to think that such a seemingly pleasant and kind couple like Robert and Anna could be so cold-hearted, so casually horrible. She shivered at the thought and double-checked the lock before heading towards the stairs.

Her thoughts drifted a little too easily back to the handsome captain, and she felt another smile tug at her lips. There would be a lot of excitement over the next few days, and she'd doubtless have to testify or at least give another formal statement, but then things would quiet down again.

It was probably just as well; the next week would start off one of their busiest seasons. Her parents would need her focused on the inn, not bank robbers, killers, and handsome cops. She felt herself redden and quickly banished that last thought.

She walked slowly up the stairs, giving herself time to calm down before her family plied her for the details of her encounter with the Gilfords. She wondered if she'd get any sleep at all.

CHAPTER TWENTY

"I can't believe you did all that." Tony shook his head in complete wonder as he stared at Maiden.

"I can." Amelia looked smugly pleased as she stood beside him at the desk, which reached almost to her shoulders. "Women are tough, my son, I keep telling you that."

"And I've never argued with you. But trapping killers is next level." He slid her a smiling look, but then turned back to Maiden. "They actually admitted to everything?"

She shrugged and nodded. It was early and Tony was still working, although he'd been standing around the lobby for the past ten minutes while he and Amelia prized as much information from Maiden as they could.

"How did you even hear about the arrests?" Maiden asked curiously. "It only happened last night."

"My first stop this morning was the police station." He smiled happily. "Boy was Greg in the mood to talk. He was finally in on a big arrest and he got to hang around you for hours and watch you trick the killers; he was giddy."

"And naturally Tony called me straight away." Amelia gave a satisfied nod. "I told him to bring me right over. I can't believe Gloria didn't tell me herself. She and I are gonna have words."

"Mom didn't know about the plan until the last minute," she assured her. "She wasn't thrilled about it either."

"So how did you figure out that it was the Gilfords?" Tony leaned closer.

"A lot of little things." She shrugged. "And the idea that Vera was involved with Creevey never added up."

"What's your theory about Reg Varney?" He quirked a brow.

What's my theory? Maiden tried not to feel too flattered that they were waiting so eagerly to hear her thoughts on the matter. It wasn't easy, though.

"I believe he would have murdered Vera if Robert hadn't gotten to her first," she said with calm certainty. "Emily told me how shocked he was when he learned that Vera died from barbiturates, he was expecting cyanide because that's what he'd used to sabotage her sedatives. That's why he broke into her room, to get those pills back, he knew the cyanide tablet was still there waiting to be found."

"But why would he do all that?" Amelia held her gaze sternly, silently forbidding her to leave out a single detail.

"He and Vera had been having an affair for months. She had pictures." Maiden raised her eyebrows suggestively. "She was blackmailing him to stop him from breaking things off, but he couldn't risk it because she was getting very antagonistic and indiscreet around his wife. And his wife's family had the money. Robert at least suspected the affair and took advantage by putting a gift tag with Reg's name on it on the bottle of poisoned wine."

"But the police didn't connect that to Reg," Tony said.

"No, they didn't get the chance." Maiden shook her head. "What Robert didn't count on was Vera taking the bottle to dinner with her to show off, and rub Emily's nose in what she thought was a token of affection from Reg. After she dropped dead, Reg probably used the distraction to take her phone, the same way Robert used it to get the wine bottle."

"But how did they poison it?" Amelia raised a questioning finger.

"With a syringe. I looked at the cork and found the puncture hole that went straight through," Maiden explained. "They pierced the wax seal and the cork with a syringe and injected the poison. All they had to do after that was warm the wax enough to melt it and hide the puncture."

Tony let out a low whistle. "To think, you figured the whole thing out before the cops."

"I never said that!" Maiden waved it away. "They did a great job, I just happened to see a few things that they didn't, that's all."

"'That's all'? *Ha!*"

Maiden jumped as Vonny's loud voice resounded behind her. She looked back sharply and threw her a quelling look.

"Are you trying to give me a heart attack?" she demanded only to be ignored as her sister crowded in beside her.

"Mae knew from the start that the cop's suicide theory was garbage," Von said proudly as she wrapped an arm around her and gave her a squeeze. "She told them, but they ignored her."

"They didn't exactly ignore me; they just didn't agree." She winced when Von clasped a hand tightly over her bruised shoulder. "And the theory wasn't garbage, it was just incorrect."

"It was designed by the Gilfords to cover their tracks. To essentially get rid of both the people that were causing them trouble and have them implicated in each other's deaths. It was a set up, and the cops fell for it." Von smiled mercilessly as she released her and folded her arms. "Isn't that true?"

Maiden stared at Vonny as she struggled to deflect the assessment without lying. She started to speak a few times but nothing came out. She glanced at Tony and Amelia to find them watching her with knowing smirks.

"That's excessive." She finally grabbed hold of the word that had been dancing just out of reach. "I came up with a few plausible ideas and it happened to work out. The police did a fine job and the criminals were arrested. Everything was resolved and that's all there is to be said about it."

Tony raised his hands in surrender, but Amelia smiled quietly. She stepped away from the desk and headed toward the door.

"That's very interesting, girls," she said mildly. "I have errands to run now, but tell your mama she's having lunch with me today, I'll be back."

"Bye, Mrs. Ferris," Von said nicely as the older woman moved to the door with remarkable agility considering her spherical figure. She then glanced at Tony and stared owlishly. "You got a haircut!"

He smiled faintly and put his cap back on, covering his short curls. She held her hands out expectantly.

"Where is it?" she demanded with a pout. "I could've stuffed a cushion."

"You're not stuffing a cushion with my hair. It's disturbing," he laughed. "And it wasn't *that* long."

"Your mom isn't going to go around telling everyone that I solved the case, is she?" Maiden ignored Vonny's flirting and gave Tony a look, as though it was his fault or he had the slightest chance of slowing the juggernaut that was Amelia Ferris.

"Of course she will," he said mildly. "You did, didn't you?"

"I...helped. A little," she allowed, somewhat awkwardly. "I don't want anyone to be offended though."

"'Anyone' in particular?" Vonny grinned.

"Oh?" Tony gasped in feigned shock. "You mean the other rumors are true too?"

Maiden's eyes widened and her mouth fell open. If Tony knew about her flirtation with McAlister, *a lot* of people knew.

"What other rumors?" she asked tightly.

"A bit of speculation, that's all. You think a station full of people trained to investigate won't notice that much interest? On both sides?" Tony tried not to laugh at her obvious embarrassment. "Don't ever play poker, by the way. You blush too easily."

"I do not!" She knew she did.

"Greg said you and the captain would've been all over each other if you hadn't been in the middle of the lobby," he said lightly.

"Greg needs to shut up and stop exaggerating," she replied flatly, ignoring the betraying warmth in her cheeks. "Don't you have letters to deliver?"

"I do actually." He collected his mailbag and edged towards the door. "I'll talk to you both later."

He gave them a cheerful wave as he left. When they were alone, Maiden turned to her sister with an irate look. Von lifted a shoulder and shook her head a little.

"What?"

"Why did you swoop in and start making me sound like little baby Sherlock?" she asked uncomfortably. "It's going to make me look like I'm desperate for attention."

"No, it won't." Von rolled her eyes. "Maiden, you risked your neck and dug for the truth. And you were right. If you hadn't kept pushing, McAlister would have accepted the fake evidence and closed the case. You stopped two heartless killers, it's okay to feel good about that."

"I know, and I do but..." she sighed and looked down at her hands.

"I know you like the guy, but he got this one wrong," Vonny said with a gentleness that she showed far too rarely. "You shouldn't gloat, but why should you pretend that you did nothing? It won't change the facts."

"Maybe," Maiden allowed and slipped into thought. She supposed it was okay to enjoy the situation a little.

They both glanced up as Gloria emerged from the kitchen with a broadly smiling Emily Varney and a slightly less fretful Kylie.

Emily was almost unrecognizable. Gone was the matronly dress and plain, mouse-brown pageboy. Her hair was now a rich shade of glossy auburn and was elegantly styled. She wore a fitted—and blatantly expensive—burgundy pant suit that showcased a slender figure that no one had guessed was there.

"Emily! I almost thought you were someone else." Maiden smiled at her.

"I am someone else!" she laughed. "I can't believe how much I'd faded away over the last five years. But I finally feel like myself again."

"It's great to see you looking so happy," Maiden said genuinely.

"I have plenty of reasons to be happy," she said with a stubbornly cheerful nod. "My marriage may have been a sham but, as Kylie pointed out, I can hold my head up high because I know I gave it my all."

"Kylie said that?" Von glanced uncertainly at the pale chef.

"She did, and she was completely correct." Emily grasped her hand and patted it before turning to Gloria. "I have to congratulate you, Mrs. Harlow. You have an excellent chef who is also a wonderful human being. If I hadn't spent the last few days in the kitchen pouring my heart out to this amazing lady, I'm sure I'd have lost my mind."

"Really? With Kylie?" Gloria stared at Kylie incredulously, but her smile soon wriggled back to the surface. "Well, that's just lovely!"

"She certainly is! Never let her slip away from you, she'd be impossible to replace," Emily said happily and then released Kylie and clasped her hands together in front of her. "Now, I'd better go and pack. I hate to leave you ladies, but there's so much I need to do. My father is sending a car to pick me up this morning and I have to get myself sorted out."

"I'm glad you'll be with family again." Maiden smiled.

"Yes, so am I," Emily sighed. "The marriage to Reg put a bit of a wall between us, we have a lot of time to make up for. And of course, Father will look after the legal side of things."

"Of course," Gloria tut-tutted. "Even with the Gilfords' confession Reg still has to face the attempted murder charge, doesn't he?"

"Oh yes." Emily nodded. "It won't be working out for Reg this time, or whoever his old contact was that supplied him with that pill. I can only imagine what would've happened to *me* if he could have gotten to my inheritance."

She gave a delicate shudder, but then looked at them all with a smile.

"Thank you again for everything, ladies," she said with a sheen of tears in her eyes. "You helped me through some of my darkest moments, I'll never forget that."

"You go and be happy, darlin'." Gloria smiled and gave her a hug before shooing her gently towards the stairs.

They watched her disappear up the staircase and then turned to each other. Gloria arched a perfectly penciled brow and looked Kylie over.

Maiden held her breath; she knew Emily had gushed about the awkward chef out of kindness. She hadn't missed her conspiratorial wink as she walked past. She hoped it was enough to convince her mother to keep an open mind.

"Well, Miss Kylie," Gloria braced her hands on her wide hips, "I must say I'm pleased with how much you helped dear Mrs. Varney. If you keep up that sort of friendliness and consideration then...I have no real complaints."

"Thank you, Mrs. Harlow," she managed shyly. "I'll do my best."

"That's fine. *However!*" She held up a silencing hand. "I want you to start spendin' more time with the rest of us. It helps the runnin' of the inn when we know each other well."

"Yes, Mrs. Harlow." Kylie paled at the notion and pressed her lips together.

"And it starts immediately." Gloria pinned her with a hard stare. "You'll have dinner with the family tonight. In our apartment."

"Oh but..." Kylie's face flushed, and she started shaking her head, but one look at Gloria stopped the refusal in its tracks. "That would be really nice. Thank you, Mrs. Harlow."

"Atta girl," Gloria chuckled and patted her on the shoulder. "We'll have to try gettin' a glass of wine in you, honey. You're timid as a baby deer. You just get your little fluffy tail to our door at 8 o'clock."

"Yes ma'am," Kylie murmured even though Gloria had sauntered off already. She turned reluctantly to the others. "That's great...I'm looking forward to it...Should be fun."

"It will be," Maiden laughed. "Relax, you're among reasonably decent people."

"Oh, I know." Kylie smiled weakly. "But I'm bad in social situations. *Really* bad. That's why I try so hard to avoid them."

"We'll teach you how to bluff your way through." Vonny winked. "Tonight is a good time to start."

"Absolutely." Maiden nodded. "The murders are solved, the killers are locked up and Harlow House's reputation is safe. Everything can get back to normal now."

They all smiled in agreement. But as Kylie headed towards the kitchen and Vonny went to make a pot of coffee, a tiny part of Maiden wondered if things would ever really get back to normal again. She kind of hoped not.

JOIN THE FUN!

If you'd like to receive updates, bonus content and a FREE copy of the mystery novella **Blood and Money,** a fun and twisty mini-mystery, please visit my website www.camillesharpbooks.com and sign up!

<u>Blood and Money</u>
A Maiden Harlow Mystery Prequel

When a beloved guest arrives at Harlow House carrying a dangerous secret, Maiden Harlow's peaceful life is thrown into chaos.

Maiden has always taken pride in running her family's charming, small-town inn, where every visitor is treated like family.

But when a favorite guest arrives acting anxious and evasive, Maiden's instincts tell her something is terribly wrong. The guest refuses to involve the police and won't reveal who's threatening her. As unsettling clues surface and danger creeps closer, Maiden must uncover the truth herself. If she can't convince her guest to accept help, the consequences may turn deadly.

Step into Maiden's very first brush with mystery and danger in this gripping prequel to the *Maiden Harlow Mysteries* series. Perfect for fans of dark cozy mysteries, amateur sleuths, and strong female leads who won't back down when lives are on the line.

THANK YOU

Thank you so much for reading Murder Checks Inn! This book is very dear to my heart. I actually wrote it just after my brother passed away. It was a traumatic time for the whole family and he went far too young, but he was very unwell. Writing about Maiden's adventures gave me a mental escape that I desperately needed.

So, the fictional town of Golden Glen is an oasis for me. It's a haven of fun and adventure. Thank you for coming along, I hope you really enjoyed it.

I pour a lot of time and effort into my books trying to give you the very best that I can. It's a labor-intensive process and it never feels like it's truly done. But as an author you get to the point where you know you have to step back or you'll never move forward.

My goal is always to present stories for your enjoyment that are as smooth and polished as possible. I'm also very grateful to my sister, the first and ultimate beta reader, for her honest feedback and continuous support.

If you have a moment and feel inclined, it would mean so much to me if you'd leave a review.

Reviews make a huge difference to authors and they help fellow readers too. I appreciate your time and look forward to hearing what you thought of Maiden's adventures!

Warm regards,

Camille

Also by Camille Sharp

A Little About Me...

I write warm and funny dark cozy mysteries filled with sharp-witted heroines, atmospheric small towns, and secrets that refuse to stay hidden. Storytelling has been part of my life for as long as I can remember; born from long car rides, a battered notebook, and a soundtrack of country, Motown, and 80s hair bands.

My writing journey amped up in my teens, hidden away in my room with stacks of handwritten stories and a determination to build new worlds. At nineteen, I bought my first laptop, an indestructible brick of a machine that felt like magic compared to my pencil-cramped hands. I've been creating mysteries, alternate realities, and complicated characters ever since.

I love writing from every angle—heroine, hero, side character, and sometimes even the villain. My stories often follow smart, capable, slightly chaotic women who solve crimes, navigate danger, and protect the people they love. While romance often threads through my books, I'm equally drawn to the bonds of friendship, found family, and the complicated ties that shape us.

I believe books are essential, imagination is sacred, and boredom is the birthplace of creativity. And when life offers no clear way to conquer or surrender, stories give us a place to escape, rebuild, and breathe.

If you enjoy dark cozies with heart, slow-burn suspense, quirky characters, and mysteries with emotional depth, you're in the right place.

www.ingramcontent.com/pod-product-compliance
Lightning Source LLC
Chambersburg PA
CBHW061535210726
48287CB00006B/1964